V. Mahanenko

CONDEMNED

Lord Valevsky: Last of the Line

A Progression Fantasy Series
Book 10

Magic Dome Books

Condemned Book 10: A Progression Fantasy Series
(Lord Valevsky: Last of the Line)
Copyright © V. Mahanenko 2025
Cover Art © Lunar 2025
Cover Design V. Manyukhin
English translation copyright © Taylor Elise Margvelashvili 2025
Published by Magic Dome Books, 2025
All Rights Reserved
ISBN: 978-80-7702-580-5

This book is entirely a work of fiction.
Any correlation with real people or events
is coincidental.

All Series by Vasily Mahanenko:

The Way of the Shaman LitRPG Series

Dark Paladin LitRPG Series

Galactogon LitRPG Series

Invasion LitRPG Series

World of the Changed LitRPG Series

The Alchemist LitRPG Series

The Bear Clan LitRPG Series

Starting Point LitRPG Series

The Bard from Barliona LitRPG series
(with Eugenia Dmitrieva)

Condemned
(Lord Valevsky: Last of The Line)
a Progression Fantasy series

Law of the Jungle
A Wuxia Progression Fantasy Adventure Series

The Selected
A LitRPG Action Adventure Series
(with Yuri Vinokuroff)

"Earth" Release
A LitRPG Adventure Series
(with Vladimir Koshcheev)

Table of Contents:

Chapter 1

"My response hasn't changed since the last time, Heir. I have nothing to teach you. You need to visit another one of the ancient cities. Only there can you find a worthy teacher. You have the coordinates of the hidden cities. "Go on your way. Since you do not wish to fulfill your destiny, take up training. Become great and prepare a true heir who will be able to fulfill what you did not have the spirit to do..."

MY CONVERSATION with the sixth-generation interactive neural network was less than fruitful. Yuri, as the machine called itself, hadn't eradicated me on the spot for not completing its task. In this regard, the Abyss had been right — all I needed to do was collect five dictionaries for the *Author* skill to turn from a useless errand boy, fit only for destroying the planet, into just an errand boy. Fit to raise a descendant who would destroy the planet. The ancient mechanism did not consider leaving our world alone a viable option.

However, the neural network could do nothing to help me — its database, as the memory was called on these devices, proved exceedingly limited, and because of this Yuri had to constantly delete low-priority information. Moreover, the longer the mechanism survived, the more information about the lives of the ancients it had to delete as it was replaced by new images and events. The *Author* skill was the least of its priorities — after all, something similar to this skill is already possessed by geniuses who have become part of Chaos and accepted its power. In the week since I had taken out the Wave led by the beast carrying *Tainted Blood*, I'd had a lot to think about. Including the fact that I would not have become any kind of "slave" if I had acquired a new ability. On the contrary, I would stand in the same ranks as those ancient geniuses who had lived at the edge of our world. I could come to them as an equal and ask to become their pupil. They were still just people, after all. If I'd managed to reach an agreement with the white seraph of the Abyss, why not do the same with the people who had betrayed their world? Every day I liked the idea more and more, but getting *Tainted Blood* was no longer possible — both the Inquisitor and the Interrogator flatly refused to communicate with me without payment. No free advice, offers or anything like that.

If I wanted to get something from them, I had to pay. In my case, to become an errand boy again. How often I used this phrase. I didn't like that it was popping into my head more and more often. I hoped I wouldn't normalize it to myself and come to terms with my unenviable status. No, enough of such thoughts!

"Are you ready to reach further heights, my mentor, who is currently so mired in the mundane?" Kimal Sarento entered my office without knocking. For several days he had been hard at work with the Kalimans, constructing logistical chains for our trade relationship, but for the past three days he'd been hanging around Hearth, twiddling his thumbs and having no idea what to do with himself. He didn't want to participate in the construction, he didn't like treating people, and paperwork made him yawn. Even our new guests (the emperor's youngest son and the daughter of the chief emir of the Kaliman Empire) were able to occupy Kimal Sarento's attention for only a day. Then he lost all interest in them, handing them over to the omnipresent Eleanore.

"Depends on which ones," I replied, putting aside the draft contract for the supply of food. The Shurghan Empire was being cunning, demanding that I sign the document, not Eleanor. Perhaps they were trying to get around my manager, thinking that I would review the papers myself, but the Shurghans had clearly miscalculated in this regard. Not a single document reached me without Eleanor's signature. My woman had a whole department of lawyers studying all the papers up and down, so that they came to me crossed out from beginning to end. All that was left was to sign the list of disagreements and send a messenger to our partners, offering them to make changes. Kostrish had reached the level of development where we could, instead of rushing after every supplier, carefully choose those with whom we would work.

"Any! Aren't you sick and tired of sitting in one place?"

"It's strange to hear such words from a man who spent fifty years sitting in his tower," I couldn't help but be sarcastic. "You only left the magic academy on high holidays!"

"And? What is your response? I can state plain facts to myself without your help."

"My response? Alright, no, I'm not sick and tired of sitting in one place. I enjoy the peaceful days and sleepless nights with my Naira."

"Spare me the details," Kimal Sarento grimaced. "So you're not going to Pharapho now?"

"Do you want to come with me?" I asked, surprised. "Are you ready to risk everything to see a second-orbital power in real life?"

"I don't think that Pharapho will appear to you personally. The Abyss, as I understand it, also sent one of its vassals to talk to you. A human is not capable of adequately perceiving the speech of higher powers. Remember the lithoids — the main beast was clearly incapable of holding any reasonable conversation. I'm sure the situation was the same with the offworlders. You could interact with ordinary lackeys, but not with the leader."

"Before we go to Pharapho, you need to pass through the rift that is near the Black Mountain. It would be right to meet this entity by showing your usefulness. I think it takes too much power for the fog creature to hold back this hole in the ground, considering that there is a device for growing rifts down to the seventy-first level."

"So you're not worried about the fog spreading? You do understand that as soon as the rift disappears, there will be nothing left alive within a radius of several hundred kilometers?"

"First of all, why should I care about the lives of the dark ones who are always throwing a wrench in my works? Secondly, nothing will happen to the fog. It has already swallowed up the entire area. Thirdly, there is not a single large settlement within a radius of three hundred kilometers, so no one will suffer. And fourthly, we can always come to an agreement. If Pharapho is even half as sane as the Abyss, then there should be no problems negotiating with him."

"The Abyss needs the essences that Skron took from it. That's why it's so docile. No one took anything from Pharapho. I'm not sure that he will even let you in."

"Well, we'll see. In any case, I'm not going anywhere now — I'm waiting for messengers from the Temple of Skron. Today or tomorrow they should give me the human modernizing device, and I'll need to hand it over to the pope. And it wouldn't hurt to drop in on Father Urg and warn him about what happened. I want to see his face when he finds out that his plans to become pope are ruined. If he thought me some poor sacrificial lamb, ready to meekly fulfill all his whims, then I have unpleasant news for him."

"I like you more and more, my bloodthirsty mentor," Kimal Sarento smiled. "My presence definitely has had a positive effect on you."

"By the way — I'm actually glad you came to me. I know perfectly well that I'm sticking my nose where it's none of my business and that you have the right not to answer, but I promised Naira that I would ask, so I have no choice. After Elor finally went over to the Orthodox and started an open war not only with the light, but with the other dark factions, there is no longer any point in being married to Adeline. You are not obliged to fulfill the conditions you have assumed. In fact, my wife asked me to find out what your plans are with Adeline."

"You are right, my mentor who has become codependent with his wife, that you are meddling in something that is none of your business." Judging by the cold smile that had spread across Kimal Sarento's face, he did not want to touch on this topic. However, I'd completely forgotten any sense of shame lately.

"Just don't pretend to be someone you've never been. As for me, it's better to ask directly once and get an answer than to beat around the bush for a hundred years without reaching any conclusion in the end. Relations with the Bartolomeo Clan are important to me. They are not only the current leaders in the Kerux area, they are also our strategic partners. That's why I try to maintain close relations with Naira in order to benefit in the future. We don't have so many partners among the dark ones that we can afford a stupid quarrel because of someone's unrequited love or incomprehensible grievances."

"I repeat, my presence definitely has had a positive effect on you," Kimal Sarento grinned warmly now. "Your question caught me by surprise — this morning I received a letter from Adeline containing the very same query. My wife and erstwhile pupil are both extremely invested in how our relationship will develop further."

"In that case, I rescind by question," I said, which took him by surprise. "What? I promised that I would ask, and I did. I gave my motivation and explained why it was important to me, among other things. I wouldn't want your relationship to interfere with Hearth. But if the process is ongoing, then I definitely don't want to get involved in it. I'd like to sort out my own relationship. Naira has already said that she doesn't really want to share a bed with another woman, Alia keeps saying that she needs to go back to the church, and I don't want to let either of them go."

"But bigamy is not welcomed among the light lands," Kimal Sarento reminded me.

"Therein lies the issue. Sooner or later, I'll be forced to choose in favor of one of the girls, and..."

"Allow me to interrupt, my befuddled mentor,

and repeat once again: bigamy is not welcomed among the light lands. Mind your words carefully."

"Not welcomed doesn't mean forbidden," I said, surprised.

"Isn't it obvious? It's not welcome to drink alcohol, but it's not forbidden, right? Many things in this world are not welcome, but we do them calmly, receiving approval from above. Or we give it to ourselves."

"I cannot give myself such permission. No one will accept it, even in Hearth."

"So you need to find someone who will not oppose your desires. Our lovely empresses, for example. I do not think they would refuse two people in love. Or the pope, who you will be seeing again very soon. His Holiness dreams of putting you on a leash that he can yank when you are disobedient, so he will easily approve of the marriage with Alia, even despite Naira. I can even formulate a justification for why you would be allowed to do this right away."

"Naira is dark, Alia is light." I could see what the clever man was hinting at. "In theory, it could work. With the pope, in any case. The only thing left to do is discuss this issue with my ladies. I doubt they would jump for joy at the prospect."

"It all depends on how you approach the conversation," Kimal Sarento grinned mysteriously. "For a fee, I'm ready to give you a few lessons and advice."

"A separate fee? Do I pay you too little?"

"Pay me? What are you on about, my greedy

mentor? You pay me nothing!"

"Doesn't Eleanore give you a monthly salary?"

"Of course not! All my expenses I pay out of pocket, on my own. At least you take me out and let me see the world. But, jokes aside, you really need to seriously prepare for the conversation with the girls. Force — your modus operandi — won't work. But don't despair, my saddened mentor! That's what you have me for! I will teach you, give advice and take some of your burdens upon my shoulders. You know that you must give each of your girls a gift that would make it impossible for them to even think of contradicting you, right? Judging by the look in your eyes, the thought occurred to you, although not in such concrete terms. So it always is: you live with a person, break bread with them, but have no idea what interests them, what they value. You know, my callous mentor, that you must make this change within yourself. If you're going to live with two wives, you need to learn to take care of them. You need to treat them as if they were an important part of your world, not an obligatory component that is there as a matter of course. Only then will you be able to avoid conflict and get your grubby paws on two stunning women at once. Oh, don't look at me like I'm butting in. I wasn't the one who brought it up!"

Kimal Sarento once again showed a new side of himself. The last thing I'd expected in this life from my egotistical pupil was a heart-to-heart talk about women and how to properly communicate with them. Even my parents did not like to talk to me about such topics. It was believed that a person should comprehend the mysteries of relationships on his own, getting their own bumps and bruises along the way. All my father did was hire two twins as maids to initiate me into the wonderful world of sex. This was the beginning and end of my education on interpersonal relationships.

"I think you should consider my words. We will return to them a little later, when you receive consent for bigamy from the Pope and our future empresses. By the way! It completely slipped my mind: in three weeks we need to be in Turb for the coronation ceremony. Refusing is out of the question. I understand that you may have certain doubts about this. After all, the previous event you attended turned into a complete calamity and outright war with Count Vyazemsky, but now times have changed."

"Did I say a single word about not going to the coronation? I dare someone to look at me wrong or say anything about my wife. We will definitely attend and cast ourselves in the best light before the highest aristocracy of the Zarak Empire. However, my cunning pupil, now I really began to wonder what you plan to do with Adeline. In my opinion, anyone who is giving advice on relationships should have his own relationships in order."

"Isn't the answer obvious?" Kimal Sarento grinned. "Of course I'm going to get a divorce. What else? You think I don't know about the letters that some lowly baron sent to my still wife? I know perfectly well that Adeline didn't give her chosen one even a hint of her feelings after the wedding and honestly accepted the difficult burden of Countess Sarento, but I really don't need that. When you live to be eighty, like me, you'll understand."

"Almost a hundred and fifty," I corrected, causing Kimal Sarento's face to turn stony. "You think I don't know your true age? Or why the hell you still look forty? Of course, I'm surprised by your attempts to conceal the truth, but I've long understood that Kimal Sarento can't do otherwise. So I don't even pay attention to it anymore."

"However, this does not change the fact that it is time to start being more productive," he retorted, quickly pulling himself together and pretending that nothing special had happened.

"Sir, the servants of the Temple of Skron are waiting for you at the portal." There was a knock at the door, and my secretary entered. Eleanore insisted that I have my own personal assistant to handle all the red tape, and I have to admit, she was right. Having a single communication node through which all information flowed proved indispensable within the first week.

"There's the answer, my hasty pupil." I couldn't help but be sarcastic. "Everything should happen in its own time. Including productive work. Let's go and see this miracle of mechanoid technology."

One still had some surprises up his sleeve. When he had said that the modernization device was stationary and that improvements were needed to make it mobile, I assumed that there was a huge hangar somewhere where people are taken and have to pass through mechanisms, and that the improvement consists of turning this hangar into, say, a cart. Just as large, but on wheels and capable of moving in space. The reality turned out to be much more interesting.

"One presents this gift to Hearth and reminds that it is time to fulfill your promises. Karina Fardi is able to hold Skron for twenty-five minutes already, and with each day that passes, this will only increase. According to forecasts, it will be no more than six months before the vessel finally becomes self-aware and is able to control the power granted it. You know what will happen then."

Only now did I notice the small suitcase that the temple servant was holding. He placed it in front of himself and pressed the activation button. The only button. The suitcase opened up like an umbrella, turning into a two-meter-long hollow transparent flask with a door. It seemed that the walls and the door were made of glass, which amazed me — I didn't know glass could fold like that. The temple servant pointed to the control panel:

"The main parameters of the upgrade are set here. The device works on dorim, which is mined from rifts above level fifteen. Instructions on how to use, set up and charge the mechanism are included. The Temple of Skron has fully fulfilled its obligations and expects the same from the Hearth. In six months, any agreements we make will be rendered null and void — Karina Fardi will declare herself as a new force."

"I don't think the open teleportation platform is the right place to discuss such things," I stopped the temple servant. "The agreements are in force. The Abyss has already given the go-ahead, all that's left is to meet Pharapho."

"The Temple of Skron relies on you, Archduke Valevsky. To return the mechanism to its original form, press the activation button."

He demonstrated where it was, and the "umbrella" collapsed, turning back into a small suitcase. Without another word, the temple servant turned and walked into the still active portal. The minotaur silently followed his guest with his gaze and deactivated the shimmering veil as soon as it was no longer needed. One had fulfilled his part of the agreement, now it was up to me.

"Now to the pope for a blessing?" Kimal Sarento nodded at the suitcase.

"No way!" I was amazed by his words. "Only after I get the book from him! As practice shows, if I give something to someone before I get paid for my work, I will never see that payment again. So I will wait for the dictionary that His Holiness must somehow cunningly take from Father Urg, and only then will I hand him the suitcase."

"You can't trust anyone in this world," Kimal Sarento agreed. "If the high priest is stubborn and the pope can't confiscate the book, I'll have to give the suitcase to Father Urg. That's the right decision. I'll take the suitcase to the treasury. It shouldn't be lying out there on the street."

Kimal Sarento was clearly up to something — he grabbed the device too quickly. Knowing him, one could assume that he wanted to test the mechanism on some doomed soldier who happened to be nearby. Or, alternatively, on the Evil Engineer. My former mentor had relocated to Hearth, where he'd begun training a sabotage group. They trained from morning until evening, trying to meet the high demands of the former dark one. I happened to be present at one such training. The way my gloomy mentor mocked grown men made the hair on the back of my neck stand on end. Honestly, the preschool program Karina Fardi and I had gone through was nowhere near the full gamut. Even now, after receiving a bunch of enhancements and significantly surpassing the Evil Engineer in speed and strength, I was not sure that I could defeat him without magic. To each his own in this world.

Kimal Sarento left, and I embodied one pre-prepared line from *Author* skill, opening a red portal next to me. Before moving on, we needed to get a mechanism to accelerate the growth of rifts. Plus show Pharapho that we were on his side and ready to cooperate. Did I need to somehow establish contact with this huge pile of flesh?

The fog enveloped me from head to toe, but this time I was ready for it. The supreme converts sent by Naira were unable to reach their target — the fog destroyed them before they got close, and they'd been forced to open a portal where they stood. According to the map, it was several dozen kilometers to the rift, which only worked to my advantage. I had emptied my immaterial backpack in advance, leaving only food and water in it for my upcoming conquest of the rift. The rest of the space was intended for bone armor, which I was going to fill my backpack with to the brim. I needed to form several more full mithril armor sets. My sabotage group would be fully kitted. People like the Evil Engineer were not to be simply thrown away.

There was not a single moving Pharapho spawn left within a hundred meters of me. The creatures had frozen, having fallen under the influence of the twenty-fifth level ousel. It had been the right decision to switch it on to maximum from the get-go. The proximity to the seventy-first level rift, which had recently been infected, had had an effect — the creatures had become more tolerant to the dark aura.

Development crystals, cutting stones, bone armor, several unidentified artifacts — I was moving so slowly towards the rift that I began to doubt that I would even make it there before the end of the night. Which, by the way, hadn't even fallen yet. However, I wasn't going to give up my greedy business — everything that was mined in the Pharapho fog had "unique" status. I even came across an ancient device that looked like a book! I had to spend my daily limit identifying artifacts to find out the good news: the device really was an artifact of a past era. The screen was locked, of course, but I had a Defender at my disposal who would easily select the correct sequence of buttons. In fact, because of the artifacts, I was moving as slowly as possible, trying to peer through flickering in the fog surrounding me. When another sergeant exploded, the section I had passed was completely cleared of fog for some time. I had to return to land that had not seen the sun for almost a thousand years, and I did not regret it, as if I had found myself in a field of shimmering artifacts. Yes, most of them were production materials, but there were also several golden recipes and figurines that clearly had some value. All of this had to be studied, assessed and, if possible, sold for a higher price.

Kimal Sarento didn't even ask where I was going. He was quite adept at drawing the right conclusions and didn't bother me unnecessarily. Although his concern was sometimes irritating. I didn't understand why this sly fox treated me like that. He probably needed something from me, but what exactly was unclear. The eternal life he was granted under Magister Meram was something he definitely couldn't expect from me.

"I knew you would come here, Valevsky!"

The sun had nearly set when I heard a completely unexpected voice call out. The remains of another sergeant had just scattered all over the area, so I had to hide behind the bone armor to avoid getting covered in huge chunks of flesh. Apparently, the guest took advantage of this moment to get close to me. A few dozen meters away from me stood Karina Fardi, radiating with unhealthy strength. The girl had changed. She had become even more frightening — the dark fog was now emanating not only from her eyes, but even from her hands. The dark holes in her eyes, despite the distance, pierced me through and through. It was extremely unpleasant, to say the least. And what I noticed right away was that my level twenty-five ousel had no effect on Skron's vessel at all. Karina Fardi had become the ideal rift conqueror.

"You were warned, Valevsky. If you go into the lands of the dark ones, you'll have only yourself to blame. You didn't listen to reasonable advice. You started to stir up trouble. You encouraged the dark one to betray you. The pyramid will definitely suffer the punishment it deserves, but first I'll deal with you, you nimble little worm. You'll never meet Pharapho. Do you know why? Because you're going to die right here and now!"

With these words, Karina Fardi released the power of Skron, and the surrounding area was blanketed in death.

Chapter 2

TWENTY-FIVE MINUTES. I only had to hold on for twenty-five more minutes and then things would get a lot easier.

"Stop, Valevsky!" Karina Fardi roared. "Face your death like a man!"

I wanted to respond with some clever, nasty retort, but I didn't have the chance. All my attention was focused on not stumbling and sprawling on the ground following another *Dash.* The damned fog hid all the unevenness and stones scattered around the area, so any wrong move could be fatal.

As soon as Karina Fardi announced that nothing but death awaited me, I was already *Dash*ing away, getting as far away from the crazy girl as possible. I had no desire whatsoever to get involved in hand-to-hand combat or, Light forbid, a magic duel. Moreover, I knew I wouldn't be able to open a portal and escape — this would require precious seconds that I simply did not have. Skron's aura hit me as I was in mid flight. It only took a moment while I was flying for my body to turn into a bloody cabbage. I wasn't exactly sure what a bloody cabbage would look like, but that was how I felt. It was as if I had been shredded into tiny pieces. Even *Tainted Blood* had been more gentle. The blow was so strong that my heart and veins were torn inside my body. How I managed to cast *Heal*, I cannot say. I don't remember landing. The world went dark for a moment, only to return in a blinding flash as my body recovered. My body carried me of its own accord, without consciousness. Even my subconscious was screaming that I needed to get as far away from this place as possible.

But escaping wasn't that easy. Instead of being taken aback by my impressive speed and freezing on the spot, Karina Fardi rushed immediately after me. I had long ago established through experience that the maximum distance that *Dash* could throw me was fifty meters. Then there was a pause of a few moments before the ability became available again. That is, in a second I could cover a hundred meters without any particular problems or consequences for my body. I always believed that *Dash* was the ultimate ability, capable of carrying me away from any trouble.

Only I'd forgotten to tell Karina Fardi this, so Skron's mad vessel moved after me with the inevitability of a tsunami and the speed of lightning.

Somehow, she managed to significantly surpass me in speed, although, as I understood, she did not use *Dash*. She did not even run. She simply quickly moved from one point to another without using teleports. The surrounding space near Fardi exploded and cleared of fog, so I was able to determine the radius of the deadly darkness quite quickly — no more than twenty-five meters. One meter for every minute that Fardi could hold the power of the first-orbital creature.

But such an insignificant distance didn't do anything for me, for, as has already been said, Karina moved with preposterous speed. With another *Dash* I found myself at the very edge of her ability range and managed to slip away at the very last moment. Not straight ahead, as I had been moving all this time, but off to the side. Karina Fardi flew on, naively believing that I would only move on a straight path, and I heard her scream of rage. She was standing where the next *Dash* should have taken me, but I wasn't there.

"You'll still die, Valevsky!"

"Only after you," I muttered, starting to zigzag like a hare. Moving in a straight line was too dangerous, as practice had shown.

Within a couple of minutes, it became clear that I might not hold out until Skron's aura died. A few times, nothing short of a miracle had saved me from Fardi's clutches. She was monstrously fast and had somehow begun to predict my movements. I had barely chosen the direction of my next *Dash* and Karina was already flying in that direction. I was forced to perform incredible feats of dexterity at the last moment to change my trajectory. It was barely anything, but it was enough to avoid falling under that deathly aura. I was discouraged to find that I was right: I simply didn't physically have enough time to activate a portal. After a few near-fatal misses, I abandoned the idea. Now, only speed and the final buzzer could save me. Twenty-five minutes…I wondered how many had already elapsed. It felt as if Karina and I had been playing cat and mouse forever.

Night finally fell heavy on the scene. The Black Mountain, which seemed to absorb the surrounding starlight, contributed to the pitch blackness. It wasn't completely dark, but it was enough to make me slip up and choose the wrong move. Fardi, it seemed, was completely unfazed by the dwindling light. She stayed right on my tail, flying after me and breaking all conceivable and inconceivable laws of physics as she did. Living beings cannot move at such speeds without magic. Why without magic? Because any normal being would have run out of mana long ago. If not for my *Praxis*, disaster would have certainly befallen me — the act of popping open a potion and drinking it also took time.

However, the darkness didn't work in everyone's favor. Without my light crystal, I could barely see an inch in front of my nose. I was leaping without looking, hoping that I landed on flat ground that was devoid of large pits or rocks. It killed some time, but I knew full well that sooner or later I'd trip up. And I did. One *Dash* sent me soaring straight into a rock face and I nearly lost consciousness. Stars swum before my eyes and I heard Fardi's cry of glee nearby, who had seen me stumble in this impenetrable darkness, and then I did something that I would never have done in a sane state of mind. I raised my head to the sky and used activated *Dash* once more to flee from the enraged vessel of Skron.

The spell flung me fifty meters into the air and left me breathless as I began to fall back toward the earth. Slowly at first, and then with gathering speed. Somewhere below, I heard another irritated scream from Karina Fardi, so I simply had no choice but to use *Dash* again. The hulking mass of mountain behind us truly did absorb all light, so the only thing I could see now were the dim points of distant stars. And once again, having reached the highest point, I began to fall. Deciding to give myself a few seconds to come down, I used the ability to move again, throwing myself another fifty meters into the air.

It worked. Astoundingly, it worked! I was flung up and down in the air, with Fardi screaming furiously below, unable to follow, her vessel inexorably approaching its limit for holding Skron. I was even able to touch my head and activate the Gourfan light crystal. The space was illuminated by light, and as I turned the brightness up to maximum, my stomach clenched and I almost forgot that I needed to activate *Dash* every two seconds. I wasn't just high, I was soaring in the atmosphere! My light barely reached the ground, where Fardi was screaming and flailing her arms. Apparently, she was trying to fly. But Valevsky was the only one flying today. Even if he had a strange way of doing so.

On the tenth or twentieth *Dash* (I lost count almost immediately), I finally had the courage to look around. The rock I had crashed into somewhere below turned out to be none other than the Black Mountain, rising vertically into the sky. For some reason, Karina Fardi wouldn't go near the mountain, maintaining a distance of a few dozen meters. In fact, this was the reason she wasn't pursuing me. I had no doubt that the girl would be able to climb even the slickest of vertical surfaces. During training with the Evil Engineer, we practiced gripping and crawling on surfaces with a negative angle of inclination. But if she wasn't approaching the Black Mountain, there must be a good reason for that. What was it? The answer, in my opinion, was quite obvious: Pharapho. The second-orbital power did not want to invite one who had not yet become a force to be reckoned with into its personal chambers.

"You're still going to die, Valevsky!" Karina eventually grew tired of waiting. "I'm calling open season on you! Now, no matter where you go, I will be there! I won't just kill you, I'll kill everyone you hold dear! Do you hear me, freak?! Anyone connected to you in any way will be destroyed! I'll start with the Bartolomeo Clan!"

Fardi stopped screaming and froze in place. I didn't really want to see what she was doing down there, so I looked up, trying to find a good landing spot. I urgently needed to talk to Kimal Sarento — he would have to employ the Interrogator, no matter what it cost us. We needed to protect the dark ones. It seemed like being an errand boy was apparently in my blood. I couldn't just sacrifice the entire Bartolomeo Clan. They were too profitable for Hearth. I would have to negotiate with Chaos — a meeting I was not at all looking forward to.

Dash took me higher and higher. I was no longer waiting for gravity to start pulling me back down. As soon as the ability became active again, I cast it, taking me further and further into the sky. But there were no flat areas, just a solid, bare, sheer wall of black stone. I began to fear that I would not find anything at all, but I brushed the thought aside. In any case, the Black Mountain must have a peak, and I could cling onto it. I needed only a few moments to activate the portal to Hearth and begin the work of reining Fardi in. She had finally gone completely mad, fancying herself the punishing hand of justice in this world. Thinking that she could do whatever she pleases. She needed a reminder of who really ruled our planet.

I couldn't tell you how many *Dash*es it took to get to the small cliff edge. Yes, at around a kilometer high, I spied a relatively flat area where I could sit and rest a moment before portaling back to Hearth. The constant flight exhausted me more than training. Apparently, the ability was not intended for vertical movement and using it in this way had a negative effect on the body. I was shaking uncontrollably, and even the *Heal*s that I poured into myself did nothing to help.

Falling lightly onto the platform, I simply lay there for a few minutes, trying to catch my breath. My head was spinning, my nose was bleeding, and my general condition was getting worse with every passing second, but there was nothing I could do about it. My healing abilities were useless. Belatedly, I realized why I was feeling so poorly — the Black Mountain. Pharapho who was sitting inside, probably had some kind of aura that negatively affected all living things. It was no wonder that Karina Fardi couldn't approach the rock. I recalled my first trip to the Abyss, in which I had obtained the Abyssal Gem, which reduced the effect of the white seraph's influence. Evidently, there was something similar going on here: I needed some sort of object that would keep me from perishing. If that was the case, I needed to get out of here fast. In my current condition, there was nothing for me here. Gathering my last strength, I activated the portal to Hearth with the remnants of my sanity. That was it, enough adventures for today. Now I needed to lie in bed for a week under the watchful eyes of Naira and Alia.

"You should not leave, human," I heard a voice say. Turning my head, since I was unable to jump to my feet, I saw a projection of the Fog Stalker floating in air in front of me — an eyeless face, toothy mouth, four multi-jointed arms that could turn in different directions, clothes made of fog that hung in tatters and covered an unpleasant pale body. I never linked the Fog Stalker's appearance. There was something alien about it. Inhuman.

"This aura is killing me," I wheezed, flipping over onto one side. Another heroic feat awaited me: crawling the half meter to the portal. But the Fog Stalker had other plans:

"Use this stone." A large hunk of purple, sparkling rock covered in symbols was carelessly tossed in my direction. Despite the apparent nonchalance, it rolled over the other rocks and landed perfectly in my open palm. My fingers automatically clenched around the loot and a message popped up before the eyes:

Flesh of Pharapho. Unidentified object.

I had no choice but to identify and examine the properties of my new acquisition.

Flesh of Pharapho. *Description: Integrates into the development model cell. Available properties: Inures you against the Fog Stalker's influence, allows you to adapt to the aura of Pharapho.*

I didn't have any free slots in my development model, so I had to quickly pull out one of the crystals and integrate Flesh of Pharapho. The name was certainly creepy, and the stone itself proved stingy with any additional properties. Take the Abyssal gem, for instance: it allowed me to avoid the aura and also increased damage for each inlaid gem, but this one only protected me from Pharapho's influence. Considering that the development model originally belonged to him, he could have been a little more generous.

However, despite my obvious disappointment in the gift, it came in very handy. It was as if a huge burden had been lifted from my shoulders. It became easier to breathe, my head cleared up and my nose stopped bleeding. Several *Heals* transformed me back to normal. I even managed to get to my feet without swaying.

"You have lead Skron's vessel to the Black Mountain." The Fog Stalker nodded meaningfully toward the cliff. There, somewhere far below, was Karina Fardi, waiting for me to descend. Or had she already died and gone to be reborn? It was a shame that Skron had granted her eternal life. It was much harder to fight those who kept coming back.

I felt so fantastic that I was even able to *Analyze* the Fog Stalker, although this didn't reveal anything of note. Only the most ordinary development model, one that could be found in almost anyone. No secret abilities, no amplifiers, nothing unique. How did he fly? Was this a natural feature? The Fog Stalker projection in the arena also flew, but the longer I communicated with the current representative of Pharapho, the more I noticed the difference between him and the creature I had grown accustomed to. They were similar, no doubt, but in this similarity there were also striking differences, making each creature unique. In front of me stood a different Fog Stalker than the one that met me in the stark nothingness of the arena. However, I had to answer, so I just shrugged:

"I didn't have a choice. The vessel wanted to destroy me, so I was forced to improvise."

"The current vessel has demonstrated amazing results. In just a month, it was able to hold Skron for twenty-seven minutes without its own ego dissolving. This is amazing. It is worthy of the interest of higher powers. I know that Chaos resides within your city, human. You bear the seal of both hypostases of Chaos. Why do they not stop Skron's vessel? It has lost touch with reality and is capable of destroying the fragile balance that has befallen our planet."

"The current balance is a myth. It's strange that an omniscient being doesn't know about this. That's why I'm here. To restore balance."

"How do you intend to do that?" Curiosity appeared in the lifeless voice "The offworlders and the lithoids have been expelled from the world. In order for the system to stabilize and the ancients' weapons not to work, it is necessary to either reduce the number of forces of the third orbit to four, or add two more forces capable of replacing the ones that have left. The echo of the mechanoid and Karina Fardi are the ones who want to get this role.

"Chaos has made its position clear: it will not allow the Skron vessel to become one of the forces. It is currently unable to resolve this issue on its own — all its forces are directed at keeping the ancient's bomb stable. The two methods you already voiced will indeed work, but the system will still only be in a suspended state. There is another way that I recently proposed to Chaos, and which it approved."

"Creating a new second-orbital force," the Fog Stalker once again demonstrated his omniscience. I was a little surprised — how did the creature that had settled in the Black Mountain know everything about our world?

"I spoke with the white seraph. The Abyss agrees to give up part of its power to give birth to a new second-orbital being. Chaos promised to fulfill its demands, which I know nothing about. However, the Abyss will not make this deal unilaterally. Only if Pharapho agrees as well. There is only one way the planet can stabilize: if both second-orbital forces agree to give up part of their power to the new being. One, which you called an echo of the mechanoids."

"You want me to relinquish part of my power to another?" The Fog Stalker permitted himself a small show of emotion again. "Human, you have lost touch with reality!"

"Don't hassle me about it. I am here as a herald of Chaos. He guarantees that Pharapho will receive significant compensation for meeting the planet halfway. I'm not the one you need to bargain with — talk to Chaos. I'm not the one who should be accused of madness, but Chaos! For my part, I can only say that the idea is not without merit and as a gesture of goodwill, I will rid you of the annoying splinter that has been stuck in the base of Black Mountain and tormenting you for a thousand years. I will close the seventy-one level rift."

"Close the rift? You?" He hovered closer to me. "An ordinary human, who was nearly killed by the aura of the Black Mountain alone?"

"You know very well that I am a rift conqueror. Yes, my maximum level is still far above the depths of this rift but that is why they say it's the deepest the Abyss has ever generated. I do not know how long it will take me to close it — a week, two, maybe a month or more. But the fact remains: I will do it, and in the very near future. I have all the resources I need."

"And also the vessel of Skron, which will follow you as soon as you enter the rift. You will not be able to escape from there, even using the magic of the ancients. Are you ready for this? Unlike you, Karina Fardi has already adapted to the darkness of the hundredth level. The only thing that will slow her down are the dark rift beasts. Are you ready to face death, human?"

"The ancient portal doesn't work in the rifts?" This wasn't the happiest news to me, but it wasn't the kind that would make me start planning out my headstone either. "No big deal — I'll go visit the Abyss."

"Whenever you leave the Abyss, the enemy will be there. The Skron vessel will be waiting for you.

"This is a level seventy-one rift. If I adapt to

this depth, I'll slip rings on to block the influence of darkness and escape. The difference between me and the vessel will only be twenty-nine levels. This is considerably less daunting."

"You don't understand, human. Each new level is harder to pass than the previous one. Sometimes by an order of magnitude. It will take you more than one year of being in the rift to adapt to the hundredth. This is provided that you don't leave and constantly pour healing magic into yourself. The rings received from the metamorph will not help you. Their level is too weak to cope."

"If the metamorph rings are weak, then there must be something that will help, right?" I wasn't liking what I was hearing. By all indications, I would not be able to close the seventy-one level rift, and if I started gearing toward the hundredth, Karina Fardi would come to finish me off.

"No, human, there is no magic pill that will help you quickly adapt to the darkness. The only possibility is that you may become a new vessel of Skron. Accept the essence of the first orbit, surrender to it entirely, body and soul. Only in this case will you gain instant immunity to the darkness. Any other methods are tied to enduring and changing your body, adjusting it to new adversities. Even if you cover your fingers in rings and adapt entirely to the seventy-first level, without any crutches, you will still be torn apart by the absolute aura of level one hundred. You recently experienced the full immensity of its power. You managed to survive, but the vessel of Skron will not give you a second chance."

"If the situation is so futile, why are you still talking to me? Why did you stop me? You knew why I came here. you knew I planned to destroy the gaping wound beneath your mountain."

"Pharapho is not omniscient. The deeds of Chaos are beyond his reach — they are beyond his powers. It is difficult for him to access the deeds of Light and Skron. The forces of the first orbit carefully guard their secrets."

"But not well enough," I surmised. "There is a way to block the rift. No, that won't help. Fardi will be waiting for me at the exit — inside the rift, the ancient portals won't work. So there is some way to block not only the rift itself, but the lands around it as well."

"It is gratifying to see you picking up the right train of thought. Yes, there is a way to do this. As soon as you enter the seventy-one level rift, the Skron vessel will become aware of this. He will appear and destroy you. However, there is a way to stop him."

"How?" I asked with bated breath.

"Not so fast, human. First, I need to find out from Chaos what he can offer me for this crazy idea of restoring balance in the world, and agree on my participation. Only after that can we begin the second part of our negotiations. The part where you pay for my responses."

"What is the payment?" His words were unnerving. "Gold? Essences? Resources?"

"Who needs material goods in this world, human?" he asked. "You will pay the standard price that everyone who wants to learn something from Pharapho gives. You will pass through waves in the arena. All forty waves. Only then will you learn how to protect yourself from the encroachments of the Skron vessel and close rifts without it being there."

"But you, too, benefit from the seventy-one level rift being destroyed!" I exclaimed fervently.

"The disappearance of the rift will be one of my conditions to Chaos. They will have no choice but to agree to destroy it. There are not many beings in this world right now who can do this. More precisely, only one: you. So the forces of Chaos will simply give you a task and oblige you to carry it out. Whether you want it or not. The balance of power in the world is more important than the life of a single person, especially when both Pharapho and the Abyss are still at the negotiation stage. Your participation in this process is no longer required. You can easily be sacrificed. You will have to go into this rift anyway, so I have nothing to lose."

"I may die in the arena."

"In that case, Chaos will find me a new conqueror. It will just take a little longer. I know all the humans who are dark mirrors. You are not unique, human. You were just lucky to be in the right place at the right time and take advantage of the situation. If you die, others will come. I have waited a thousand years, I will wait longer."

"Why the arena? What is the purpose?"

"Complete all forty waves, and you will receive the answer to this question, human. Go now. Pharapho needs to meet with Chaos and discuss the future of this world. Prepare for the arena. You will enter in exactly two weeks."

Chapter 3

"ESSENTIALLY, THE MAIN QUESTION IS: what do we do now?"

The emergency meeting in Hearth took place thirty minutes after my return, despite the late night. The sleepy leadership of the city gathered in my office, but after ten minutes they were all wide awake. Except perhaps Kimal Sarento. He continued to sit there with his eyes closed, nodding off, regardless of the meeting agenda.

"She must be stopped! She must not be permitted to destroy my clan!" Naira was overwhelmed with emotion. The girl was ready to tear apart with her own hands the impudent fool who had decided to threaten her family.

"We need to contact the Inquisitor!" Eleanore suggested. "Yes, the creatures of Chaos may demand too high a price, but this way we can protect our partners. Too much is tied to the Bartolomeo Clan. We cannot turn a blind eye to what Fardi is planning to do."

"Is there anything we can do?" Alia wasn't sitting on the sidelines. "Even Max couldn't handle her. Count Sarento, stop sleeping! We have a problem, and you act as if nothing is happening!"

"Is something happening?" Kimal Sarento opened his eyes. "Just to clarify, gentlemen: why are you all so alarmed? Did anything terrible happen? Any irreparable damage? Only one conclusion can be drawn from what my mortally frightened mentor has said: Pharapho is an exceedingly repugnant being who loves to pull the wool over young and naive eyes."

"I wish there was just a bit more information in that river of words," Eleanore frowned. "Have you heard something that we missed?"

"Oh, youth! Tell me, great manager of this autonomous city, who is Karina Fardi? Other than the fact that she is Skron's vessel, and we are not taking that fact into account."

"A human being," Eleanore answered cautiously, not understanding where Kimal Sarento was heading. He gestured for her to continue, and she began generating descriptions: "A mad girl who has seized power. Someone who believes that the whole world lies beneath her heel."

"No need to describe her character, we all know what a shrew the young Fardi is. Facts, Eleanore. Naked facts. Who exactly is Karina Fardi?"

"A twenty-year-old woman. The heiress of the

Fardi family. Possessor of several dozen enhancements that have been shoved down her throat since childhood. This made her strong, fast, dangerous. A student at the magical academy of the Zarak Empire..."

"Finally!" Kimal Sarento even sighed with relief. "A student of the magic academy. Even though she trained under the guidance of the Evil Engineer, her foundation cannot be changed so easily: she is a mage. And she was raised as a mage from childhood. Now the main question, for everyone: how do you fight mages? Do you engage them in hand-to-hand combat, as my naive student tried to do?"

"They are destroyed from afar with steel bolts from crossbows," Eleanore said thoughtfully. "I don't think Skron's vessel can be destroyed with simple steel."

"The Chaos beast that our wonderful Inquisitor and Interrogator embodied could be destroyed with simple steel. Any force that exists in our world can be destroyed with steel, even Skron himself. Why would a vessel that hasn't even reached full power yet suddenly become an exception? The radius of Karina Fardi's deadly aura is twenty-seven meters. Remind me, what is the aim range of a combat crossbow?"

"One hundred twenty meters," Naira answered.

"Let's say, let's just imagine that Karina Fardi has some kind of protective aura that can easily deflect the bolt. Maybe two or even ten. But the eleventh, twentieth, maybe even the hundredth will pass through. The Bartolomeo Clan is capable of defending itself. Just like us, if Fardi showed up outside of Hearth's walls. You just need to prepare for this and understand in advance that you shouldn't get involved in hand-to-hand combat with this horrorshow."

"Are you saying that I shouldn't have sweat it so much and should have just shot her with a vyrma arrow?"

"Vyrma most likely won't work. Like it or not, this metal is the Abyss' domain. A second-orbital force. Fardi channels a higher-level entity, so to fight her we will need to use what the ancients invented. Or, me."

At the last sentence, a satisfied grin broke across his face.

"Fifty-third-level magic born in subordination to the Light. Yes, that could work," Eleanore nodded understandingly, to which Alia and Naira shot him a quizzical look. Unlike Eleanore, who had full access to our stats, the girls did not know how strong Kimal Sarento was.

"Not only that," continued Kimal Sarento. "What my mentor, who was scared out of his mind, did is completely outrageous. Tell me, great warrior, how you had no problems fighting a creature of Chaos, a zero-orbital being, and somehow come out on top, but have failed against a simple girl who is not even half as strong as you? Where did all those combat tables go? Why did you decide that running from Skron's vessel was better than imprisoning it in an impenetrable cube?"

"In order to use *Author*, you need a source to draw resources from. I can't create something tangible from fog."

"What does that mean?" Kimal Sarento said. He had clearly decided to get even for being woken up in the middle of the night. "That you need to constantly carry around a certain supply of material from which you can form what you need in emergency situations. Why didn't you take care of that?"

"Because I've never encountered anything like this before!" I flared up.

"It is called selective consciousness, my enraged mentor. I have long been surprised by the fact that you are ready to fight anyone with ease, but as soon as the conversation turns to Karina Fardi, who promised to finish you off, you become a complete wimp. It's true that you won't be able to kill her now. I have serious doubts that it's possible to kill a vessel of Skron with steel. Stopping her and sending her back to the rebirth cycle, sure, but completely eliminating her, probably not. That's what close combat is for. You need to tear out her essence."

"Can mithril pierce her body?"

"Why not? Stop thinking of her as an invincible monster who is going to terrorize the entire planet. If that were the case, Karina Fardi would have long ago sat on the throne of Kerux and commanded that all the dark forces be sent in our direction. But for some reason she doesn't do that. Does she really love the light ones so much that she doesn't want them all to perish? No! It's because she can't! Because she can't even control One. He will be punished, he will pay for his betrayal...A complete show-off that only the most narrow-minded people can buy into. Including my naive mentor, of course."

"Okay, let's say you're right," Eleanore said thoughtfully. "We can handle Skron's vessel with steel. Why do you think that Pharapho was deceiving us?"

"Because it benefited him to do so! Instead of clearly explaining how to handle the rift, he began to wax poetic about the meaning of existence! Pass forty waves, if you can't, then I'll find a new conqueror, I can wait a little longer...He can't wait, otherwise he wouldn't have given my mentor, who has now become quiet and begun to put the pieces together, a chunk of his own flesh. I have no idea how he learns information about our world, but he knew perfectly well that Chaos wanted to form a second-orbital power. So it bargained for more favorable conditions, simultaneously intimidating my naive mentor."

"This is all well and good, of course, but how can we ensure that the rift near the Black Mountain stays secure? We can't put crossbowmen there: the fog creatures will devour them in a matter of minutes."

"I think I understand," Alia said. "With the help of *Author,* you can create a protective dome, hiding the entrance to the rift. If the dome is thick enough, Karina won't be able to break through it. In any case, she'll have to try really hard to do so. It'll take an unacceptably large amount of time. By the time she breaks through your defense, if she can do it at all, you'll be done with the rift and will meet her fully armed. With your tables, for instance. Stick four legs into her stupid head, and that's the end of it. Let's see how a creature with the borrowed power of a first-orbital force can survive the magic of the ancients."

"You should keep your ladies close," Kimal Sarento said, looking at Alia with respect, making her feel embarrassed. "If you yourself lack brains, employ the help of those who have them. Karina Fardi is not as scary as you imagined. Do not forget: she only claims the power of the third orbit. How many of them have we destroyed? I can't even count! I hope this is all? Can we go to bed? Or do we have some other urgent and important matter to address?"

Judging by how relaxed the others were, Kimal Sarento's words had an effect. Indeed, what is there to fear from Skron's vessel if it can theoretically be stopped with a banal crossbow?

"I'll go to the clan," Naira stood up first. "We need to warn our family that they are being threatened by a crazy young lady."

"I'm with you," Kimal Sarento said, causing everyone to be surprised. "Come on, don't you get it? There's a ninety-nine percent chance that Karina will show up at the Bartolomeo Clan's estate in the next two days, consumed by the desire to get even with those who once sheltered my nimble mentor. Steel bolts are good and reliable, of course, but it's always good to be on the safe side. I want to see with my own eyes how our great heroine, who imagines herself almost a god, will fight against high-level magic. Besides, it's high time to grant Adeline her freedom. Let her build her own happiness. Not everyone is given the chance to find their soulmate, especially if that soulmate belongs to the opposite side of the conflict. There are only a few people like my lucky student and his beautiful wife in the entire world. One request, my overly nimble mentor: while I'm off visiting the Bartolomeo Clan, don't screw things up. Just sit here in Hearth, heal people, inform the pope that you already have the modernization mechanism, let him hurry up with the book. You should work on your personal development as well. Try to work on your own personal development. Try to pinpoint the flaw in your syntax. Basically, do whatever you like, but don't leave the city. Your trips beyond the walls always end in problems that the whole world has to solve."

"I completely agree." Alia sat closer to me, which she hadn't done for several weeks. "I'll look after him until you get back."

Naira's eyes flashed, but she remained silent. The emergency meeting ended there. It was amazing how big fear's eyes could be. What I perceived as a planetary-scale problem, others saw as a minor nuisance, eliminated by quite a standard means. It was a shame that I gave in to panic and didn't try the magic of the ancients on Fardi. It seemed that I needed to shed the past and perceive reality from a position of strength.

Naira and Kimal Sarento immediately went into the portal, and Alia went with me. Climbing under the blanket and occupying the spot where, just recently, my wife had lay, Alia shivered from the night chill and smiled.

"Are you going to stand there like a statue? Come to bed, it's a long time until morning."

"You haven't been in my bed for a while." I lay down next to her, not understanding how to react to such a strange transformation in the girl.

"How could I, when Naira is taking my place?"

"You disappeared long before she appeared," I reminded her.

"Max, what's the point of talking about what was? I suggest we think about what will be. Our child will be born soon, and I will have to make a difficult choice."

"So you haven't decided yet? I don't want you to go back to the Church of the Light. I need you."

"The Inquisitor forbade our relationship. Besides, you already have a beautiful wife. Why do you need me too? To get in the way and constantly remind you of our failed wedding?"

"I'm going to go to the Pope and ask for his blessing for bigamy. Then I'll make the same request to our empresses once they've taken the throne. I don't care what the Inquisitor thinks or how he'll react to disobedience. I want you to be my wife. Officially."

"Bigamy?" Alia's eyebrows shot up. "Max, it's forbidden!"

"Can you name a decree that prohibits this? Any regulation? At least one regulatory document that says that it is forbidden to have two wives in the Zarak Empire? You can look, of course, but there is no such document. Just as there are no other restrictions. Bigamy is not encouraged, but not prohibited. Tell me, will you be my wife?"

"Max, I..."

"We have two empresses on the throne. This is something never before seen, and yet it is happening. Alia, I need you. I feel awful without you. I have no idea how Naira will feel about me taking you as a second wife, but I can't let you go either. Because without you there is no me. And there never will be."

"Divorce Naira," Alia suggested. "If you need me so much, why do you need her?"

"Because I am no longer Maximilian Valevsky, rank-and-file doomed soldier who conquered the rifts and the heart of his personal attendant. I am the Archduke of the only autonomous city in the world officially recognized by the Church of the Light as a communication hub with the dark ones. We need them, whether we like it or not. I cannot reject Naira. Hearth depends on our union. After all, it is the dark ones who are building our city. But I cannot reject you either. Because you are all I have. The one who has been by my side from the very first moment and even went to the stake for me. Who carries my child. The one I love.

"But you love Naira too. Max, I saw how you look at her. Not just as a burden imposed by the dark ones. She is dear to you. She makes you feel good. I don't want to interfere with your affairs, Max. Bigamy is forbidden for a reason, even though you claim the opposite. It is impossible by its very nature."

Little by little I started to boil. Alia's sheepish stubbornness was infuriating. Kimal Sarento had been right a thousand times over when he'd said that I must prepare for the conversation and that it wouldn't be taken by force. But I couldn't go back now — the cat was out of the bag and now the situation required closure. Alright then, I'd have to get it out of the way now.

"Alia, I'll say it again: I need you. I want you to be my wife. I'll change all the laws in the world to achieve this, if I have to. I will rewrite them so that no one will even dare to *think* anything bad about us. You will not interfere with me or Naira. You will be my only light wife, she will be the only dark one. If suddenly another color appears, green, I will have another wife, and she'll be the only green one. Hearth unites two worlds, which means that its ruler should have two wives. This is the only logical solution. Or are you trying to say that Hearth should become dark? After all, both Naira and I are dark."

"You're light!" Alia protested.

"Tell that to the Inquisitor, whose every word pummels me into the ground. Yes, I have a special feature: I can become both dark and light, depending on whether I have *Golden Dome of Protection* or not. But this does not mean that the head of Hearth should be dark. Or light. Both will be negatively perceived by the opposite side. Remember what Naira's visit to the Vyazemsky estate turned into? A war that almost ended in total catastrophe for the city. But I cannot take you to the Temple of Skron either. They will not accept you there. Therefore, the head of Hearth needs two wives. Both dark and light. Skron take them all, but this 'balance' they talk so much about is actually relevant to this situation. I will have to take a light wife anyway, but I want her to be the one I love. I want it to be you."

"I hadn't thought about it from that angle," Alia said pensively. Judging by her face, she had been stunned by my improvisational argument. I was sure that Kimal Sarento could have sorted everything out at the very beginning of the conversation, but I was incredibly happy that I had managed to turn such a sensitive topic in the direction I needed. The fact that Alia was thinking said a lot. The girl internally agreed with my arguments, but with the sheepish stubbornness for which my overseer was famous, she resisted the need to admit the obvious.

"How are Naira and I supposed to get along?" Alia asked after a long pause. "Share your bed according to a schedule?"

"Let's decide this issue right after I get the approval of the pope and our empresses, okay? The three of us will sit down: you, me, Naira — and decide how we will live from thereon out. I need you. I need her. Hearth needs you both. We'll come up with something. Is this the first time we've gone outside of the status quo?"

"I need to think." Alia wrapped herself tighter in the blanket and stared off into infinity. "Turn off the light, please. You need to sleep, tomorrow is a tough day for you — there are a lot of patients in the hospital. I think their money will help Hearth a lot. As for your offer...I need to think."

Turning off the light and lying down next to Alia, I hugged her and almost immediately fell asleep. Already drifting off, I remembered that I hadn't even taken off the mithril armor that fit like a second skin, but I was too lazy to get up and take it off. Sex wasn't in the cards for me anyway.

I spent the whole next day in the hospital, receiving patients. Zarakians, Shurgans, Kalimans, dark ones — I had to treat them all. Rumors that they worked real miracles in Hearth, even returning lost limbs, had long since spread throughout the world. Many people came to me without any money at all. All they could pay for the restoration of limbs or getting rid of incurable diseases was work for the good of the city. And there was a lot that still needed to be done: the teams of dark construction workers constantly needed cheap labor for delivering materials. Eleanore completely freed me from the process of payment and contracts with the people — only those who passed the strict vetting process made it into my office. Those who paid a very large sum or signed a contract for work. From one to five years, depending on the degree of damage. My assistants even managed to create a gradation of diseases and injuries, as if something depended on it. It made no difference to me whether I used *Heal* on a person who simply had a toothache or had all their limbs torn off by dark creatures. The result was the same in both cases. As was the mana consumption. Thanks to *Praxis*, I forgot about any restrictions. Although I was being disingenuous. Limbs were not restored with one use of *Heal.* It took up to ten casts to accomplish the impossible. But the essence did not change: it cost me nothing, so the triage system was incomprehensible to me. But if people were willing to pay, it means they'd accepted the rules of the game. Who was I to change them?

"Precisely what I wanted to show!" That evening, Kimal Sarento, happy as a cat with a full belly, pushed through the throngs of people and burst into my office. "Alright, my hard-working mentor, finish up — that's enough for today. You can continue tomorrow. Today, we have a reason to celebrate! Maybe two!"

"What are you going on about now?" The monotonous work was driving me crazy, so I was actually glad that he had interrupted. Did I need another excuse to escape my monotonous duties and the countless earnest expressions of gratitude given by those who I'd healed?

"What do you mean? Isn't it obvious? As of today, your one and only beloved pupil is officially divorced! Cedric Jode dissolved our marriage, the

Temple of Skron easily confirmed the decision of the clan leader, so now I am as free as a falcon soaring through unclouded skies. Is this not a good reason to drink a bottle of the fine wine stored in the top drawer in your desk?"

"This, as I understand it, is the first reason. What about the second?"

"Karina Fardi did not disappoint our expectations and finally showed up at the Bartolomeo Clan estate. Can you imagine how predictable this poor girl is? I even feel sorry for her. So naive."

"The crossbows?" I waited with bated breath.

"It took twenty-two shots to penetrate her defense. I was starting to doubt that it would work, but the Bartolomeo Clan fighters know their business. The twenty-second bolt went straight through her forehead and sent her back to her master. You should have seen Karina's. There was so much disappointment and childish resentment that I even felt sorry for her. She thought herself a powerful, invincible thunderstorm and she died at the hands of ordinary humans. Okay, not quite ordinary — the supreme converts are serious warriors, but the fact remains the same. The only thing she accomplished was scorching a path in the lawn as she walked to the estate."

"You do know she'll prepare before her next visit?"

"Naturally. Cedrick Jode understands this as well. As the head of the Bartolomeo Clan, he is a reasonable enough man, my doubting mentor. He is well aware of what is happening and hopes that you will manage to complete your business before the enraged Fardi harms their clan. And the whole world in general.

"That's it, finish it. I can't wait to drink some wine. By the way, I talked to Naira and explained the bigamy situation to her. She understands entirely and agrees that Alia would be the perfect candidate for your light wife. All that's left to do is have a conversation with Alia and we can head to the pope for a blessing."

"Alia and I talked everything over yesterday," I admitted, afraid that Kimal Sarento could do harm without having all the information. "She promised to think about it, but overall she agrees."

"Then we have a third cause to drink to, my risk-taking mentor!" Kimal Sarento clapped me on the shoulder, causing me to stagger considerably. The blow was so strong that even the mithril armor couldn't absorb all the inertia. If it weren't for the armor, I could have been killed by this friendly blow!

"Sir, the Pope's envoy has come to see you." My assistant ran into the office where I was seeing patients. "He says he has some kind of package for you, which His Holiness ordered to be handed over personally. And also...the churchmen brought devices! Many devices! The defender is already working on them."

"We're going to get so drunk today!" Kimal Sarento exclaimed, but suddenly fell silent as another man entered the office. My assistant bowed to him, then explained:

"Sir, I asked the Pope's envoy to wait, but I have no right to stop him…"

"It's fine, Richard, you don't have to worry. You're free to go."

My assistant disappeared. The representative of the Church of the Light sat down on one of the guest chairs and, groaning like an old man, said:

"Count Sarento, did you say something about drinking? Frankly, I wouldn't mind having some of your wine, which is famous throughout the world. And I'd also like to hear the story of how two swindlers tricked the High Priest of the Zarak Empire, handing him straight over to the Pope."

"Father Urg, what a pleasant and unexpected meeting," I said as the pause began to drag on.

"Max, let's leave all this bowing and groveling for later. I admit that you won this round, but this little game called life is far from over, and I still have the chance to win again. So invite me to the table where delicious wine is poured and divulge the reasons behind your actions and, of course, tell me how you beat me."

"My friend, you won't believe it," Kimal Sarento finally came to his senses. "It's not us. It's life! The pope himself sold you out, we have nothing to do with it."

"Now I definitely need details and wine." Father Urg's gaze became like steel, capable of cutting through any obstacle. "Who?"

"You will have to find out for yourself. We were not given names. But the fact remains: your own people are betraying you. Enough work, my hardworking mentor. It's time to retire to your office and satisfy the curiosity of the high priest. Father Urg, you brought the book, right? The pope assured us that we would definitely get it. But I never thought that we would receive it from your hands."

Father Urg said nothing, but I had no doubt that this man would definitely take revenge. He was so vile and dangerous that I would surely regret many times over that I did not finish him off there and then, when I had the chance. But these were all problems for future me. Right now, all I could do was smile and enjoy the pope's victory. Father Urg had been put in his place. Sometimes even other people's victories bring pleasure, so Kimal Sarento is right: there is no reason not to have a drink! Today is a holiday in Hearth!"

Chapter 4

HIT! THE SPEAR CRUMBLED into dust and another wave of rigidity rolled over me. Several casts of *Heal* were able to restore me to my normal state, but each unsuccessful attempt made me more and more displeased. Never quite right! Always a little off! I was nothing more than a talentless schmuck who had gotten ahold of stolen power and was incapable of anything other than throwing tables at the enemy! And even ordinary tables had a negative effect on my condition when destroyed. Everything was stacked against me.

"Alright, Valevsky, pull yourself together and get back to work!" I practically yelled at myself, getting up from the floor. The testing ground had suffered greatly from my attacks: deep holes had appeared in the walls where spears or table legs had struck. The stonework was unable to withstand the magic of the ancients. I had to form a wall from bricks using *Author*. And this posed another conundrum: after another spear strike, several bricks cracked and crumbled into stone chips. I braced myself for a kickback, but there was none! For some reason, *Author* decided that the brick creation was worthy of being considered perfect, even after I had destroyed another dozen bricks. Meanwhile, the several spears and tables that splintered against the wall demonstrated my incompetence in my mastery of ancient magic.

What was I doing wrong?

A few more unsuccessful attempts forced me to sit up to at least maintain an upright position. I wanted to lie down on the floor and forget about everything, as if it was a bad dream. But I couldn't just abandon the venture: if I didn't understand what my problem was, I would be unprepared for my next battle with Fardi. Which in itself was a crime. A delicate cough was heard behind me — my omnipresent assistant reminded me of his presence:

"Sir, the food is served. Would you like it delivered here or would you like to go to the dining room?"

"I'll take it here. No need to bring a table. I have plenty to choose from here, as you can see."

"Yes, sir. If you will permit us, we will still bring furniture. Your tables are made of stone, it is not the best idea to dine at them. They are too cold. Lifeless. After all, a table is an object made of wood, rarely metal, but never stone. It is not proper for an archduke of a great city to eat at such a table."

"Alright, bring a table," I agreed, although my thoughts were already hovering in a completely different plane. The line that formed the table was before my eyes again, and I turned it back and forth, trying to understand what had caught my attention in his words. The table must be made of wood. Rarely of metal. Never of stone, and especially not of earth, as I had built it during the battle with the creatures of Chaos. Now, a brick — sure, it can be made of stone. Of course, you could make it out of wood, but the result wouldn't be the same. So, once again: a table of wood, a brick of stone, a spear...a spear of metal and wood, and not just metal, as I had done before! What if the transformation of space created by the ancients had its limitations in the manufacturing material, and if you used the wrong material, there was a kickback? When space itself let you know that you were doing something wrong?

Apart from the summoning sentence, there were no other explanations about how to form a table. As if the ancients had an implicit understanding of what objects needed to be designed from. As if they were trained in this...Hey, that was an idea! What if the point of training was not to teach you how to formulate sentences correctly, but what type of material to use? That raised the question: was it possible to cheat?

"I need a cubic meter of wood and a few ingots of pure steel," I told my assistant and, while he ran to fulfill my order, I began to slowly chew the food I'd packed, my thoughts hovering over the *Author* skill. Consider my ill-fated spears. What if I made changes to the command spell related to the material it was made from? For example, adding the conditions, "tip-make-steel, shaft-make-wood." This would greatly restrict my options, as these materials couldn't be found everywhere. That meant I needed to carry them in my inventory and use them when necessary. I'd have to test this theory!

The result exceeded all expectations. When I formed a spear with these new conditions in place, it was a complete revelation — it came out perfect! Exactly as I had originally intended it to be. The first stone wall couldn't stand up to my new weapon, but the second shattered the spear into small pieces. My body reflexively tensed up, preparing for pain, but my mind knew there would be no consequences. I was right: destroying the weapon had no effect on me whatsoever. Sending my assistant away, I plopped down on the floor and continued to tinker with the command prompt. In the process of testing my first theory, I'd come up with a few more ideas I wanted to try out right away. It seemed that I was slowly beginning to understand the basis behind the ancient methods of transforming space.

"You've been sitting here for too long, my hardworking mentor," Kimal Sarento said when he arrived a couple of hours later. By this time, I had finally finished working with the spear and began to form a defense at the entrance to the rift. I needed a ten-meter dome that could withstand an attack by a furious Fardi. That is, not only durable, but also impenetrable, with the ability to delay the influence of Skron. The dome caught my pupil's eye, and he nodded at it and asked:

"How durable is it? Will there be a kickback?"

"There shouldn't be. One second, I'll make the final adjustments now and then I'll have to test it. I propose you do the honors. If you manage to destroy it within a minute, I'll grant you a wish. If you don't, I'll get a case of wine produced at the Sarento estate. It seems like a worthy wager."

"Can I use any means available to me?" Kimal Sarento asked, watching with curiosity as the solid structure crumbled into fine dust, but immediately reformed into perfect stone blocks.

"You can," I said. "The task is to destroy the dome within a minute. You can even bang your head against it, if you think it would help."

"You think too highly of your achievements, my suspicious mentor. Get ready to grant my wish, young man! Now you will learn the true power of Kimal Sarento!"

This last phrase my pupil practically shouted to intimidate me. But he was no Karina Fardi. I had inured myself to his taunts long ago. Adding one small condition to the sentence forming the dome, I set my leftover piece of pie from lunch on the floor and sequentially activated four phrases. One formed the base, another was responsible for the strength, the third for impenetrability, the fourth linked all the blocks into a single whole. Once again, the joy of a well-crafted sentence rolled over me, and the dome itself seemed to emanate blue light. But considering that Kimal Sarento did not react to this in any way, I was the only one who could see it.

"Ready? Your time has started!"

Two branching lightning bolts broke from Kimal Sarento's hands and crashed into my creation. The smell of ozone wafted through the air. The dome disappeared under the bright flashes of lightning running across it, and I sincerely began to doubt its structural integrity. The mage wasted no time and struck with everything he had. He put all his available strength into the streams of lightning, and at one point even took one hand away to replenish his mana supply.

"Time!" I said as soon as the timer I'd set hit zero. Lightning continued to shoot from Kimal Sarento's hands for a while, but soon he calmed down. The dome was still standing. No, not standing — floating in a lake of molten rock that almost instantly solidified as soon as the preposterous amount of energy being poured into it had dissipated.

"Still standing," Kimal Sarento remarked pointedly. "How?"

"Because it's perfect?" I suggested and deactivated my creation. It crumbled to the floor as fine dust, and then my pupil burst into loud laughter. Not even ashes remained from the pie I had placed under the dome — the energy that Kimal Sarento had used had melted not only the floor only around it, but everything underneath it as well. The dome held up, but it would have been impossible to survive under it.

"Evidently, there is some factor I forgot to take into account," I said thoughtfully. "Never mind, I'll definitely figure out how to eliminate the influence of external conditions on the internal contents of the dome over a glass of excellent wine."

"Are you hinting that I owe you a case of wine? No way, my cunning mentor — you've only formed a meter-wide dome. You can't hide the entrance to the rift under that. If you want to win our wager, you must make a decent-sized shield, not this miniscule masterpiece."

Judging by his displeasure, Kimal Sarento was furious that he couldn't handle my creation, so he was spouting complete nonsense. Although, admittedly, there was some truth in his words: a meter-long dome required much less material and was more compact, and therefore more durable. Whether all this would work on the ten-meter cap that I planned to use to close the passage to the rift was still a looming question. Pulling out my special bell, I summoned my assistant.

"I need rock — at least three cubic meters, no less."

"Yes, sir, it will be delivered to you now."

Kimal Sarento silently looked at the servants who were hauling huge boulders to the training ground, while I tried to change the design once again. How could I prevent external influence on the contents? Moreover, Kimal Sarento's attack had rocked my dome like a boat on a raging sea. In this case, of course, the sea was molten stone, but this made me think that the dome, although strong, must be quite light. Karina Fardi would not destroy it — with her strength, she would simply lift one of the edges and scoop the contents out from underneath. Increasing the mass of the dome would not help: Skron's vessel has enough strength to lift even an elephant. Anchor it deep into the ground? An option, but how could I then protect whatever was under the dome from her furious attack? I needed to think. There was still time...

"Ready? Begin!" After the servants had hauled in the stones, I'd built a ten-meter dome around another piece of dishware. What was I supposed to do, use a living test subject? Kimal Sarento didn't make me ask twice and unleashed a stream of level-fifty-three *Chain Lightning* again. But this time, something immediately went wrong with his plan: the stones around the huge structure didn't heat up. The ten-meter dome absorbed the energy, distributing it over its huge surface area. A minute passed, then two, then five. Kimal Sarento attacked tirelessly, constantly using mana elixirs, but it didn't bring any results: the dome held.

"Enough!" I shouted, putting an end to the bedlam. The testing ground might not be capable of withstanding such a furious attack and collapse. Where would I conduct my tests then? Making sure that the lightning had fully dissipated, I crumbled the dome into dust and barely held back my cry of glee — the dish was intact. Covered in dust, sure, but far from deep fried. Now, if I added anchors that went five meters into the ground, not even Karina Fardi would be able to break through my defense.

"It held," my pupil agreed, but then went to search for weak spots: "What about tunneling? Even if you can't break through the dome, you can still easily get inside that way."

"Yes, I thought about that — I'd need to make some kind of floor. And long pins delving into the ground so that the structure can't be lifted."

"Finish it, and we'll test it in the open air. Let's invite the Evil Engineer. He's a master at getting into various confined spaces. If he can't do it, you can safely head into the rift. How much time do you need to alter the syntax of the sentence?"

"Just can't wait to get rid of me, eh?" I chuckled.

"The thing is, my mentor, who I think is trying to be sarcastic, that you and I have no time to warm up and prepare for this fight. Don't forget: the coronation is in less than two weeks. By that time, the seventy-first level rift must be closed. Or do you have other plans for it? Do you want to work hard in the Fog Arena? Are you ready to pass through forty waves?"

"To be honest, I want to understand why Pharapho needs these waves. It can't just be because he's got a pugnacious attitude. There's a reason he put up forty waves as a means of payment for help in blocking Karina Fardi."

"The answer is quite simple, my presumptuous mentor. The reason for Pharapho's incomprehensible behavior is that he understands perfectly well that a person is not able to pass all the waves. No way. You miraculously crawled to the thirtieth and were practically broken by it. It gets even more difficult after that. You cannot defeat two Pharaphos without *Tainted Blood.* You don't have it, and Pharapho knows this perfectly well. That's why he is now setting you a deliberately impossible task, so that he can then start trading on his own terms. So that you agree as soon as you hear some other offer, in which you simply need to share resources. This is a classic example of what negotiating with the powers that be looks like."

"And if I pass the forty waves?"

"Then all honor and glory to you. Pharapho will silently curse himself, but nothing critical will happen — he will observe how you passed through, and next time he will adjust his creations in such a way that neither you nor anyone else can use this method. So our foggy friend will win in either case."

All I could do was sigh — I was still far from being able to draw such correct conclusions based on two or three events. Sitting down, I delved into the *Author* skill to attach anchors and anti-tunneling measures to my dome. It proved quite easy: when there is a ready-made structure, attaching something additional to it does not require much effort. The only thing that irritated me about the skill was the need to constantly pull materials out of my immaterial inventory. At some point, I freaked out and tried indicating my personal storage as the source. Having hidden the steel rods that I used to strengthen the stone structure, I embodied a new version of the dome and immediately regretted it. It worked, and it had no problems drawing the materials from the immaterial backpack. But due to the fact that the dome now had five-meter legs, they raised the upper part to the level of the ceiling and, as it turned out, a little higher. Immediately, stones from the collapsing ceiling began to fall, there was a crunching sound, cracks appeared on the ceiling, and just before the huge stone blocks fell to the floor, I managed to escape from the room with a *Dash.* There was a deafening roar behind me, and there was one less building in Hearth — my training ground, which was intended for secret testing of the most dangerous abilities, could not withstand the load and collapsed, burying my structure underneath

People came running to the sound. They were shouting something, waving their arms. I could only smile, watching the top of the dome I'd created rise from the ruins. The structure withstood the building collapsing on top of it, telling me that the entire day wasn't a waste after all.

"Max, how is this possible?" Eleanore came running to assess the scale of the tragedy with her own eyes. She had sincerely believed that the training ground was the pinnacle of her creative energies: three-meter walls capable of withstanding any known or unknown magical attack. But not the magic of the ancients.

"It was an accident," I sighed. "I need the Evil Engineer and his crew. There's somewhere we need to infiltrate."

"Where?" Eleanore asked with interest. She personally overlooked anything concerning secret attacks, not trusting any of her assistants with such things.

"There." I dispelled the dome, causing another wave of rubble and dust, and immediately created a new structure, covering one of the nearest bushes with it. "The task is simple: there is a bush under the dome. It must be destroyed by any available means. By 'any' I mean everything that is in his arsenal. If he needs anything, we must provide him with it."

"All this noise and there's not even a battle?" Kimal Sarento asked as he joined us. Seeing the destroyed training ground, he only grinned: "So that's it, the secret training is over? Tell me, my mentor who brings chaos to this world, has this dome been modernized to my specifications?"

"There's a bush under it," I repeated. "The task is to destroy the bush. By any means necessary. No time limit. Shall we place bets?"

The people around us heard the word "bets" and went wild. Less than ten minutes after the Evil Engineer arrived, the odds that he would break this flimsy structure dropped to one to two. At the same time, the odds that the dome would hold up and nothing would happen to the bush were one to ten. Apparently, people didn't believe in me at all. Or they believed in the Evil Engineer too much.

Soon my former mentor arrived. He didn't come alone — his entire personal guard, including the son of the Kaliman Emperor, came in tow. Everyone wanted to take part in the popular pastime of "break the archduke." No one remembered that literally half an hour ago one of the city buildings had been destroyed. Everyone was interested in only one question: would this curmudgeonly gray human be able to do the impossible? Kimal Sarento brought the Evil Engineer up to date and stepped aside. Ostensibly so as not to interfere, but I knew perfectly well that he stepped aside so that he would not be inadvertently offered to take part in the destruction of an innocent bush. My cunning pupil had already realized that his magic was useless against my construction, and he did not want to lose face in front of the people. As if there was someone to lose face in front of...

It took the Evil Engineer thirty minutes to admit defeat. Eventually, the spectators even forgot that they were spectators and rushed to help the warriors, trying to tunnel underneath, shift the dome from its spot, or break it with a ladle. Despite the evening encroaching, everyone was having fun. Of course they were — the head of the city was such a powerful mage that no one could defeat his magic. How could they not rejoice that they had made the right decision to stay in Hearth? When I dispelled the dome, the bush remained intact. Sure, it had toppled, since the bottom of the dome cut off its trunk — I had not foreseen that a passage was needed. However, such a small detail didn't bother me. I'd only have to make a few minor adjustments and it would be perfect. The throngs of entertained townsfolk had been unable to dig under, or even move the dome an inch.

I was ready to pass through the rift!

Looking around at the happy faces of the townsfolk as they gleefully hugged each other, I realized that what they lacked was mundane, everyday joy. Ordinary human happiness, when you can have fun without thinking about the hard work that must be done or about the fact that there are scary dark humans in your city. Or that an entire army was besieging it.

"Eleanore, may I have a word with you?" I made my way over to my city manager, who was also standing in a state of strange pensiveness, looking at the people. Now they had forgotten who was light and who was dark. They were all simply residents of Hearth who had failed to break through their leader's shield.

"The people need a holiday," the manager suddenly said, anticipating my thoughts.

"They already have the carrot and the stick," chimed in Kimal Sarento, who had somehow snuck up on us. "They need a spectacle."

"Actually, that's what I wanted to talk to you about. We need to introduce some holidays."

"Great Light, what holidays, my hasty mentor?" Kimal Sarento even grimaced, as if he had swallowed something sour. "Eleanore, will you not listen to your superior and instead heed my voice of reason? We do not need holidays. There are enough of them in the Zarak Empire. What we really need is our own arena! Battles, circuses, theatrical performances, city events — there are many things that can be done in an arena. I'm surprised that it wasn't included in the original city plans."

"I agree. An arena with tens of thousands of seats will solve the issue of where to hold mass events. That's more or less what I was thinking. But the arena is a long way off, and people need to be entertained now. Tomorrow morning I'll send messengers to Turb, Al-Khorezm, and Olro to invite wandering musicians, comedians, harlequins, and other such wretched riffraff to Hearth."

"Eleanore!" Kimal Sarento exclaimed dramatically.

"That's my name, don't wear it out! And yes, they are hooligans, even in the Kaliman Empire! Useless corruptors of the populace, only able to amuse the crowd and nothing more. How can you take anyone seriously who has chosen the fate of a jester?"

"Not to be rude, my dear city manager, but you should rid yourself of your rift-conquering habits. I understand that eight years don't just fly by, but buffoons and jesters are also an important part of society. Without them, no matter how you look at it, it's hard to control the crowd. Because people are weak by nature and do everything in their power to avoid overwork. Right now, Hearth is more united than ever. Construction is still ongoing and we face external problems, but if we put even more pressure on the people, they'll start to break. Rest is just as important as work."

"I understand that perfectly well!" Eleanore snapped. "It's just...They're useless, Kimal! Parasites who leech off of a successful society! And the more successful the society, the more brazen these bastards are, trying to do things that have never before been seen. About twenty years ago, one such troupe came to our palace. Do you know what they did? They drew paintings with their asses! The people laughed as if they had never seen anything more hilarious in their lives. But this is nonsense. Complete nonsense, multiplied by madness! However, that artist seriously demanded that his creations be hung in the main halls of palaces, so that people could enjoy high art. So don't tell me that I don't understand something about entertainment. I don't understand why the crowd likes any nonsense. And it infuriates me beyond words."

She fell silent, looking on as the people cavorted. I just sighed, realizing that there was nothing more to say about the matter. Nevertheless, I had to say something. Something that the whole world seemed to be waiting for me to say:

"I'm going to the rift. I have food and water. I don't know when I will return. I'll try to make it before the coronation, but I can't promise anything."

"Not so fast, my hasty mentor. Before you disappear for who knows how long, you need to resolve two issues. The pope and your wives. You owe one a mysterious suitcase, and you need to discuss your future life with the others. You can't leave these issues for the future."

"Wives?" Eleanore asked, surprised.

"Oh, you still haven't heard," Kimal Sarento smiled. "I'm about to give you a juicy piece of gossip that will make all the artists in the world look like saints. So here's what our great Archduke has come up with…"

Chapter 5

AN IMPENETRABLE DOME covered the entrance to the rift, cutting me off from the outside world. Absolute darkness descended, but I was in no hurry to turn on the light crystal. It seemed I had reached a place where I could take a brief pause. Time to think over everything that had happened to me and decide how to live with it all now. Lying down on the ground, I closed my eyes, running through my three fateful meetings in my head again. The first had taken place this afternoon with my pope, the second had been with my wives, and the third with the Inquisitor. Yes, they were now my wives — I'd received permission from His Holiness to marry the light Alia, without breaking off my relations with the dark Naira. The pope even managed to surprise me by saying that he himself was considering the fact that I would need a light wife, but did not yet know how to approach this issue. The fact that I was concerned about him myself, and even planned to connect my life with Mother Alia, a protégé of the Church of the Light, made him incredibly happy.

After coming to an agreement with the pope and confirming it with a firm handshake, I went to Hearth. As it turned out, my two ladies hadn't waited for my return, and had already figured everything out amongst themselves. They pushed me against the wall and demanded I answer questions about how life would now proceed. I'd spend even nights with Alia, odd ones with Naira. No joint nights. Any decisions regarding the relationship could only be made collectively, no obligations or surprises. Whenever I was in the city, I was obliged to spend at least an hour with each of the wives. I can combine the meetings and see them both at once, but in that case, the time doubled. Each of my wives had the right to a two-month vacation to be alone or with her family. In addition, I must not forget, or rather, I was obliged to remember such important things as gifts and flowers. Both girls, it turned out, were extremely unhappy with the fact that in all this time I gave them only one set of jewelry. The one I stole from the Nocturnal Guild. Good husbands, as I was told, are obliged to take care of their wives and provide them with everything they need. And some small things: all social outings in Hearth would only take place with all three present — Alia on my right and Naira on my left. I would visit the dark ones with Naira and light ones with Alia. And I would try my best not to go anywhere at all. Anyone who needed something from me would be obliged to come knocking on their own. And the most striking condition was the library. A mandatory requirement of both wives. Hearth needed a library, where they would teach writing and languages (both light and dark), mathematics and other important sciences. Neither Naira nor Alia saw themselves as acting city leaders, but taking care of children, raising them to be kind and bright — that was always welcome. My women did not make concessions, they supported each other in every possible way, and in order not to fan the flame of conflict, I had to agree to their demands.

My third, and perhaps most important meeting had taken place not but twenty minutes prior. A conversation with the Inquisitor, for which I had to remove *Golden Dome of Protection*. The creature of Chaos clearly had some kind of grudge against me. As soon as I voiced my desire to take Alia as my wife, it immediately turned to aggression: it would punish me, kill me, destroy me — basically, I was forbidden from even breathing in Alia's direction. The Inquisitor's protests were moot. After I'd had to acquiesce to the demands of my wives, I didn't have much else to lose. I went on the counter attack. Chaos wanted balance? Let it create balance itself, Hearth washed its hands of the business! Chaos wants a human to act as a mediator between it, the Abyss and Pharapho? Let it find another, if it refused to allow this human to enjoy his fleeting life. Or did Chaos have plans for Alia? Did it want to place her on the snow-white throne of the Church of the Light? No? Then what was the reason for this refusal? Just because it can? We had a good screaming match. Or rather, I screamed and the Inquisitor played the role of an impenetrable rock, easily repelling any attacks. In the end, I could not stand it and, realizing the futility of further conversation, simply declared that I would take Alia as my wife as soon as I closed the level seventy-first rift. Whether the Inquisitor agreed to this or not made no difference to me. I, as the archduke of the only autonomous city in the world, was not going to ask permission to act from everyone I met. The Inquisitor continued to announce the terrible punishments that would befall the heads of those who disobey, but I did not listen to him. I activated the teleport right in front of the creature of Chaos and, without saying another word, left Hearth...Enough! I'd like to see them try to forbid me from doing something! I would involve His Holiness, and I would still end up getting my way!

My emotions subsided and I finally got to my feet. There were only a few minutes left before the rift opened, so I wondered if the metamorph would appear or not. On the one hand, Karina Fardi had recently been here, and she'd squashed a dangerous level-fifteen beast like it was a field mouse. On the other hand, the eternal fog that had enveloped these lands could force the metamorph to stay underground and not come out unless necessary. I really wanted the latter to be true — after all, the metamorph's rebirth time was seven days. I had only one unidentified ring and an amulet left, which would be used to adapt to invert and twist, whatever they were. The rot that began at level twenty-five was no threat in a full suit of mithril armor. Since I was fully protected, I planned to get to level forty, where the mysterious "invert" would begin, without any issue. Except that every five levels, I needed to catch another ousel to stuff in my steel box. Practice had shown how useful they could be. Twist would be present starting at level sixty and would prove another complication, and although it didn't apply to this rift, at level eighty-five I would encounter filth. According to the Abyss, filth is the pinnacle of its creativity. It is capable of destroying almost any material object, so I would have to crawl through the last fifteen levels of the level hundred rift completely naked. Filth would eat through mithril armor with ease.

Checking that my dome was stable and not going anywhere, just in case, I entered the rift. The difference between this rift and the other holes in the ground was immediately apparent: the lighting wasn't blue, but a filthy shade of green. All the rift crystals were coated in an unpleasant substance that looked like mold. Since this mold was everywhere, I scraped it off the crystal closest to me. Underneath it was a standard blue stone, but the mold immediately began to grow over the hole I'd formed. Moreover, the small piece that was on my finger tried to grow over my skin and envelop me entirely. The mithril armor did not allow it and the dirty green muck easily slid off. Looking at my legs, I saw a similar picture: my feet were sludgy with the mold, which was trying hard to seize me with a vice grip. It was as if it was alive and wanted to devour any person who fell into its clutches. But it didn't have the opportunity: Pharapho's flesh completely protected me.

In the first cave, the only dark creatures were a couple of rapses hiding on the ceiling, so I boldly delved in further. The dark mirror had been in its rightful place for a while, so I didn't expect any special problems. At least not at first...

What the Skron-damned soul of the Light!

My heart nearly broke when a monstrously distorted creature jumped from the ceiling at me. One might feasibly call it a rapse, but I couldn't bring myself to do so. While my mind was frozen in fear, my body reacted and with one deft blow pulled the essence out of the monster flying at me.

Obtained essence of a level 1 invert rapse.

The corpse thudded to the ground, where the dirty green mildew immediately began to engulf it. If this was a rapse, then I was Karina Fardi! What was a rapse? A small creature about the size of a medium dog, with a pillow-like body and four legs with three joints and tenacious fingers that allowed the creature to feel as at home on the ceiling as on the floor. The monster had no eyes, but it had a huge mouth filled with several rows of shark teeth. Once long ago, my first trophy from the rift had been the tooth of a rapse I had impaled with my spear. But this had been a rapse, beautiful and familiar. The creature that had just leapt at me looked like...like nothing. It was as if a mad butcher had taken to a rapse with a huge, blunt axe, hacking it inside out. How this creature was still alive, I did not understand. Naked bones that could not be pierced by ordinary steel, a bunch of organs hanging on veins or meat, rows of teeth like spikes that no longer served any purpose. The creature looked terrifying and at the same time did not look like easy prey at all. Even though most of its internal organs were now on the outside.

The green mold finished consuming the body, and the mound quickly flattened out. A few seconds later, there was no trace of the slain monster. I scraped off the mold to make sure. Even the solid bones were gone. The green infection continued its futile attempts to break through my defenses, so it was time for a small experiment. There was no point in hiding any longer anyway: the dark mirror had been useless against the invert beast.

My *Amplified Healing Aura* filled the space and I prepared for battle. I didn't try to limit my aura, setting the maximum radius. Auras didn't penetrate to other caves anyway — I'd checked many times. The rift jerked as if there was an earthquake. And not the tiniest of tremors. I think I even heard a distant roar of pain. The cave filled with the usual blue light — there was no trace left of the dirty green mold. But the most amazing thing is that the invert rapses no longer had any thought of attacking me, despite my light aura. Even when

I stood under one of them, the creature continued to hang on the ceiling, pretending with all its might that it was unbothered by the shift in circumstances. Jumping up, I thrust my glove into the creature, wanting to check whether it was alive or not. Judging by the fact that I got another essence, as well as a bunch of different alchemy materials, it had been. But for some reason, it didn't even think about attacking me. As if the *Healing Aura* not only didn't work to harm it, but also hid me from it somehow.

I began to form an idea of what the invert was and how to handle it. Everything I'd known about the previous rifts had been turned upside down and inside out. The dark mirror no longer hid me, but on the contrary, prompted aggression. *Heal* and *Healing Aura* no longer injured the creatures, but rather calmed them down and allowed me to hide. At the same time, there was still a dirty green mold threatening to fill the entire available space. The mold did not touch the rift creatures and burned under the influence of *Healing Aura.* Did I miss anything? If this had something to do with twist, then the mold alone would not do.

It was actually quite strange. Technically, infected rifts didn't exist anymore, so the boundaries between the different rift mechanics should be clear. I'd already gone through a level thirty rift — there wasn't even a hint of rot until level twenty-five. But this rift had all the mechanics you could possibly encounter from level one. Rapses belonged to the first twenty-five levels, the white fog

I just noticed was rot, the inside-out rapse was invert, and the dirty green mold was twist. This was normal for infected rifts, but clearly not for a regular creation of the Abyss. Although...technically, this rift had once been infected. Maybe there hadn't been time since the offworlders left our planet for things to return back to normal. Damn it! Once again, so many questions, so few answers. Everything I hated most in the world! Maybe I should pay the Abyss a visit? It probably knew what was going on here. No, still too early. I needed more input data.

I stood up and moved on. There was no point in sitting still and thinking about the meaning of existence. Even if everything was mixed up here because Pharapho was trying to stop the rift from developing, I still needed to get to the Riftmaster as quickly as possible. The rift wouldn't disappear on its own.

But the surprises just kept on coming. When I entered the second cave and cleared it of dirty green mold with *Healing Aura,* causing another earthquake, four kronas rushed at me. Regular kronas! Without any "inverted" features. But to keep me on my toes, in addition to the four standard kronas, there was also a group of invert kronas. I immediately recognized these creatures by their disgusting appearance. They didn't react to me in any way, continuing to stand silently to the side. They even ignored the aggressive behavior of their ordinary kin.

I couldn't ignore the attack. Yes, four level one

kronas wouldn't be able to harm me, but I couldn't let them gnaw at my armor. I had to spend time finishing off the toothy dogs, then free the cave from the invert kronas before plopping back down on the floor, feeling discouraged.

It seemed I had a temporary problem. The problem was that no matter which aura I turned on, dark or light, some of the creatures would immediately rush at me with a desire to devour me. In principle, it was not a problem, as the mithril armor offered a feeling of security, but my speed would be reduced to an absolute minimum. As if I was part of a group of ordinary rift cleansers, clearing cave after cave to make sure no beast was left alive.

Alright, there was one more method I was going to test in practice. I had a level 20 *Phantom* in stock, reinforced with several important support stones. This stone is what had allowed me to sneak into the papal palace, so I was confident in its quality and reliability. Why not use it in the rift, especially since the dirty green mold cast shadows everywhere? I needed to test it.

I switched *Healing Aura* off, and mold immediately began to crawl into the cave. *Analyze* said nothing about it, as if it did not exist at all, however, this nasty thing behaved as if it was controlled by a living creature. An extremely hungry and angry living creature. I activated the camouflage stone and went to the third cave. This time, the mold behaved strangely. When I stepped on it, it did not immediately rush up to absorb the unexpected guest, but bubbled near my feet, like boiling resin. The creature did not understand what to cling on to. It was as if it had eyes! The mold felt that someone was walking on it, but it did not see where exactly. So it bubbled in the hope that it could cling to the invisible body. If I didn't have mithril armor, this would have happened. This rift carefully guarded all its secrets and was ready for any type of conqueror. Dark, light, invisible. What it was definitely not ready for was that all three would be rolled into one, wearing a full armor of Pharapho flesh. The fog spawn conquered all!

The crowns and rapses, both regular and invert, didn't pay any attention to me. My *Phantom* was too high level. Leaving the monsters alive, I began to go through cave after cave, looking for a descent to the second level. It seemed to be going well! Of course, at level twenty there would come a time when my stone would be useless — the level twenty creatures would see me, but I would need to reach that level first.

It was as if I had seen into the future! When I reached the descent, I hung there for a while, assessing the unexpected obstacle:

Twist Plop. First-level rift creature.

There was no passage down. Or rather, there was one, but it was hidden beneath a huge dirty-green seething mass, similar to my dome from a distance. The plop generated mold and filled the entire level with it. This creature had no mouth, no eyes, no limbs of any kind. However, *Analyze* suggested that with a high degree of probability (because someone had encountered plops before, but not twist plops) this creature had three hearts. Just like a Metamorph. So, the blow had to be lightning fast, with both hands at once, to be sure to remove two of the three essences. Then it would be the plop's turn to attack, and my task was to survive.

Wait! Why was I thinking from the perspective of a melee fighter again? It had already been proven that the twist creature had a negative response to *Healing Aura.* In this, it was similar to the creatures I'd met in the arena of the Fog. Why should I get enmired in hand-to-hand combat if I could step back and do what I did better than almost anyone in this world? Heal!

I saw no point in putting off my amazing idea any longer. Skirting around the beast and moving back a bit, I aimed my palm in its direction, though this had stopped being necessary for me long ago, and I cast two *Heal*s, one after the other. The rift trembled again, and this time I understood why: the plop had been extremely insensed by my vile and treacherous blow. Instead of engaging in hand-to-hand combat, I'd snuck up and attacked from behind. If that creature even had a behind.

The creature wet mad. It was twitching, emitting an unpleasant high-pitched howl, which even caused my armor to temporarily turn off external sounds, it was stretching up several meters high, then falling almost to the floor. I was in no hurry to use more healing magic. I wanted to see its reaction. After thirty seconds, all the mold was sucked back into the plop, clearing the level, and the creature began to pulsate strangely, expanding more and more with each passing moment. I had already seen something similar before — Pharapho sergeants always exploded before they died. scattering the remains of their bone armor around the area. A kind of last-chance bomb. Such was the case here. At one point, the plop's twitching reached a critical frequency, and it exploded, scattering its flesh around the cave. *Golden Dome of Protection* held back the main mass, not allowing it to reach the body, and the green fog that mixed with the fog of rot blocked the mithril armor. The blue crystals that the flesh of the plop fell on began to melt, as if a whole bucket of strong acid had been poured on them. I could only gulp: any person who would have come to this level in standard steel armor would have died from poisoning. I was so used to the fact that the blue crystals were an invariable part of the rift that I did not even think that it was possible to interact with them and somehow harm them. The twist plop had given me new information, and I couldn't say that I was happy about it.

On the first level of the rift: 142 nox, 43 chrone, 12 chabre, 1 yem were found. Would you like to absorb?

It was hard to describe my surprise. The first level of any rift was known for containing only green nox crystals. Everything else was mined from higher levels. Chrona from the third, chabre from the fifth, and yem was a resource mined from guards! Where did all of this come from? However, *Devour* didn't make mistakes. It assessed the level that I managed to pass and displayed all the resources available for absorption. Deciding that there must be an accidental error in the description, I agreed to absorb, and the entire list, exactly as described, fell into my inventory. This was when I lost any mental grip I'd had on the situation. If this wasn't an error, what was it? How could this rift be so muddled and mixed up? It was as if some madman had added all the mechanics and levels into one big jar, shook it vigorously and poured it into the ground, calling the result a level-seventy-one rift. There was no logic, none of the usual rules, no order whatsoever. And the exploding plops capable of destroying every living thing in its wake were just level one! That wasn't how it was supposed to work! The difficulty should increase from floor to floor, but instead it immediately made me aware that I was not welcome.

Sighing, still not having drawn any helpful conclusions, I approached the passage. The mold hadn't crawled up from the second level, but for some reason, I had no doubt that everything would be similar on the second level. The same mold, two types of creatures in each cave, a white fog of rot capable of eating away at everything living and inanimate (except for the beasts themselves, for some reason), as well as a pulsating plop in the last cave. And I still had seventy floors of the same ahead of me, diluted with all sorts of metamorphs, guards, splashes and Wardens. I'd likely spend the next week and a half in this endlessly exhilarating environment.

On that thought, why I hadn't I considered it before: how was I supposed to eat while completely surrounded by rot? I'd have to open my visor and the mold would definitely take advantage of the opening...Damn it! Another problem to be solved. But not right now. First, I needed to reach at least level twenty. And do it without the rings that I've already stuffed into my immaterial backpack. I needed to adapt to the darkness without crutches, as Pharapho had called them. That was the only way I could fight Karina Fardi on equal terms.

I wondered if she could survive here. If so, how?

Chapter 6

WHAT COULD BE SAID about my progress through the next thirty levels? Only that Pharapho was a being with whom, if I was going to do business, I'd have to deal very carefully. Why? Because he'd had the audacity to say that I would not be able to escape from the rift, since the magic of the ancients didn't not work here. In part, he had been right: forming a portal to escape wouldn't work. Apparently, only the supreme converts had an operational system for moving throughout the rifts. But everything else worked flawlessly! Especially my spear, which pierced through the poor dark beasts without a question about their origin. Common, infected, inverted, twist — my weapon easily dealt with each. I even stepped out of the shadows and ceased to be invisible, as I no longer saw any need. I walked into the room with *Healing Aura,* burning through the dirty green mold, and then launched my spear. The dumb beasts paid no attention to the weapon — a flying stick, who cared? They were punished for their ignorance. On average, I had to spend about thirty seconds per cave, forcing the spear to fly from one to the next, forming fairly large holes through their bodies. However, even despite their serious wounds, the monsters did not die — they fell to the floor, suffered from the immediate rot infection, and yet still they struggled to reach me. I simply ignored them. More precisely, I skipped over the ordinary ones, stopping only near the magical, elite and exclusive ones. Essences and alchemy materials fell into my inventory, after which I moved on. Only once did I decide to linger to see what would happen to the creatures of the Abyss. If there was an ordinary rift here, nothing would have happened to them, but in this upside-down world, where all the mechanics were mashed into one, it did not leave its damaged offspring the right to salvation. Rot did its dirty work, corroding still living bodies. And, as unpleasant as it was to admit, my spear as well. It only lasted two levels, after which the white fog achieved its goal and my creation fell to the floor as a pile of decayed remains.

The metamorph, as I found out, was alive, and was in the last cave of the level, along with a twist plop similar to the one I'd already encountered blocking the passage to the next floor. I had to spend some time examining the creature, trying to understand from which side to approach it. It was invert, meaning that all its internal organs were positioned on the outside. It looked like a boiled sausage with a split skin. All that considered, its dark aura had increased. I'd found it on just the fifteenth floor, but the aura nevertheless weighed on my body as if it was at least level thirty. I didn't find it necessary to deal with adapting to the darkness at that exact moment, so with a *Dash* I was by its side, thrusting my hands into the center, trying to avoid the organs. I didn't like the hue — it was far too unhealthy. They looked less like organs and more like tumors filled with poisonous rot. Who knew what I'd find in a rift like this!

This was how my descent generally went: I'd clear the room with a spear, skewering anything with a valuable essence inside, and move on. And this continued until I stood rooted to the spot, unable to continue the descent. Another spear broke and was swallowed by rot, so the rest of the creatures in the level thirtieth cave had to be finished off with *Dark Thorn* and the mithril glove. I even took a few steps into the last cave, where the plop that closed the passage was located, but my body was instantly wracked with monstrous pain — the darkness had finally caught up with me. I didn't have any rings to block the influence and had made it to level thirty on sheer will alone. But everything had a limit, including my heroism. Switching on *Healing Aura* to drive the mold out of the cave, I sat down by the wall and wearily closed my eyes, periodically illuminating my form with *Heal.* According to the Abyss, the support stone combined with the ability should ease the suffering, but I hadn't noticed any difference. With or without the healing magic, I felt equally terrible.

"How are you faring?" I heard Kimal Sarento's voice in my ear. "Already at level fifty, I suppose?"

"Thirty. I'm sitting and taking in the local fauna."

"Yes, I saw the notebook. Eleanore is showing us the pictures and reading out their stats like a fantasy novel. Not great that you haven't reached level fifty yet, but getting through only thirty of such an unusual rift isn't bad for the first day. What about the loot?"

"Are you serious right now?!" I said angrily. "Can you ever think about anything but profit?"

"But you feel better now, don't you?" Kimal Sarento chuckled, making me shut up. Indeed, anger helped me cope with my current state. I was even able to take a deep breath. Of course, anger was not the best way to conquer rifts, but it helped me out in a pinch. I was finally able to get to my feet and, checking the lists in my immaterial inventory, created a small dome around myself. It was dark, but when I turned my light stone on, I liked what I saw. There was no hint of fog inside. Just in case, I cast *Healing Aura* several times, driving out all the remnants of the corrosive stuff, and opened my visor. There was no burning sensation. Pulling out a piece of bread, I held it in the air. If the rot was hiding somewhere under the dome, it would definitely pounce on the food. Nothing happened: the bread remained whole.

Thus the food problem was solved, but I couldn't enjoy the peace under the dome for long: the thirtieth-level rot ate away the dome I had formed in an hour. By that time I had managed to do everything vital and even lie down to get a little rest. By the time important things and lie down to rest. When the dust fell on me, I was already asleep. Thirty levels in a day was really a good result for any rift conqueror. Especially since I'd had to work, and couldn't stroll past all the dark beasts as usual. The next seven days were more of the same: work. Hard with a hint of sadomasochism, but still just work. On average, I managed to pass through five levels a day. My body couldn't handle more. On top of that, I had to sleep at a level higher than what I could currently handle, and where my body had not yet fully adapted, I could not rest. Starting from the thirty-fifth level, I declared open season on ousels, but the very first attempt showed how futile this undertaking was. At such a depth, the rot was so concentrated that the steel box was corroded before I had time to stuff the yellow orb inside. After losing all of my boxes, I kicked the poor ousel in frustration, causing it to attack me. The ousel, which I had nicknamed "flying death" for its speed and miniscule size, gave me a few minutes of unpleasantness as it deftly dodged my blows and constantly struck sparks from the *Golden Dome of Protection*. It seemed I was consistently unlucky in this regard, and I would continue to be in the future. In order to find high-level ousels, I'd need to create an additional device for the mithril to integrate. They couldn't survive in separate boxes, so they'd have to be stored in the armor itself. Now I just had to figure out how to limit their dark aura, as the mithril armor didn't protect against darkness.

At level forty, new creatures began to appear. Those that were directly related to invert mechanics. Unlike the disfigured kronas, rapses, and even the metamorph, these ones looked practically normal. In any case, they didn't make me want to puke. However, the speed, strength, and durability of these bastards was so enormous that it required one spear for every cave. I had so few materials left that I had to go back to my original version and make a spear from what was at hand. I was already feeling poorly, and now after each cave I had to take a long break to piece myself back together. This slowed down my already sluggish descent even more, but I had no other choice. Starting from level forty, the beasts had no reaction to either my dark mirror or *Healing Aura*. As soon as I appeared in the cave, everything in it dropped whatever important business they were attending to and tried to eat me whole. It wasn't ideal, of course, but it was perfectly tolerable.

At least, it was tolerable until level sixty, which I reached a week into the process. As soon as I entered twist territory, my speed dropped to barely a crawl. As soon as I descended the spiral staircase into the first cave of level sixty, my body locked up. Neither rage nor healing magic helped. Nothing helped. My only saving grace was the fact that the cave was practically empty. The only thing there was the mold, which had turned from a dirty green to just green. Bright, acidic and poisonous. The dome I placed around myself lasted only ten seconds. However, those ten seconds allowed me to turn around and take a few steps back up to level fifty-nine. Of course, I didn't go far and as soon as the dome dissipated, I fell face down, but I was on the right track. My head fell into the upper part of the pathway, where the influence from the sixtieth level was not as great.

It took me a day to come to my senses and crawl back up. I spent most of that time unconscious, and as soon as I left the darkness of level sixty behind, I felt a wild hunger. The dome on this floor lasted five minutes, which allowed me to gobble up a ton of food and also assess my condition. I was once again barely more than a desiccated mummy. Even *Heal* didn't help: my body was dehydrated to the point of exhaustion. It was a blessing that I had a lot of fluids — they drained into my body as if into desert sand. The gap between these two levels was truly colossal.

"In case you've forgotten, my absent-minded mentor, the coronation of our beloved empresses is set to take place in four days," Kimal Sarento's voice rang out in my head. He had been careful not to bother me for several days, knowing perfectly well how complex the process of rift conquering could be. All information about my suffering (actually, just information about new beasts, environmental features and the loot I'd obtained) was automatically transferred to the notebook kept in Hearth's treasury. Eleanore, as its keeper, recounted my progress, so everyone was aware of my successes. Only Alia and Naira periodically contacted me and told me how much they loved me. Apparently, Kimal Sarento demanded that they express their support.

"I'm afraid it will have to go on without me," I tried to say, but no articulate sounds came out. Only a wheeze.

"I see the feats of heroism have begun," he said with a note of concern. "How bad is it? On a scale of one to ten where one is, 'I'm more alive than I've ever been,' and ten is, 'so bad that it's already too late to write a will,' how would you evaluate your condition? Cough the appropriate number of times."

Thinking for a moment, I coughed nine times. Speaking was painful and nearly caused my throat to spasm. Even breathing ached.

"You know, my heroically inclined mentor, my words will probably sound unusual and unconventional, but you should come back. Sit for another day on the last level available to you, try to acclimatize, then come back. The rift will still be there tomorrow, as well as the day after. The world will not collapse, regardless of whether you choose to conquer this now or a little later, once you've recovered. From the sound of it, you may not be long for this world. You've already done what your distant ancestor could not. His limit was level fifty-five. You're already on fifty-nine, and twelve floors remain, but you need to approach them with more time to spare. Apparently, Pharapho was right when he said that adaptation would be more difficult with each new level. And I am not the only one who shares this opinion. Your wives are silent, of course, but the way they look at me, mentally begging me to get you out of there, speaks volumes. And don't forget: we have found the perfect way to fight Fardi, despite her monstrous speed. So stop pretending to be the savior of the world and get out of that rift tomorrow."

Kimal Sarento's words were so surprising that I even felt a little better. Apparently, my body hadn't been able to relax because of the constant thoughts about the last twelve levels. It was embarrassing to admit, but my wise pupil was right: in my current state, level sixty was impossible for me. And this was despite the darkness blocking rings that I'd returned to my fingers long ago. If it weren't for them, I wouldn't have even gotten here. And not only because of the darkness, but also because of the monsters. As it turned out, true invert beasts had the extremely unpleasant ability to worm into your brain and generate images there, driving you crazy. Only a miracle allowed me to survive the first such attack. A miracle called mithril armor. Pharpho's flesh proved its worth as the ultimate suit of armor. If it could also block darkness, it would be priceless.

In that vein, what could block darkness? I already had one solution — the shield I'd used to stop Karina Fardi. The stone dome appeared around me, and for five sweet minutes, it was as if a granite boulder had been lifted from my shoulders. The rot began to devour my creation, but it was too slow. Five minutes of absolute calm. Of course, there were some serious flaws in the design: it was impenetrable, meaning that even oxygen didn't pass through and, as has already been stated, it was susceptible to the effects of rot. Nevertheless, even five minutes away from the level fifty-nine influence was a miracle. I wished I could slap a pair of legs on the dome and send it into the rift...Hold on! That *was* an idea, no matter how wild it may seem!

Okay, let's figure this out. I had an impenetrable dome that could protect against the dark influence up to level 100. At least, that was what it was designed to do.

Problem: the dome was static and not designed to move. Solution: actually there was one option: I could use the same flight syntax I had used for the spear.

Problem: In order to use the flight syntax, I needed to see where to send the object. The dome was impenetrable. Solution: I'd need to make a small hole.

Problem: the darkness would seep in through the hole. Solution: use a system of mirrors. After all, the darkness from the lower levels does not penetrate through the descent? It is only active near the passage, but a few meters from the stairs it is not so mobile. So if I moved as far away from the hole as possible and peered out through the system of mirrors, it should work.

Problem: The lifespan of the dome I created at level sixty was only ten seconds. Solution... I needed a solid shell that would protect my creation from the harmful effects of rot, invert and twist. What should I make it out of? The answer, as much as I would have hoped otherwise, was obvious: mithril. I would have to indicate my armor as the source of the material, covering the entire structure with a thin layer. It should work.

Problem: even if I was able to maneuver around the level, all the descents were caulked shut by plops. Solution: in addition to the dome, I'd need to be able to control the spears. Since I wouldn't have mithril armor, I'd no longer have my immaterial inventory. This meant that in addition to the mirror system, I'd have to house a huge pile of spear-making materials under the dome.

Problem: the spears would dissolve before they reach their target. Solution: craft them from rift materials mined at high levels. I'd just have to make it past level sixty and absorb all the materials from the level. This would be horrendously wasteful, since no one had ever collected resources from so deep, but I didn't have much of a choice. This would reduce the amount of material I'd have to keep under the dome.

Problem...Solution...

It took me a while to convince myself that this plan would work. I even had to recruit a group from Hearth to help. Kimal Sarento, Eleanor, and even my wives tried to dissuade me from the idea, but when they realized the futility of this undertaking, they began to help. They even brought in the Defender, who designed the mirror system. Eleanore passed it along to me by adding a new paragraph to her notebook. We considered every angle, from the amount of air available, oxygen conserving breath techniques, to the optimal shape of the dome. Mithril was a fairly strong material, of course, but if it was constantly grating against rock and defending against beasts trying to rip it apart, the *Integrity* would instantly drop to zero. Given the circumstances, and the creatures surrounding me, the ideal shape would be a sphere. That way, I could roll in any direction, and if something obstructed my visibility and I couldn't see the next point to travel to, I could roll out of the way like a hamster in a ball. Moreover, when used midair, my *Golden Dome of Protection* formed a perfect sphere, which would surround the ball and allow me to somehow protect the *Integrity* of the mithril. When I naively asked how a level thirty-one protection would fare against level sixty rift beasts, Kimal Sarento only smirked and asked me to carefully study the artifacts I had obtained.

Were the golden pieces of paper on which the recipes for creating level-raising elixirs that the Temple of Skron had given me really useless? They had been before, as no one alive today had the resources from which these elixirs could be created. But now, with fifty-nine levels under my belt, all which had been sucked dry by *Devour*, I had no such limitations. I could pump *Heal, Healing Aura* and *Golden Dome of Protection* all the way to level fifty, which would allow me to…well, to accomplish incredible things! Even passing through all forty waves of the Fog Stalker's arena!

The Defender redesigned the mirror system again, and also found the most efficient construction for my sphere. Particular attention was paid to the viewing hole and protection from the dark influence that would break in. The mechanoid decided to take full responsibility for the design. Soon, Eleanore had drawn a diagram of a small, closed box with a mirror system. Considering that my design could, at any moment, be flipped over with the viewing hole on the bottom, I would require at least four of them.

Plopping down next to the descent to the lower level, I started crafting. First, the most difficult component: the boxes covering the viewing holes and the built-in system of mirrors. The syntax for the mirror I found among the *Author* recipes, so I had no problems constructing the phrase. What proved more difficult was placing all the sentence elements in the correct order. The mechanoid indicated the necessary angles, but for a long time I could not find a suitable verbal construction to ensure that these angles were maintained. I spent a whole day on the box alone, however, when the result was finally achieved, building it in was no problem. As well as turning the dome into a sphere. I put off the final touch for as long as possible — covering my ball with mithril. I even had to conduct several tests, creating the *Thunderer* set and, before the rot devoured it, covering the hull with metal. It seemed to work, but in my case the mithril still needed to be made transparent for my viewing holes to work.

In total, it took me almost three days to finally make sure I was prepared to do the impossible. Kimal Sarento delicately hinted several times that the coronation would take place tomorrow and that not attending would be tantamount to political suicide, so either I would destroy the rift or I might never return from it again. He did not give me any other choice. Just in case, after forming the final version of the dome, I tried to eat all the remains of food that I had in five minutes. My body had even slowly begun to recover, and in the three days I'd spent on level fifty-nine, I'd stopped resembling a hollowed-out mummy. Now I was just someone in the advanced stages of anorexia. The rot once again devoured the stone, and, taking a deep breath, I began to work magic. Or madness — whichever you prefer.

Jumping up to ensure that I was in the center of my structure, I began to craft one phrase after another, starting with the outer shell. My body was immediately enveloped in bitter cold. The temperature at such a depth was bone-chilling. It was dark for a few moments, but soon light began to break through the four holes and mirror system. I landed on the stones that formed in the inner layer of the sphere. It was still freezing, but I was glad for it. It distracted me from fear. Regardless of my preparations, I was terrified. There was no turning back. If my plan didn't work and the darkness of level sixty broke through, there would be nothing left of me. The rings would not help. But I couldn't sit there waiting for long. According to the Defender, there was only enough air to last eight hours. Barely enough to pass through twelve hours.

And we were off!

I didn't use the *flight* syntax right away, instead rolling myself forward like a hamster. *Golden Dome of Protection* was already in place, enveloping my ball with an additional layer of protection. After I grew accustomed to the controls, I was able to find the next descent quite quickly and, resting my hands and feet on the stone, used magic to pull myself to the steep slope.

At that point, gravity and physics came into play. It was like I was a kid again, a decade ago when my brothers and I used to push each other down hills in barrels. Of course, I was always the guinea pig, but my brothers would also take turns. The feeling was not entirely pleasant, but quite familiar. The only factor I didn't account for was crashing into the wall at full speed and, despite bracing myself with my legs and arms, being smeared across the inner surface of the sphere. *Heal* helped — I wasn't interested in moving forward with broken arms and legs. I spent a few minutes trying to figure out my current position, whether the darkness was affecting me or not. Currently, it didn't seem to be. There was no burning in my chest, my head was clear, my body was responding to my commands. Perhaps the cold grew a little more bitter, but the difference was minor. With the help of mirrors, I managed to unlock the map of the cave and, having located the exit, I began to roll my ball in that direction. Turned out, I'd make a pretty good hamster!

The beasts paid no attention to me. I didn't even have to use the spear: the monsters were indifferent to the incomprehensible two-meter stone sphere that had rolled into their cave. It rolled by, and continued rolling — what was so special about that? The protection I created not only blocked the darkness, but also protected me from the monsters, even better than the dark mirror. I only had to defend myself once, when I accidentally caught an unknown beast in my *Golden Dome of Protection* — here, on the sixtieth level of the rift, there were no common dark beasts. The spear helped, but it only lasted for a few seconds. Just enough to make a hole in the nimble creature. I had to switch the stone off so as not to provoke the others, once again orient myself in space and move on. On the unpleasant side, my communication device had disappeared along with my mithril armor, so I could only relay my experiences through my notebook. But of course, I had no time for that. Nor any desire.

In the final cave of the floor, as on all the floors above, there was a twist plop. I solved this issue in the most banal way: I simply drove over it. The plop was completely unprepared for the load and simply burst. I barely had time to rest before I was on the sixty-first level, and *Devour* happily informed me that it was ready to absorb a mountain of unusual resources with names I had never even heard before. There were no recipes that mentioned them!

Half an hour per level — that was my top speed. The Warden, who was located on the seventieth level, turned out to be a huge snake that encircled the entire cave. I moved forward and ran into it several times, forcing the rings to twitch. Like all the creatures above, this one did not see me as a living being. Just some kind of stone that rolled from wall to wall. The only place where I lingered was the cave with the guards. It could barely be called a cave — it was a massive and completely unoccupied space that was so rugged and twisted that it was impossible to drive through. I had to use my improvised flight: choose a place, move the structure there, choose the next place. The roar was terrible: the stones under my ball were crumbling, several times I had to crawl out of deep holes, but fortunately, the beasts continued to ignore me. Even when I entered the last room, where the Rift Master of this insane creation was located, they paid no more attention to me than if I was inanimate rock.

You already have a map of this location. Due to the fact that the rift level is greater than or equal to 70, a map improvement has been added: places of origin of magic stones, ruins with an active Pharapho core, minerals, habitats of altered creatures, transport hubs, stor-

age of ancients, locations of artifacts. Total improvements: 7 out of 10.

Obtained 7 *Amplify* stones.

The map updates and new magic stones were certainly useful, but the most valuable loot was the small metal cylinder that appeared in my hand.

A device for increasing the level of the rift has been obtained. To begin working with the mechanism, you must undergo preliminary training.

The ball crumbled into fine dust. All the dark influence had disappeared along with the Rift Master. There was no rot, no invert, no twist. Nothing at all, except for the mithril crumbs on the floor, which I gazed upon sadly. I feared it would be impossible to collect. I'd have to ask Kimal Sarento to work to turn thirty units of bone armor into mithril armor with all the improvements. Without them, as practice shows, it was difficult to do any work. The rift had lost whatever property had blocked the ancients' magic, which allowed me to create a portal to Hearth. But I didn't portal there yet. Above me were at least thirty floors with frozen creatures of various mechanics. I could no longer obtain essences from them, but the resources, especially such high-level ones and in such quantities, would do my city good. So it was time to get to work. This rift wouldn't plunder itself!

Chapter 7

"I, ZURGAN THE FIRST, abdicate the throne in favor of my daughter Marisa Shub and niece Miralda Vyazemsky. Rule with dignity and achieve prosperity for the Zarak Empire!"

The ceremonial abdication and coronation took place on the same day. In the same minute, essentially. As soon as Zurgan abdicated the throne, the masters of ceremonies — of which we had to hire many — placed crowns on four heads: Marisa the First, Miralda the First and their spouses, Herbert Shub and Georgy Vyazemsky. Both weddings, as I learned, had taken place in the presence of an intimate circle of family members several days ago.

I was there alone. Alia had gone to Father Urg and was enthusiastically discussing something with him, not paying attention to the ceremony.

Kimal Sarento had disappeared into the hall half an hour ago, and during this time I'd only caught a glimpse of him a couple of times. He was basking in the attention and enjoying arranging his next insidious schemes. It would have been stupid to interfere with this. Several times, strangers intended to approach me, obviously with the goal of starting some particularly important conversation, but when they crossed the "forbidden line," they ran into my glowering gaze and the darkness of a fifth level of ousel. The radius was small, only two meters, but this was enough to create an empty space around me. People weren't keen on standing in a space where they lost all control over their bodies. It had been proven in practice: one naive young man had already been carried away. Clearly unable to adapt to the darkness of the rifts. And I wasn't in the right condition to be holding all sorts of meetings. The fact that I'd shown up for the coronation was already a miracle — it would take my dried-out body several weeks, if not a month to recover, and there was nothing I could do about it. Neither *Heal* nor the abundance of food helped.

But, to be honest, there were few who wanted to talk to me. For the Zarak Empire, I was a dangerous and little-studied entity with monstrous powers. For example, I had already called over the colonel of the secret chancery of His Imperial Majesty, Slovan Usminsky, twice, and indicated a high-born guest to him. I had no intention of showing pity or covering for anyone: if the converts were so stupid as to show up for the coronation, that was their problem. *Analyze* allowed me to identify the creatures who had sold out to Skron without fail. The investigators of the Empire and the Fortress approached the people I had pointed out, took them aside, and no one saw these corrupt freaks again. Tomorrow, there would be two new fires blazing in Hearth, if not more. I was sure that the inquisition would thoroughly investigate the converts' families, searching for traitors to the Light. It had been a huge blunder, allowing converts to infiltrate the solemn ceremony. A disgrace and dishonor to our Dark Inquisition. Although, considering that Father Nor was not among them, it was not surprising that they were unable to cope with such a task. Sniffing out converts required a special nose.

"Ladies and Gentlemen, it's time to greet your empresses!"

Here it was, the moment for which Kimal Sarento had dragged me here — time to hand out gifts. A vital and intrinsic part of the event, rooted in nothing more than human greed. In fact, as the master of an autonomous city, I didn't care much for the ceremony. I wouldn't give up Hearth, I didn't need to seek the favor of the empresses or their families, so I shouldn't go out of my way. However, my persistent and meticulous pupil had convinced me that I absolutely must prepare gifts, and that they must be the best this world had to offer. So extravagant that all the clans of the Zarak Empire would understand the greatness of Hearth and its inhabitants. So that they would fear us and at the same time want to work with us. Because we were unique!

The first to arrive, of course, were the representatives of the families. Counts Shub and Vyazemsky needed to demonstrate their power to the entire upper echelon of the aristocracy, who currently ran the show in the Zarak Empire. As soon as the herald's call sounded, the central doors opened and servants began to drag chests with various valuables into the room. Gold, jewelry, trinkets, and in a separate, smaller box, they even brought several level-ten magic stones. Level ten! How much had the counts spent to acquire such precious gems? Tarra Loyd, the current head of the magic academy, was extremely unwilling to part with her property. Somehow, she surpassed even her predecessor in greed. Rumors of her tight-fistedness had reached Hearth, about how it was impossible to squeeze any decent, high-level stone out of her. Not to mention any facet-adding or level-raising elixirs, of which Hearth had recently established a trade supply. It wasn't a huge supply, of course, since my recipes were very limited, but the fact that the magic academy received something of such value from us, and at a reasonable price, finally made them our ally. Although Tarra Loyd was already considered one of Kimal Sarento's people.

To the enthusiastic roar of the crowd, first Count Vyazemsky, then Count Shub began to list the gifts from the families. Clearly, this was part of the ritual — all the proceeding gift-givers had to voice their contributions aloud. The servants continued to carry chests and trunks into the main hall. I couldn't help but shift slightly to peer back through the open doors, where a line of servants bearing gifts stretched around the corner and was lost somewhere in the bowels of the palace. Apparently, there was some kind of unspoken order of greeting the empresses that had been established before the ceremony. As was easy to guess, there was a hierarchy among the donors. The Vyazemsky and Shub families were first, the highest aristocracy, the common aristocracy, large industrialists, friends, servants, beggars and the disadvantaged, pets, sewage, and at the very end, the representative from the autonomous city of Hearth, Archduke Valevsky. I could not explain what was happening in any other way. Those who had coped with their task walked away contentedly, joining the group of people that was growing larger and larger with each passing minute.

Finally, there were only three people left. Myself, Alia, who had come here as my companion, and Kimal Sarento.

"It seems our turn has come, my patient mentor," Kimal Sarento said cheerfully, as if nothing out of the ordinary was occurring. Everyone craned their necks to see what the servants would bring into the hall, but no one rushed inside bearing chests or velvet pillows. Especially impatient guests, despite their rank, even went to the door and looked into the corridor. There really was nothing there.

"Marisa and Miralda the First!" I came closer to the throne and delivered a speech that had been prepared for me in advance. Kimal Sarento had to get his kicks somewhere, while I was rolling in my hamster ball along the seventy-first level rift, didn't he? "You are taking the reins of the empire at a very difficult time. A time of change. A time when monstrous and unprecedented events are taking place, the likes of which have not been seen since the time of the first emperor. You must become strong. And no, I did not misspeak: I meant 'become.' Right now, you are not strong enough. That is why I am here. To make you strong."

A deathly silence fell over the room. It wasn' every day that someone tells the heads of state that they were weak. The look that both empresses gave me was too pointed. They had apparently already grown accustomed to their role and accepted it completely. It was an unpleasant look. A look of submission. Resignation to their fate. And now I suddenly said something that stands out from the orderly row of their future gray everyday life. Strength! What was this strength? What was this crazy Valevsky talking about? What was the man who saved us talking about now? Ensuring that my words were understood correctly, I continued, trying not to smile.

"Please accept this gift from Hearth, my empresses!"

With these words, I drew two red velvet cushions with magic stones, glowing with a bright, crimson light, from my new immaterial inventory.

Two for each. Judging by the way the faces of the people standing in front of me lengthened, the effect was achieved. Both Shub and Vyazemsky, the old foxes, could hardly restrain themselves from snatching the gift from me and running away with it to a secret room, where they could sort everything out in peace and safety. If it were possible to move objects with a glance, I was one hundred percent sure that they would already be in the hands of these greedy advisers. Double "no" and triple "ha" to you, gentlemen. Let's see how straight a face you can keep after the next one!

"As everyone here knows, the Zarak Empire was recently attacked by the lithoids. My great disciple and I had to intervene to stop them, but as practice shows, we cannot be everywhere at once. Sometimes, various situations occur that require my presence and I have to leave. I can't even imagine what would have happened to the Zarak Empire if we hadn't appeared in time, but now there won't be such a problem. We have solved it. Hearth gifts each Empress two exclusive level-fifty magic ability stones with eight facets, as well as instructions on which support stones are best suited for improving them. Moreover, Hearth presented the empresses with these very stones, although only of the thirtieth level, but even this is enough to create *Diamond Defense*, allowing you to block any magical, physical or poisonous damage, and *Spear of Light* is able to hit and destroy any enemy that stands in your way. I understand that the current magical power of the empresses may not be enough to actively use these stones, so Hearth has solved this problem as well. Each of my empresses will receive a hundred gallo stones. In ten years, you will be able to completely integrate all of them, using the altar of enhancement, which is in the treasury of the imperial palace, and you will become the strongest mages in this world. No one will ever be able to threaten you. You will become empresses who rule the Zarak Empire wisely, without casting a second glance to any external influences.

Kimal Sarento and Alia each took another velvet pillow out of their backpacks. My pupil had support stones, my future wife had the gallo crystals, each of which gave ten development points. It was established through experience that no more than ten crystals could be used per year, but even a hundred development points would make the empresses the strongest people in the empire, capable of resisting the influence of their new relatives. However, our performance did not end there. Simply giving gifts to the empresses was like handing them over to the old foxes who would pocket our gifts and say that they had earned them. Servants rushed to us to take away the most valuable items, the cost of which was comparable if not to the entire Zarak Empire, then certainly to half of it, but no such luck. As if by magic, our gifts disappeared, returning to the immaterial backpacks. The final round had begun.

"My empresses, I don't beat around the bush, so I will be straight with you: the gifts of Hearth are too valuable and dangerous a resource to be given to anyone for uncontrolled use. Even you. Therefore, for now, the stones will remain with me. As soon as you decide that you are ready to integrate them into your magical field, we will appear and help you with this process. Our gift is intended for you, and you alone. Not your husbands, not your advisers. If you decide that you are not ready to accept such a heavy burden, my gift will remain with me. Hearth recognizes the authority of only three people. Its immediate ruler — me — and my empresses. Now, instead of stones and crystals, each of you will receive a communication device. With its help, you will be able to contact me at any time and express your will. Hearth will be ready to fulfill it."

Kimal Sarento embodied the next pillow, on which lay two oblong objects made of mithril. Yesterday, my eternally lazy pupil had been forced to sweat a little as he created me a new set of armor and additional devices for it. Including remote communication devices. A similar item was also given to Father Urg (Alia had given it to him), as well as Tarra Loyd, the rector of the magic academy. The ability to communicate remotely was worth a lot, and Hearth was going to actively make money on this, issuing devices to new participants. But first, I needed to advertise, which the empresses, Father Urg, and Tarra Loyd would do for me.

"What is this, some kind of joke?" The menacing roar of Count Vyazemsky Sr. broke the deathly silence of the throne room. "Are you out of your mind, Archduke? A gift that is not a gift? Return the stones immediately!"

"Integrating level-fifty eight-sided stones without the proper experience and equipment has a ninety-percent probability of killing the host. Irreversibly. Healing magic will be useless. I am not handing over these gifts now, as I fear for the lives of my empresses. Because someone might decide that they are an expert in integrating stones and harm them. As a valiant son of the Zarak Empire, I have no right to expose my empresses to even the slightest risk. With the equipment that I have, as well as the experience of my student, Kimal Sarento, the integration of the stones will have a one hundred percent probability of success. Those who wish can verify the correctness of my words by asking the Inquisitor. For this reason, the stones will remain with me until the empresses contact me and say that they are ready for integration. We will deliver the equipment to the place of their choosing and carry out the process."

"Do you want to force the heads of the empire to carry out orders, running from one point to another?" My answer had angered Count Vyazemsky. "Their task is to govern the state, and not to plug up holes in the ground!"

"Let me remind the esteemed advisor that the first emperor, the founder of the Church of the Light, carried out his orders without any anger or desire for reward. He protected his people, his lands. That is why his deeds are still honored by us. My empresses have the right to refuse the gift. But if they accept it and follow the path of valor and justice, their deeds will go down in history and will be spoken of even after a thousand years!"

"I agree!" Miralda the First rose abruptly from the throne. She knew her prospects and saw the danger in her husband and father's constant overwatch. But now I gave her hope that she would turn from a worthless appendage into an independent force. The girl did not want to lose such a chance and, until her husband or one of the advisers said otherwise, she made her choice.

"I agree!" Marisa the First jumped to her feet a second after her cousin.

"We are ready to carry out the integration right now!" the empresses answered almost in unison. "Such is our will!"

Here I couldn't help but grin with satisfaction: the two old foxes' faces spoke volumes. They wanted one thing — to grind me into dust. Crush me. Destroy me. Throw me away. But they didn't have the chance — even if they risked ignoring the highest aristocracy and ordered the empresses to shut up and sit back down, Father Urg, who was looking thoughtfully in our direction, would not allow it. I was actually glad that the Fortress had begun to gain strength in our empire again. Even such strong players had to reckon with it.

"As you wish, my empresses. I would ask you lead us to a room where we may do this. The integration procedure is shrouded in secret. Even if everyone present here today has already undergone the process, tradition is tradition. We guessed that this might be your decision, so we brought the necessary equipment with us."

A few minutes later, we were in a small side room. It was me, Kimal Sarento, Alia, both empresses, the advisors, husbands and Father Urg, of course — where would we be without him? Kimal Sarento pulled a few devices from his immaterial inventory and began activating them, one after the other. No one spoke for some time. The empresses were visibly trembling, their inner emotions bursting out, unable to deal with the tension. It was a chance! A chance to turn the situation to our side! A chance for independence!

"You are making a grave mistake," the elder Count Vyazemsky said. "The stones and crystals should be given to our sons, not these..."

"These empresses," Father Urg said softly, stroking his clean-shaven chin. "I will admit that Valevsky's gift shocked me just as much as it did you, respected adviser, and at first, I, too thought it would be impossible, but now, having thought his decision over, I must bow to the wisdom of the Archduke and his people. It is the ideal solution. Both for now, and the future. However, we can't just give the girls the stones. Situations can change quickly, and life is long. Archduke Valevsky, the Church of the Light has a request for you. Don't take this as impudence or rudeness, but our empresses need mithril armor. Like the set you wear, all three of you. It will protect them from accidental troubles while the power of the stones is inactive. As we know, it won't be possible to maintain it forever. Even you, esteemed Archduke, can do it with the help of Praxis."

"What is *Praxis*? Why don't the empresses have it? Explain yourself!" Count Vyazemsky demanded immediately. Surprisingly, I had always seen him as a calm and reasonable man who was able to admit defeat. Now, however, he looked just like an old granny in the marketplace!

"*Praxis* is an extremely interesting stone the then-doomed soldier Max managed to get his hands on. It significantly reduces mana consumption. The Church of the Light decided to leave it in his possession, so that he could continue to do his great deeds."

"Get his hands on? You mean he stole it from the empire? He must return the stone!"

"That is not for you to decide, adviser," Father Urg said. His smile could freeze a man. "Or have you suddenly ascended to the position of High Priest of the Fortress and now have the authority to distribute magic stones? The decision has been made, and the Church of the Light does not intend to change it."

"Miralda, if you would be so kind." While everyone was talking, Kimal Sarento was busy with his own affairs. Using three mechanisms in sequence, he activated the stones, and after some time, the eyes of the first empress widened in amazement. The old magic stones were removed as something superfluous and unnecessary, and eighteen new ones took their place. Two abilities and sixteen support stones. Miralda the First became the third most powerful person in the Zarak Empire and the entire light world as a whole. In the dark world as well, if you didn't count Karina Fardi. But she could hardly be called a person anymore.

"Marisa, if you wouldn't mind," Kimal Sarento said to the second empress, but Alia intercepted.

"Please, have a gallo," Alia handed the girl ten crystals, and at that time I pulled another giant object out of my inventory.. If we were going to start the process of pumping up the empresses, we need to do it as efficiently as possible. It was stupid to expect that Miralda or Marisa would be allowed to access the altar of development. Those evil old men they called advisers would come up with a myriad of reasons why the altar was currently unavailable. That was why I'd brought not only the integration equipment, but also Hearth's altar of development.

"Now we will open your development model, where you will choose the optimal development path," continued Alia. We'd discussed this point for quite a long time — we did not want to hand over the process to the young empresses, so we needed help. Alia, under the guidance of Eleanore, Kimal Sarento and Naira, underwent express training in managing the development model and, I dare say, became the world's leading expert in the subject.

"What's this?" Miralda asked, dumbfounded, when Alia handed her another gift. One we didn't want to present in front of the courtiers and guests.

"A development crystal with five useful properties. You can read them, but you shouldn't say them out loud. These parameters belong to you, and only you. No one in the world has the right to know them, and the bonuses they bring will make you strong."

"Great Light!" Miralda said in awe when the crystal was in place. She had been raised in the palace and knew all the key parameters and what they were for, but she couldn't even imagine that there were development crystals with the five most important parameters for any light person. *Magic Power, Vampirism, Split Consciousness, Indestructibility, Maximum Limit* — these five in combination would make someone an extremely dangerous adversary with no mana problems. I'd had to use a whole pile of cutting stones to create these two crystals. One for Miralda, the other for Marisa. But it was worth it!

"I wouldn't be surprised if you already have the mithril armor on you," Father Urg said. For not the first time today, something like respect had crept into his voice.

"How could we leave our empresses defenseless?" Kimal Sarento said, offended, as he pulled out the next secret present.

Our independence must be unquestioned. Marisa had already been passed into Alia's clutches and was busy distributing a hundred development points, so we had time. Miralda was playing around at the time, creating *Diamond Defense.* I pulled these stones out of a level seventy-one rift, and I must say responsibly that the decision to give them away had been extremely difficult. If I hadn't remembered that I had twenty more of them back in Hearth, I would never have agreed to it.

The defense these stones gave was practically impenetrable! Even in its pure form, without support stones, it could repel attacks with steel and vyrma for some time. That was a feat in-and-of itself.

"How do I put it on?" Miralda asked, finishing her defense and turning her attention to the armor.

"Just place it on top of your dress," Kimal Sarento said. "You can change it later. This isn't just a suit of armor, my empress. It is an adaptive device that can adjust to the user's requirements. Information on how to use all this will be found in the immaterial inventory when you put on the armor. I can give you one piece of advice: as in the case of the development crystals, it is better for you to keep this description a secret. When you start reading, you will understand why. By the way, return our amulets. You no longer need them: remote communication is part of your armor. Now, gentlemen, I can say with confidence that Hearth's wellspring of gifts has run dry. My empresses, I believe that you must discuss your future, and the future of the empire with your loyal subjects and spouses. We take our leave. Business calls. Would my great mentor be so kind as to open a portal to the Hearth? We must finally rid the Ka-limans of their ill-fated rifts. They've gotten out of control. And we won't get rich by just sitting here.

Chapter 8

"I FORBID IT!" the Inquisitor's thunderous roar seemed to echo throughout all of Hearth.

"You are free to forbid me as much as you like, Inquisitor! But there are no servants of yours in Hearth. The people who live here have the right to agree or disagree with your prohibitions. I am not going to agree with this one, in particular. Alia will become my wife, regardless of your decision."

"Mother Alia! Call her by her full title! Mother Alia is an attendant of the Church of the Light!"

"As soon as Alia becomes my wife, she will leave this order."

"No one ever leaves the Church of Light's control! It's the law!"

"There's a first time for everything. Including leaving the church."

"As soon as she gives birth to your child, she

will go to the Citadel! She will become the first female cardinal! You have no right to interfere with her destiny!"

"Destiny? Did you ask Alia if she wanted to accept the position of cardinal? Does she want such a destiny? Do you want her to become the first woman among a nest of snakes, where she will be devoured without a second thought? No, Inquisitor! Your demands are unrealistic. Alia will be mine. Eleanore, continue."

"I forbid it!" The Inquisitor even drew his sword, threatening us with reprisals. Most of those gathered collapsed to the floor under the immense pressure of Chaos' power. Only the four owners of mithril armor remained on their feet: me, Alia, Eleanore and Kimal Sarento. I did not take Naira to this event. Everyone knew that the Inquisitor would come and that my dark wife would feel ill.

"I don't want to be a cardinal!" Alia said. "I want to be with Max!"

"I forbid it!" The Inquisitor would listen to no one.

"On what grounds?" Alia said, suddenly going on the offensive. "Who are you to meddle in the lives of ordinary humans? You are the Inquisitor! Your task is to maintain the integrity of the Church of the Light and ensure balance in this world, not to forbid marriages!"

"You will become a cardinal!" The Inquisitor was adamant.

"She will become my wife!" I was already starting to get angry. "Since we can't come to an agreement, let's approach this issue from a different angle. Either Alia becomes my wife, or the respected Inquisitor can look for a new mediator between the Abyss and Pharapho! I won't stick my nose into their business anymore."

"You dare to threaten me?!" The Inquisitor grew in size, looming over the assembled group. Lightning began to strike from his Light-filled eyes, the pressure of his aura increased, and we all struggled to stay on our feet. The guests to our ceremony suddenly remembered other vital matters they had to attend to and crawled out of the hall, leaving a bloody path behind them — the capillaries in their noses couldn't withstand the pressure and had burst. Turning up the radius of my aura to the max, I activated the *Healing Aura*, reducing the Inquisitor's influence and allowing people to rise to their feet. Nevertheless, soon only four people remained in the hall. The wrath of the supreme being of Chaos was too terrible to endure.

"I dare. I threaten. I am tired of the respected Inquisitor doing nothing but forbidding, intimidating and forcing. I have not seen any benefit from you living in Hearth. When will you and the Interrogator go home and give us the opportunity to live in peace? If the forces of Chaos want the world to come into harmony, either with a new force of the second orbit or by destroying two forces of the third, they will have to find themselves a new cardinal. Because Alia is mine, and mine alone! I am not going to give her to anyone."

"You will be punished, Archduke Valevsky!

"I have already been punished by the fact that the Inquisitor and the Interrogator are sitting in my palace! Do you think you can imagine anything worse than that? Alia will become my wife, Inquisitor. Whether you want it or not. If you resist, establish the balance yourself, I will become a no one. I will grow carrots, bake bread, manage the city and won't give a second thought to what's happening to the rest of the planet. The balance will last for my lifetime, and after that, what will be will be. Are you satisfied with this arrangement?"

"You will be punished, Archduke Valevsky!" the Inquisitor said, still wound up. Apparently, he had run out of reasonable arguments, so he continued to shower us with threats. He was certainly fed up!

"Go on, Eleanore," I said as if nothing had happened, turning away from the Inquisitor. The sword was still in his hands, but now, unlike the conflict during the Wave, the Inquisitor remained calm. Or relatively so, as it was hard to come off as completely calm and collected while still visibly inflated with anger and holding a huge sword in your hands, but the fact that he refrained from attacking me was already something. As I understood it, the creatures of Chaos did not believe that I would be able to get to Pharapho and somehow negotiate with him, so they had demanded the previously impossible. For some reason, the monsters that had settled in my castle could not independently communicate with either the Abyss or Pharapho. Only respond to their calls. Which was, of course, rather strange: after all, the creatures of the zero orbit, who rule the world, must have some power over the other forces. It was there, but somehow strange and incomprehensible. Maybe I should ask the Abyss why this was so. The only thing stopping me was that its bottomless maw would suck all the essences out of me in exchange for an answer.

"Alia, do you agree to become the second wife of Archduke Valevsky?" Eleanore asked. The sword in the Inquisitor's hands shone brighter, but the force of Chaos remained silent, continuing to glare.

"Yes!" Alia looked straight ahead. However, I knew her too well not to see how nervous she was. She had the same stoic expression as when she had gone to the pyre. Now she knew that nothing actually threatened her, but at that time, she had sincerely believed she would die. Nevertheless, she did not bow or bend under the circumstances, meeting death with her head held high. I did not have the chance to be present at the conversation between Alia and Father Urg, but it was after this that she told me she did not wish to return to the Church of the Light. She wanted to stay with me.

"Archduke Valevsky, do you agree to take Alia as your second wife?"

"Yes!"

"By the power vested in me by the law of the city of Hearth, I pronounce you husband and wife! From henceforth, you are Maximilian and Alia Valevsky!"

The Inquisitor turned sharply and went to his throne. The Interrogator observed the ceremony from his throne, not even thinking of interfering. He, the ruler of the dark, was indifferent to the problems of the cardinals. He had too many of his own problems to delve into the domain of the light ones. But I had no doubt that the creatures of Chaos would definitely take revenge on me for my disobedience. This was the second time the Inquisitor had been forced to retreat before an ordinary human. I didn't think such things could be forgiven.

"Congratulations, Archduchess," Kimal Sarento approached my wife and delicately kissed her hand. "Not everyone is capable of defying the entire world order to be with the one they love."

"Thank you, Count Sarento," Alia blushed slightly. Looking towards the throne where the Inquisitor and the Interrogator were, she suddenly said, "My husband, where will Naira and I sit? Why are our seats currently occupied by these beings?"

The question was asked loudly enough for the representatives of Chaos to hear. Silently, without saying a word, both the Inquisitor and the Interrogator stood up from their seats and moved the enormous chairs, which seemed unwieldy, slightly to the side. An additional place appeared next to my throne, which should be just enough for the thrones of my wives. Alia would sit next to the Inquisitor, Naira with the Interrogator. I looked at Eleanore. She understood me without words and only nodded:

"It will be done."

"Do you have five or ten minutes, my fearless and unflappable mentor? I wish to discuss a certain delicate matter with you. Alone, if possible."

Kimal Sarento made this last clarification with a glance toward both my wives, who were eyeing us with interest. I must admit, he had managed to intrigue me as well. What did he need to say that couldn't be said in front of them?

"Prepare the feast, we'll be there soon," I ordered Eleanore, and soon Kimal Sarento and I found ourselves in my office. There were no representatives of Chaos, invisibles, or other eavesdropping creatures here. Kimal Sarento looked out the window for a while, watching the construction unfold, then turned to me and asked point-blank:

"You do understand that Chaos will not forget everything you have done lately?"

"The Wave and my marriage?" I clarified. "They will take revenge. That's a fact."

"It's good that you realize this. Only I would add to the list your unwillingness to carry out their order and destroy two forces of the third orbit. The attempt to negotiate, of course, turned into an excellent plan that suddenly came into fruition, but I have one hundred percent confidence that when the time comes, you will be reminded of this defiance, too."

"As if I had a choice! Run around the whole world, exterminating two forces — what a distinct pleasure."

"You are not speaking the right words, my uncomprehending mentor. Choice, lack of it, what have you — all this is unimportant. Tell me, when you get a dog and it stops listening to you, what do you do?"

"Are you trying to say I'm a dog?" I frowned.

"Don't be persnickety about my word choice. What do you do if your pet stops listening to you?"

"It will have a punishment coming. Animals must understand who is in control. But this is irrelevant to the current conversation. I am not a dog."

"I agree, you are not a dog. Compared to the creatures of Chaos, you are much smaller. A cockroach that got hold of a bread crumb and runs around it, happily jumping at the behest of the powers that be. If you run away from this crumb, you will either be forcibly returned or slapped with a slipper to be replaced with a new cockroach. Your only advantage over a cockroach is that others need to be taught to eat bread crumbs, and not fall on their backs, pretending to be dead. Those who set the rules of the game in our world are too busy with other things to be distracted by new cockroaches. That is why you are still alive. But I want you to understand: as soon as the balance in the world is maintained, the creatures of Chaos will take you seriously. And, as has already been said, they will remember all your sins."

For a moment I stared at Kimal Sarento, not understanding why he was voicing the obvious. In fact, Alia had become my wife because after not receiving the *Tainted Blood* and our skirmish with the Inquisitor, nothing else mattered. I knew full well that the creatures of Chaos would remember all my sins, and my only hope was that this would happen after I had children. After all, I wanted to look at all three of them and make sure that they were mine. Yes, three: Naira was also pregnant.

"It's unlikely that the wise and cunning Kimal Sarento called me for a private conversation in order to voice the obvious facts, right? You have some alternative option, right?"

"Of course," he grinned. "The ability to foresee a problem and react to it correctly is the basis for survival in high society, my still-inexperienced mentor. In fact, I have come up with several options on how to save your life after the third second-orbital force appears in the world. First, you must undergo full-scale training in the *Author* skill. As practice shows, the magic of the ancients is capable of standing on equal ground with the powers of Chaos. You just need to use it correctly. There are three places in this world where you can undergo training."

"Two," I corrected. "The location of the ancients in the Zarak Empire is not suitable for this. Its owner is too weak and does not have the skills of a mentor."

"Three, my slow-witted mentor. There are three places in this world. Two, as you correctly understood, are the two remaining locations of the ancients, the coordinates of which you already have, the third is the geniuses of the ancients. The mysterious force of the third orbit that accepted the rules of Chaos' game and forgot its own past. But I'm certain they did not forget about *Author.* Otherwise, everything will immediately lose its meaning. These are geniuses we're talking about — they need to test their theories somehow, and the space management mechanism is perfect for this. If they cannot help in the locations of the ancients, you must make a bee-line to the geniuses."

The idea was reasonable, but it had its shortcomings.

"The ancients lost, even with the *Author* skill. And they were much more experienced than me, and also had complete dictionaries. I'm afraid your option is only good for the short term. It will win one battle, but it definitely won't win the war."

"That's where the second part comes in, transitioning smoothly from part one. When you gain power, you will need to resolve the issue with the weapons of the ancients."

"That around which all forces revolve?" I was surprised.

"True. The interactive neural network was right: we need to bring the world closer to total collapse. But not allow it. I have no idea whether this is possible or not, but if you manage to close the control of the weapon to yourself, the forces of Chaos will do nothing to you. Because doing so would be a death sentence."

"Even if it all works out, I'm just a human. Sooner or later I'll still have to meet the Light."

"So you will have to either somehow extend your life, or learn to pass on your abilities to your children. Fortunately, you will have enough of them. But all these are problems for your future. First, you need to protect yourself. Although there is, of course, a third option. You approach the Inquisitor, fall to your knees and beg for forgiveness. Dissolve your marriage with Alia, ask to be given *Tainted Blood*, agree to carry out any assignment, no matter how difficult it may seem, and I am one hundred percent sure that you will be pardoned."

"No!" I shouted. This suggestion was edging on outright insulting.

"If not, then you have no business sitting here in Hearth. I believe that Chaos will need some time to agree on all the conditions between the Abyss and Pharapho, after which you will be put back to work. Since our uninvited guests cannot contact the second-orbital forces on their own, they will have to rely on someone to do it. I'll give you three tries to guess who will bear this heavy burden. That's why I think you can't rest here for long. You need to run."

"A sound plan, but first I need to get into the treasury of Padishah Bayazid the Fourth. One of the *Author* dictionaries is there for sure."

"I may be mistaken, but I think that six dictionaries should be more than sufficient for your purposes. They have everything you could need to fight back against anyone, be it the Inquisitor, or Karina Fardi, or any of the forces on the planet. All you need is to learn how to use what you already have. The rest you will get in the locations of the ancients."

"Are you that eager to kick me out of town?"

"You? The Light be with you, my joking mentor. Unlike ordinary people, no matter how far you run during the day, you will still have the opportunity to return home in the evening to start your journey from the same point the next morning. So do not accuse me of such nonsense. I am afraid that as soon as Chaos comes to an agreement with the forces of the second orbit, and this can happen at any moment, you will no longer have time for your own affairs."

"I'm not going anywhere today. I just got married, after all!"

"No one is driving you out of town today. Celebrate, rejoice, and tomorrow, with a clear conscience, get to work. I can't even imagine how much time a five thousand kilometer journey will take you, so there's no point in postponing it. We'll deal with the local problems ourselves. As well as with Karina Fardi, if she decides to stick her nose into Hearth."

"I need to go to the Fog Arena," I said. "There must be a way to form portals to the desired point. There's no way the ancients overlooked this."

"Going to see the Fog Stalker is a sound idea, of course, and fortunately you have more keys now, but this method does not seem right to me. How can the creature of Pharapho know about what happened on the planet before it appeared? No, my mentor, who is so eager to ease his lot in life. You will still have to work. Of course, you can take a risk and use the dark ones' teleport, but I have no guarantee that the Temple of Skron will take you where you want. Maybe it will hide you in places where your magic will not work. Or straight to Karina Fardi. One is a patient guy, of course, but even he can get tired of waiting for the other forces to take the next step. What if he decides that the third orbit is not so bad? You need to be prepared for every little thing. Enough, let's go. Your new wife is already waiting for you."

We had decided to have the ceremonial wedding outdoors. It was too beautiful a day to miss: the cold, autumn winds had died down and the sun was peeking out from behind the clouds, as if to join the celebration. Even Father Urg had promised to attend and confirm the validity of our marriage. Or rather, I would have to fly off to Turb after him. Having an intercom dramatically improved my quality and convenience of life.

The party ran late into the night. I had been right in assuming that residents of Hearth were sorely lacking in festivities. The townsfolk were partying as if it was their last day on the planet. We even had to call the guards in to pacify the particularly drunk and rowdy. The city guests who had come for an audience with the Inquisitor or Interrogator initially approached us with caution, but they soon relaxed, and some even joined in. Of course they did — who would refuse free food and drink? Especially since our cooks had really let their epicurean spirits run wild. Wine flowed like a river, food was gobbled up by the cartload, people fell into piles on the ground. A perfect party.

According to the agreement, tonight was Alia's night, but my new wife was too tired to do anything exciting. And her belly was already getting in the way. So she kissed me, lay her head down, and fell asleep in a matter of seconds. I lay next to her, listening to her calm breathing, and with each passing second grew more and more convinced that Kimal Sarento was wrong. The Fog Stalker knew exactly how to use *Author*. How? Because there was a high probability that the geniuses of the ancients were using this skill or something similar to it as we speak!

As I took out the key to the arena, I turned it over in my hands, weighing all the pros and cons. If the Fog Stalker didn't know the answer to my questions, then I'd be wasting a rare and precious item. And I didn't need any more information from it now. I already knew everything I wanted to know. Perhaps I could find out Karina Fardi's location, but that was a stupid question too. I could get a list of all possible upgrades for the mithril armor, but the Fog Stalker could try to be clever and say that no such list exited. A person can craft anything they can think of. What else? Exact coordinates of all the dictionaries? A way of adapting to the dark at level sixty of the rifts? What else would I ask, if the Fog Stalker claimed there was no way to help with my portals?

Wait! There *was* a question that piqued my interest. Not just that — I was dying to know!

"Greetings, traveler! I am the Fog Stalker. Those who…"

"You can save your long-winded introduction, I've already heard it more than once. I came here for answers, Fog Stalker. I have the *Author* skill. One sentence allows me to open a portal, but only to places I have already been. How do I change the sentence to allow me to teleport to any point on the planet that I wish?"

"Forty waves, traveler. The answer to this question will cost you forty waves."

"Have you lost your mind?! Why such a high price?" I asked indignantly.

"Unrestricted teleportation is an undesirable skill. It upsets the balance just by existing. Anyone who wants to do forbidden things must pay a hefty price for them. Forty waves, traveler. Only then will I be able to unstick my tongue and give you an answer."

"So Chaos is against it?" I guessed.

"I am not privy to the thoughts of the creatures of Chaos, but I am sure that they would like to remain the only creatures of our world with the ability to teleport to any point. Therefore, they will do everything in their power to eliminate any competitor, as well as anyone who gave them such an opportunity. However, passing forty waves is an immutable rule, which even the creatures of Chaos will not be able to contend. They will be forced to admit that I had no other choice, and will destroy only you."

I frowned. Just more grounds for the Inquisitor to kill me. Apparently, it was my fate. Okay, what about the second question?"

"Then another question. The creatures of Chaos already want my head, but for now they have to cooperate with me. After the balance is restored, they will have much more power. My question is, how can I avoid their wrath? How can I protect myself even if I get these teleportation capabilities? Is there an answer to this question? If so, how many waves will I have to go through to get it?"

The Fog Stalker thought for a long time. I even began to suspect that he would not answer me at all, but soon the terrible monster deigned to reply:

"It is impossible to protect yourself from the wrath of Chaos. It is the rightful master of this world, and none of the weapons that have existed since the appearance of Chaos on the planet can destroy it. None of the defenses that have existed since the appearance of Chaos on the planet can protect you from its attacks. I have no answer to your question, traveler, no matter how many waves you pass."

It would seem that I had come to the point where I should throw up my hands in despair that nothing in this world could help me, but Kimal Sarento taught me to look between the lines. The Fog Stalker had no right to answer my question. Nevertheless, it answered. And in such a way that I had no doubt that a way to escape from Chaos still exists. Because the phrase "none of those that exist since the appearance of Chaos on the plane" means that all I needed to do was use the weapons and protection of the ancients. Use what was probably stored in the last two locations still hidden from the sight of Chaos. It was unlikely that this would help me destroy the Inquisitor and the Interrogator, because they were still able to capture our world, but I would definitely be able to defend myself and keep my status as a force to be reckoned with. What was important was that at least something remained in the locations of the ancients.

If so...let's see what my Level Fifty *Healing Aura* could do. After all, what had I pumped it up for?

"I need an answer to the first question. How can I fix my teleportation? If I have to pass through forty waves, so be it. Wave!"

Chapter 9

"EXPLAIN TO ME, my dim-witted mentor, why did you have to take such a risk? Have you taken a look in the mirror? You look like a skeleton! Forty waves? How did you even decide to attempt this?"

"Did I get what I needed? I did. Am I alive? I am. What else do you need?" I asked, trying not to wheeze from the pain. *Heal* did nothing. The damage had been done on some sort of deep level that ordinary magic, even amplified by all manner of support stone, could do nothing about. Yes, I had regained use of my arms and legs, but I couldn't repair my body after two amorphous masses of the Fog Stalker had steamrolled me with all their magic and physical strength. I really hoped that over time it would recover on its own. At least that's what the Fog Stalker had promised after I completely cleared the fortieth wave. In fact, if I were asked to repeat this insanity again, citing the fact that I'd already passed through the entire arena and knew all the ins and outs, I'd have to try hard not to kill the requester on the spot. I had regretted getting involved in this venture a hundred times, but it was too late to retreat. After the thirtieth wave, the Pharapho simulacrums began to appear in pairs, which made each wave much more difficult. As for the final wave...I don't even want to cast my mind back to it. Two Pharapho bearing a hundred percent of the second-orbital force's power was an unreal experience. I was torn to pieces, kneaded like dough, several times almost thrown off the arena. The shapeless carcasses got their kicks in every way they could. Nevertheless, I passed. By the skin of my teeth, summoning the willpower from some unknown source, but still, I passed! I'd had to constantly regrow my arms and legs while shooting two or three *Heal* spells at the monsters, so by the time the last giant fell to the floor and dissipated, the integrity of my mithril armor left much to be desired. The creatures rudely ignored the fact that I was wearing impenetrable armor and tore through it like tissue paper. After it was all over, the Fog Stalker congratulated me on my first pass through the arena. In the entire history of mankind, there has not been a single case where someone had the strength and audacity to go through this nightmare and stay alive. But the reward ended with just congratulations: no super-powerful artifacts, no recipes, no resources, nothing! Only an answer to my question. But it was worth it. *Author* turned out to be an extremely unusual skill with many facets.

"You call this 'alive?'" Kimal Sarento frowned and looked me up and down once again. "Ever the optimist, my mentor with too much faith in himself! And you weren't the only thing that suffered. Your armor is in pieces! You must realize that every trip you make forces me to work harder? This is a point I'm not too happy about, incidentally."

"The Fog Stalker said that my condition would stabilize in three days. I absorbed too much of Pharapho's poison, it can't be removed that easily. The armor was damaged, of course, but I managed to take all the rings and fragments. I think one knuckle will be enough to completely restore my armor. So soon I will be fine and ready for new achievements."

"Of course you will — you simply have no other choice. You had some guests, didn't you."

"I did," I answered and shuddered at the memory. Both Chaos creatures had come to my room without even asking permission. Looming over me, they stared silently for a while, holding their bared swords. One would torture me with the fire of the Light, the other with darkness. I probably could have explained the situation to them, but after returning from the Fog Arena, I could only wheeze. Only now, a couple of hours later, had I regained the ability to speak, but even then it was difficult to breathe. In fact, both forces of Chaos stood silently near me, and then left just as silently. The only thing they managed to achieve was to frighten Alia. Although it was unclear who frightened her more: these two monsters or me after coming back from the arena. Another reason why I urgently needed to find a way to protect myself from creatures who imagined themselves to be gods of our world.

"Why did they suddenly get so excited? At one point they jumped up from the throne and started pacing the hall, as if they didn't know what to do. And when you came back, they almost ran to your room. You can't even imagine how scary it is — the Inquisitor running. Makes all your hair stand on end."

"I obtained unrestricted teleportation." I explained. "Previously, this was an ability held only by Chaos, and now I have it too. The Fog Stalker warned me that these two would not like it. As practice shows, he was right. When the balance of forces returns to our world, Chaos will have to deal with me separately. They barely restrained themselves from finishing me off today."

"So that's what it is," Kimal Sarento said thoughtfully. "So I see the option of falling to your knees and begging their forgiveness is no longer on the table?"

"I'm afraid it was doomed to fail from the start. The creatures of Chaos are too vindictive to forgive anyone. We can only hope that the negotiations with Pharapho and the Abyss will drag on for several years and..."

"Archduke Valevsky is being summoned to the throne room!" My assistant flew into my office. He looked disheveled and somewhat insane. As if the Light itself had descended upon our city and ordered me to be brought before him. I understood the reason for such behavior perfectly well: for my assistant, the forces that sat in the throne room were the embodiment of gods, so any of their words had to be carried out immediately and without question. However, an innate mischievousness awoke in me. It was not right for my assistant to put someone else's will above mine. He was my subordinate and not the Inquisitor's, was he not?

"Summoned? Who is summoning me in my city?"

"The Inquisitor!"

"Is Hearth the Inquisitor's city?" I continued. "He ordered, 'Bring Valevsky here,' just like that?"

"Just like that, Your Radiance! Word for word!"

This was unexpected. Usually, representatives of Chaos behaved with more tact. If the Inquisitor had given this order, then he must feel that he has power behind him, which worried me a bit. Why the abrupt shift?

"Any ideas?" I turned to look at a pensive Kimal Sarento.

"I do have one, but you're not going to like it. Chaos has come to an agreement with the second orbit."

"So suddenly?"

"Forty waves, my slow-witted mentor. You've passed forty waves, and Pharapho has received something as well. He's become accommodating, and the Abyss was ready from the start. Should I help you get there, or can you make it there on your own?"

"I'm afraid I won't be able to walk anywhere for the next three days," I sighed, finishing forming the sentence for the new portal. It turned out to be almost three times longer than the previous one, and twenty of the symbols were absent in all the dictionaries I currently possessed. No matter how hard I tried, I would never have come up with the sentence on my own. The Fog Stalker's help had been indispensable.

"We need a stretcher," Kimal Sarento turned to my assistant, who was off in a flash. The lazy bastard never even thought about taking me in his arms. No one remembered that after the battle with the lithoids he had carried me for several days. But the circumstances were different then. "While your overly excited assistant is running around and no one else is here, I'll ask, just in case: do you want to flee? The Inquisitor knows full well that he has no right to order you around in your city, but he does it anyway. This is bad. Very bad."

"I can escape at any moment," I assured him, and just in case, formed a portal. It opened without any problems and still had the same red glow as my previous ones. "In theory, anywhere I am, I'm only ten meters from one of the ancients' locations. Even if the creatures of Chaos follow me, they won't be able to enter. But I can't escape now and expose Hearth. Those bastards might start taking revenge for their will not being fulfilled."

"It's good that you think with your head and don't give in to emotions," nodded Kimal Sarento. "In any case, get ready. I have the feeling this won't be the most pleasant meeting."

He was one hundred percent right. My assistant brought men with a stretcher, and soon I found myself in the main hall. The Inquisitor looked at me like I was a piece of filth stuck on the heel on his perfect boots. His aura was so powerful that the servants were unable to make the full journey. They fell to the floor unconscious, forcing Kimal Sarento to rush to my aid. I am ashamed to admit, but after the Fog arena, I couldn't even stand on my own two feet. Kimal Sarento sat me on the throne and staggered away. The Inquisitor's aura crushed even him, to say nothing of me. In fact, I had no thoughts on this matter at all. The only thing I cared about right now was how to take another breath without dying.

The pressure suddenly disappeared, causing strange sounds to escape my body, similar to sighs of relief. Since I was sitting on the throne and clearly had no intention of standing up in front of the Inquisitor, he had to approach me himself. I'd already removed the magic stone that made me dark, so talking to the Inquisitor should not have killed me. Stopping a step away from me, he proclaimed in a triumphant voice:

"The fundamental agreements with the Abyss and Pharapho have been reached, we are moving on to the next phase. Now you will go to the mechanoids and take the stabilization system from them, then the geniuses of the ancients are waiting for you, who will form two carrying vessels called 'batteries.' After which you must visit the Abyss and Pharapho take part of their power from each of them in turn, storing them in the batteries. With these items, you must appear at the conjunction point into this world, where One is already waiting. There you will use the stabilizer to preserve One's mind, after which you will activate both batteries. This will make One the new second-orbital force. Go immediately."

"A few clarifications, esteemed Inquisitor," I said, and the pressure covered the throne room again. It became difficult to speak, but still possible, so I continued despite the incredible weight: "First, I am too exhausted to go anywhere now. I need three or four days before I can even walk again. If you can perform a miracle and get me back on my feet here and now, then I will be ready to work. However, there is also a second point — all the proclamations you have just made require work. And any work, as we already know, requires payment. I require payment too."

"You dare bargain with us?!" The Inquisitor was somehow stunned by my impudence.

"Not bargain — defend my interests. I do not need resources, gold or items. I need guarantees that after the world finds balance, Chaos will preserve my life, mind and freedom. I want to remain

Archduke Valevsky, the head of the autonomous city of Hearth. What is the point of me running from power to power, if after everything I have done for you, you still destroy me? What is the benefit for me and my city? Let me remind you that after the offworlders left, taking the runic magic with them, human life became temporally limited again. In a hundred years at most, which is a second by your standards, I will be gone. So what is the point of destroying me now? Are you such great soothsayers that you know what will happen five, ten years from now? What if One, having seized such strength and power, becomes too unpredictable? He will have to be replaced, since something will once again threaten your beloved balance. Even if you find someone to replace him, do you have someone in mind who can do it all over again? I'm not asking for anything incommensurate to my services, I'm not asking you to crawl on your knees before me. All I need is guarantees of security and a bit of respect."

"How long did it take you to prepare that speech?" I heard Kimal Sarento through the intercom. He had moved to the wall, but did not leave the throne room, wanting to see how it would all end. The creatures of Chaos were silent for quite a long time, looking at each other. It was as if they were communicating mentally through their intercoms, just as Kimal Sarento and I did.

"Improvisation," I replied. My fresh attempt to stand didn't yield any result. The fact that I managed to sit up without slumping over was already a victory.

"You will live," the Inquisitor suddenly declared and sharply decreased in size. "We consider you a dangerous, unpredictable and impudent person, but we cannot ignore all the benefits you have brought in the past and can bring in the future."

"So you were planning to kill me?" I asked.

"Don't overdo it," Kimal Sarento said. The Inquisitor pretended not to hear anything and continued to broadcast:

"You have five days to recover, after which you must go and carry out our assignment. The sooner balance returns to this world, the more peaceful human life can be."

"I need the coordinates of all the points you want to send me to," I said, and a sheet of paper appeared in the Inquisitor's hands. He handed it to me, but I didn't have the strength to take it. The Chaos entity frowned, considering my behavior another violation, but then Kimal Sarento arrived and took the paper.

"He can barely move right now," my quick-witted pupil explained, just in case. "Forty waves of the Fog Arena have completely drained his strength."

"We have already conveyed to the Temple of Skron and the Citadel the information that a human capable of passing forty waves of the Fog Arena has appeared in our world," the Inquisitor said, as if it were something self-evident.

"Why?" I said before my mind could shut me

up. I must have been pretty exhausted after all, since I had started speaking without thinking.

"Information or items that can be obtained in the fog stalker arena are classified as 'unique.' Both the light and the dark have a need for many things that are impossible to obtain for one reason or another. Moreover, the Fog Stalker himself is only willing to provide these items or information after forty waves."

"Don't tell me I have to work for the Temple of Skron and the Citadel pro bono! The Fog Stalker arena is not a moonlit promenade in the park with a girl on your arm. Even *Heal* is useless against Pharapho's poison which, as you see, has turned me into a vegetable."

"There is a special support stone that eliminates the effect of any poison. Including Pharapho's poison," the Inquisitor said.

"And? What's it called and how do I get it?" I asked, since the Chaos creature had fallen silent.

"Is that your question, human?" the Inquisitor asked, sending shivers down my spine. Kimal Sarento immediately started yelling over the intercom, warning me to shut up right here and now, but I knew that well enough without his words of wisdom. Asking the Inquisitor would mean paying for the answer. Knowing how harmful these entities could be, I understood that the payment could be anything. Including an order to throw myself off a cliff head first.

"I have no more questions for the Inquisitor," I said. He nodded and, before taking his seat again, added:

"The number Fog Arena keys you have also been relayed to the Temple of Skron and the Citadel. In three days, their representatives will arrive in Hearth to give you their demands. What you need to know or get in the Fog Arena. You have no right to refuse, Archduke Valevsky. Do you want to convince us of your usefulness? Prove it in action, and not with your overly active tongue. When the Temple of Skron and the Citadel get what they need, the question of your immunity can be considered closed."

With these words, the Inquisitor went to his place, allowing me to consider what he had just said.

The fact that I was doomed to lose two, or even four keys, was bad. A catastrophe. Of course, someone might think that one cannot compare one's own life with what is easily obtained from the creatures of Pharapho, but life has taught me to see without filters.

And, as it turned out, I was not the only one who did this.

"You aren't under the impression, my pensive mentor, that you just saved your own life, do you?"

"No, of course not. Today the Inquisitor gave his word, tomorrow he will take back and finish me off like a useless piece of trash. Until I have guaranteed protection from the attacks of my neighbors on the throne, I can't have any delusions of security."

"It's very good that you understand this, without any hints from me. Even if they sign some kind of agreement, it still doesn't guarantee you anything. Only your own strength and protection can grant you years of life. So our plan remains in force, despite the new input. How many keys do you have left?"

"Five. And one will have to be spent to get a support stone for *Heal*. I need protection from poison. The rest, as I understand it, will go to those in need. And I will not have the right to refuse such a high honor."

"Because it will immediately show you from a negative side and completely justify the aggressive actions of the Inquisitor," Kimal Sarento finished the thought for me. "Five arena runs. Are you ready for this?"

"No. And I'll have to do one run without a support stone. If I manage to survive, and it's quite possible I won't, I'll once again be transformed into a pile of mush that can barely muster the energy to even speak. What a nightmare. Take me back to my room. I'm so tired that I could sleep for a few days now. And make me some mithril blanks. I need to repair my armor."

Surprisingly, Kimal Sarento obeyed without saying a word. He picked me up in his arms like a child and carried my body up to the second floor. The servants opened the doors, after which he carefully laid me down on the bed.

Ruffling my head, as if he wanted to ruffle my hair (the invisible helmet did not allow this), Kimal Sarento evoked strange feelings in me. Only my mother had treated me like this, and even then only in early childhood. She often came to me in the evenings, read me fairy tales and stroked my hair, whispering words to me that my soul became warm.

The sensations after Kimal Sarento's touch were akin to that long-forgotten feeling. It was as if I had returned back to childhood, under the protection of a wise and strong adult.

"I don't think it's worth forming a level hundred rift," I said before Kimal Sarento left the room. The man turned to me and raised an eyebrow, demanding clarification.

"We need a hundred levels to stop Karina Fardi. Practice shows that she can be stopped by the supreme converts. After One becomes a second-orbital power, Skron's vessel will be useless. She will not be able to become a third-orbital power. Moreover, the freed spawns of Chaos will take care of her. No matter how you look at it, she's finished. So I see no point in creating a hundred-level-deep hole in this world. Don't you think there's a reason why, in the thousand years that these forces have existed on our planet, no such rift has ever been formed? What if this is a direct path for the Abyss to our world from the 'nothing' into which Skron drove it? And by returning the Abyss, we will create even more problems for ourselves. And not only with the Abyss as such, but also with Skron, who will lose his influence on the rifts. Not to mention the fact that it is impossible to get to the sixtieth level without a long adaptation period. When I remember those difficult minutes I spent that deep, my stomach still twists with fear."

"Sound logic," Kimal Sarento said. Returning to the bed, he sat down on the edge and began to think out loud: "Let's assume you're right and Karina is destroyed. That will make our lives much easier. If, of course, our guests from Chaos spare your life. However, there is another option: they could step aside and let Karina resolve the issue with you on her own. They themselves will remain clean and completely unrelated to what Karina will do in the light lands. What will we do if she appears, say, in Turb? The Inquisitor will say that he has no right to interfere, and the light ones have no supreme converts. The combat monks will not be able to do anything with Karina, and the commanders are extremely clumsy and do not know how to jump from one point in space to another. You, my nimble mentor, will have to move to the capital and resolve the issue on the spot. Will you be ready to meet Fardi?"

"You always know how to spoil everything," I muttered, trying to figure out a solution to this possible outcome.

"It is not me who spoils everything, but those around us. I will be nothing but glad if Chaos destroys Skron's vessel. However, one must always prepare for the worst, my mentor who is beginning to understand this difficult world. I want to note that not everything is as bad as I describe. If an open confrontation with Karina occurs, you still have your orb. Fardi is not a rift — she does not have the rot skill, so there is no need to sacrifice your mithril armor. Form a spear and run after her all over Turb. Of course, it is a pity for people that they will fall into the zone of her aura, but this is the lesser of two evils that we can do if you do not want to go through a hundred-level rift."

"It's not that I don't want to, it's just..." I began, but then fell silent. Kimal Sarento smoothly and beautifully led me to the idea that I would have to do it anyway. Whether I wanted it or not is unimportant. What's important is the result: I would be able to exist without any problem in the aura of a true Skron vessel. What were crutches for if they could be replaced with normal prostheses? Or even better — with real limbs.

"Rest," Kimal Sarento got out of bed and smiled kindly. "Recover and prepare to meet our distinguished guests. I don't know about you, but personally I'm very interested in what One and the Pope need so much that they are ready to immediately send their representatives to you. What if we need something ourselves and have to send you on a hunt to the Black Mountain to get new keys to the arena? Information, my cruciferous mentor, is vital in our world. And those who use it most effectively will rule this world. I hope you understand that I mean us? Now the Temple of Skron and the Citadel will get what they want, but I have a strong suspicion that one item or answer to a question will not be enough. This is where we will make our presence known. The Inquisitor only said that you need to go through the arena twice. Everything else is for a separate fee. Which you and I will definitely take advantage of. Or my name isn't Kimal Sarento!"

Chapter 10

"WE CAN GIVE YOU four months, Archduke Valevsky. No more. The Citadel needs this relic too much, so now that the chance to get it has appeared, we must not hesitate."

"In four months I will pass through the Fog Arena, and you will receive your treasure," I assured the commander. Kimal Sarento's sour expression eloquently showed how far the Church of the Light's demands went in Hearth. The Citadel wanted to regain a lost relic of the Light: a piece of its god, destroyed by the dark ones four hundred years ago. Thanks to this relic, the light ones ruled almost the entire world. The Kerux area, in any case, could not even breathe without the consent of the Pope. It got to the point that a sabotage group was sent to Al-Khorezm, whose task was to destroy the relic. They accomplished the task, but they themselves died, and without the right to re-incarnation. Since then, the Church of the Light had begun to decline, which led to traitors appearing inside the Citadel, who gave their souls to Skron. In general, there was nothing about this relic that did any good for Hearth. We would certainly not become another Citadel.

The dark ones had a similar story, with the only difference being that the light ones destroyed their relic only one hundred and fifty years ago. A piece of Skron himself that granted the dark ones unprecedented strength, power and other important attributes for their battle with the light. The misty servant of the Temple of Skron agreed to the four-month delay quite easily. One had already left for the conjunction point, whatever that was, so until he became a second-orbital force and chose a new leader for Kerux, the dark did not particularly need the relic. Nevertheless, they stated their demand, guided by the advice of the Interrogator: since there is an opportunity to return such a value for free, it must be used. And again, nothing of use for my city.

Mobility returned to me much earlier than expected — just a day after returning from the arena, I could move around the room on my own. There was no talk of any extraordinary feats yet, but the relative freedom allowed me to restore the mithril armor and even take part in laying the foundation for Hearth's new arena. Eleanore managed to allocate not only resources, but also several dozen construction teams for this matter, taking some workers from other sites. Our only working hotel could still cope with the flow of people, so we needed to lay the foundation before winter so that next year we could organize the first world competitions in magic, fencing and agility. Alia and Naira promised to work out the rules to equalize the participants: it would be stupid to put people in the same agility class if they all had different levels of body enhancements. In general, great times awaited Hearth. Now I only had to live to witness them.

The commander left my office. Kimal Sarento and I exchanged glances, and both shook our heads at the same time. It would not be possible to use the relics in Hearth as either light or dark. Rising from the table, I stretched luxuriously, loosening my still-stiff muscles, and headed to the throne room. In order to begin implementing my global plan, I needed to clarify a few points. The wretched experience of working with the Inquisitor made me approach his assignments differently. Diving in headfirst would be dangerous. If I wanted to survive, I needed to be prepared.

"Have the mechanoids been warned of my arrival?" I asked the Inquisitor. He looked at me as if I were a stupid child.

"We do not warn the forces about our messengers. They will know of your arrival the moment you appear before them."

"Then how will the mechanoids understand that I am an emissary of Chaos, and not just a lost man who found himself in the wrong place at the wrong time?"

"We do not bother ourselves with such trifles. You should get a stabilization system. Zero knows what it is and what it's for. If he has any questions, he can always contact us and clarify the details."

"So you can't contact him on your own?"

"You ask too many questions, Archduke Valevsky. You have been given a task. How you fulfill it is of no concern to us."

"No concern? Even if I accidentally leave this world without mechanoids?" I couldn't resist sarcasm, but the Inquisitor, surprisingly, didn't fall for the bait.

"The mechanoids are a third-orbital power. If you have to destroy them to get the stabilization system, then that is the price of creating a second-orbital power. It will ensure balance in any case, even if all the powers of the third orbit suddenly disappear."

I was taken aback: life had not prepared me for this. The ease with which Chaos agreed to the destruction of the mechanoids, as well as all the creatures of the third orbit, was frightening. As if they were something insignificant, only distracting Chaos from its main goals. However, it never even occurred to me to destroy the mechanoid. The world would lose too much from their departure. Hearth, for example, would lose the ideal security system that allows us to track all uninvited guests. Eleanore expelled several people from the city every day. This had already become a kind of tradition — Hearth treated spies with care and respect. Unless, of course, they crossed the line of what was permitted. Any violation within the city limits was punished severely, up to and including execution. But if no one violated anything, then the capture and expulsion from the city became some kind of game in which you always knew the outcome. Viscount Kurpatsky's fighters had even begun to greet some of the spies, they came to our city so often.

"So from what I understand, the geniuses of the ancients have not yet prepared the two vessels you need?"

"You understand correctly," said the Inquisitor. "You must resolve this issue yourself. If the highest hierarch has any questions, he can always ask us."

The Chaos Creature once again confirmed that communication between the forces and Chaos is initiated only by the forces themselves. The Inquisitor and the Interrogator had no ability to contact any of them on their own.

"When will One reach the conjunction point? How much time do I have?"

"Transportation will take another six months," the Inquisitor said, stunning me once again.

"Why, then, must I go to the mechanoids immediately?"

"Obtaining the necessary items and carrying out the power-siphoning procedure takes time. We are not sure that the mechanoids will easily part with the stabilization system. At the moment, it ensures that Zero continues functioning. It will require modification and copying, which takes time.”

“So the mechanoids won't listen to me at all?” The realization of what trials awaited me gave rise to an unpleasant sinking feeling in my stomach. I suddenly wanted to lock myself in the bathroom and refuse to leave for ten years. Was the Inquisitor even in his right mind, sending me to carry out such an assignment?

“We are not interested in the minor difficulties you will have to face,” the Inquisitor repeated. “You have been given a task. How you will cope with it is your concern.”

“Then I have one last question. What is the relationship between Zero and One?”

“One left the Mechanoids of his own free will, contrary to the decision of Zero. One wishes to become a second-orbital power, while the Zero will remain in the third. I think the answer is obvious, and there is no point in voicing it.”

In other words, Zero wouldn’t lift a mechanical finger to help One gain unprecedented power. The stabilization system would have to be knocked out by force. So that was why Chaos so easily agreed that the mechanoids could leave this world — they'd already thought everything through and didn’t see any other scenario except force. Neither did I, in fact. We'd have to take Kimal Sarento with us. He'd probably want to pump up his magic stone to level fifty-five, or even fifty-six.

“When are we leaving?” asked my experienced pupil when I told him the gist of the conversation with the Inquisitor. Unlike me, Kimal Sarento was no longer surprised by anything. According to him, he had expected something like this. Chaos couldn't help but throw us another curveball. It all seemed too simple — any messenger could have handled the task. However, since our services were required, it meant that everything was not as simple as it seemed at first glance.

"We can move out right now. More precisely, right after we talk to our Defender. Maybe he can suggest something useful."

No luck: our bald hedgehog wrote quickly, but his messages did not carry much meaning. Zero was a tough nut to crack, he would not compromise, all his orders are carried out by the mechanoids without question. One and, in fact, our Defender were the only mechanical creatures that had escaped his vicious circle.

"So destroying Zero won't affect you or Hearth's defense system?"

"Nor will it affect the mechanoids," the Defender wrote back. "The distinctive feature of the mechanoids from other forces is that they are a single whole. Even though the higher mechanoids have their own will and consciousness, they are still copies of Zero's mind. The physical bodies of the mechanoids are too fragile and short-lived. Metal tends to deteriorate over time, so the leader has the ability to implant his consciousness into any mechanoid available to him. The death of the leader, as happened with the lithoids and the offworlders, will not destroy the mechanoids. Only the total destruction of all mechanical creatures can drive this force from the planet. But here, too, Zero has insured himself: there are secret bunkers where the empty body of the future leader is located."

"Then it's not clear what the stabilization system is. What do the mechanoids need it for?"

"It is the life force of the leader. Without it, his consciousness would jump uncontrollably from one mechanoid to another. The stabilization system fixes the mechanical mind in one creature, turning it into a leader. Into the one who is commonly called Zero."

"This is just getting worse," Kimal Sarento said thoughtfully when we sent the Defender off to do his own thing. "As far as I remember, the Inquisitor didn't demand strict adherence to the sequence of obtaining items. The main thing is to get a stabilization system so that One doesn't lose his mind, as well as the two vessels where we'll need to pour the powers of the Abyss and Pharapho. Are you starting to get the idea, my mentor who can't seem to stay out of trouble?"

"I also think that we need to go see the geniuses of the ancients first," I said.

"Not exactly," smiled Kimal Sarento. "First, you need to visit an interesting place, access to which is only given to one person in this world. In order to communicate with the geniuses of the ancients, you should better understand these same ancients. Why did they agree to the demands of Chaos? Why did they betray their world and not activate the bomb? If the sixth-generation interactive neural network is right, then in those locations you will be able to get answers to these questions. Which, in turn, will create the foundation for your future communication. I will tell the girls that you went on business and that there is no need to bother you for some time. Go to the kitchen for food, do not leave without it. Although why am I explaining everything to you like a little child? To work, my grinning mentor. To work!"

Kimal Sarento's concern was touching. The man who had always been like solid granite was turning into a real mother hen. Although I knew his character too well. Most likely, he was not concerned about my well-being, but rather about my not accidentally dying. Kimal Sarento liked his current situation too much to change it for anything. So he had to show concern for the one on whom it depended. Yes, this was a more reasonable theory than that Kimal Sarento had turned into a kind old uncle. That the thought had even occurred to me was ridiculous.

However, I couldn't argue with the fact that he was right: you should always have some food in your immaterial backpack. You never know where your hard fate will throw you. As practice has shown, there are places where portals simply do not work. Since I am going to the location of the ancients, and then to the geniuses of the ancients who possess the skill *Author,* I needed to have some assurances.

The criteria for "purity" are not met.

Offworlder artifacts found. Clear out any foreign items to continue work.
List of items...

As with the first ancient safehold, the second did not immediately let me into its secrets. As soon as I activated the access key, a red beam appeared, scanning me from head to toe and rolling out a huge list of discrepancies. Smiling at my own stupidity, I returned to Hearth, where I undressed and took out all my magic stones. I didn't need any of it to work with ancient magic anyway. Except for the access key, which I could simply hold in my hands.

Returning to the door, I activated the plate again and received the long-awaited notification:

Access confirmed.
Welcome home, human!

Space blurred and became an ancient city. For a while, I stood there, still as a statue. I even held my breath, everything around me was so enchanting. In the previous location, the city had looked like something dead. The lifeless high-rises looked beautiful, but nothing flew between the houses. There was even a light breeze! And not just that, but also mechanisms scurrying back and forth. The city of the ancients was alive, and life hadn't stopped for a moment. There was even a smell! Dense, pleasant, tart. Nothing similar to anything that exists in our world. The only thing missing was other people.

"Welcome to the original city, Heir," a voice rang out. A middle-aged man dressed in a formal suit appeared next to me. He had a rather plain appearance without any distinguishing features, which gave reason to assume that the ancients were not much different from us. The same people, only extinct.

"I need information." I saw no reason to beat around the bush. Mandatory social protocols could be observed later, when there was time.

"What exactly do you seek, Heir? Do you wish to improve your knowledge in *Author*? As I see, your progress in collecting dictionaries is quite impressive. Seven out of twenty-five books is a worthy achievement. In a thousand years, you are the first one who has managed to advance so far."

"Can I get the remaining dictionaries from you?"

"Of those which you do not already possess, I only have two. Beginning level. All others are intermediate or advanced and were not included in my database."

"Two out of twenty-five isn't bad either," I said, doing a mental fist pump. The more dictionaries I could get, the more effective my skill would be.

"It's not bad," he agreed. "However, there is a limitation that we cannot overcome. All three outposts of ancient people remaining on this planet do not possess any material objects. I have no books, Heir. Only information. I can provide you with two dictionaries, but for this you will have to learn them. Go through each word and force it to appear in your dictionary by effort of will."

"And there will be no information that I received two dictionaries either," I guessed.

"That's right. You'll get the contents, but not the status of possessing two more dictionaries."

"How much time does it take to learn one dictionary?"

"From a week to a month, depending on your learning level."

"Got it. So I assume you won't be able to give me a weapon capable of destroying the creatures of Chaos?"

"The outposts of the ancients do not possess material objects, Heir. I believe you have already been told this."

"But you have information. Tell me, how can I defeat them? Is it even possible?"

"The only way of driving the invaders of our planet is to destroy the planet itself. The ancients, with all their advanced technology and spatial magic, couldn't do that, so why would you think that a weapon would suddenly appear a thousand years after they disappeared? No, Heir. Either this world will cease to exist, or it will forever remain under the rule of Chaos, free to do whatever it pleases. There is no other way."

"I don't need to destroy Chaos entirely. "Just one nasty representative of it," I muttered, trying to process what I had heard. It wasn't pleasant when your dreams of superweapons were shattered on the rocks of reality.

"One? When you entered my outpost, I was reading information about you. You actively communicate with creatures that are accustomed to calling themselves the Inquisitor and the Interrogator, considering them independent. This is the main mistake that people encountered a thousand years ago. Chaos is one in its essence. It has no divisions. The Inquisitor, the Interrogator, and any other monster marked by Chaos are a single whole. And they are all controlled by a single mind that surrounds the last-hour weapon."

"Then what is the point of this whole circus, of creating two different beings?" I asked.

"Humans have never managed to figure it out. Perhaps the traitors know the answer. But certainly not the interactive neural networks that control the remnants of ancient knowledge. However, I do not recommend that you communicate with those who betrayed humanity. Since they were originally mortal, they went down the path of searching for immortality. Unfortunately, as often happens, in the process of this difficult path they lost even the very concept of morality. The only thing that concerns these traitors now is the additional years of life that they can get by absorbing other creatures. They are no longer humans. They are monsters."

"Nonetheless, I need to visit them. Chaos wants to restore balance to our world. The geniuses of the ancients, as the traitors are now called, have devices called 'batteries.' With their help, it will be possible to create a second-orbital force."

"Chaos wants to draw more resources from the last-hour weapon, not restore balance," he corrected me. "The fewer fluctuations, the easier this is to do. As for the traitors, the batteries are designed to intercept the power of living beings. This is the traitors' bargaining chip. With its help, you can contain not only the power of living beings, but also, as I believe, part of the power of those who control the stabilization orbits. However, apparently, what you'll need is no ordinary battery: they depend on the volume of the contained power. You will need to find the maximum and solve the issue of survivability. I repeat: there is no morality in that society. If not for the restrictions set by Chaos, the traitors would have turned this world into a scorched desert long ago, having absorbed all life energy. They are insane and deserve to die."

"Is it possible to access the last-hour weapon? To lock it onto yourself?"

"No. It was designed in such a way as not to depend on a specific person. Inside it is an independent neural network, and already the seventh generation. For what reason it did not activate the weapon, we do not know. Perhaps Chaos is involved. We do not know."

"You can't get weapons here. You can't access the ancient bomb. You can't really get information out of here. What are these locations for anyway? How did my ancestor get the access key? It's a material object, right?"

"The access key was created, not received. If you look closely at it, you will see that it is just a piece of armor into which your ancestor invested the necessary power. But he did not do even that himself — the neural network of one of the outposts prompted him, practically giving all his power to create this key. However, it cannot be said that your arrival here is for nothing. You are a valuable enough resource that you have begun to combine the dictionaries of the *Author* skill. In order for this knowledge not to be lost, I can give part of my power — you will have the opportunity to teach this skill to others. You will be able to become a mentor and, when the time comes, choose a new mentor. The knowledge of the ancients will not be lost."

"In order to teach others, I have to understand what this skill is. Now I have to poke around all the walls like a kitten with a bag over its head."

"That's why you're here, Heir. Sit down, our conversation will be long and, I hope, maximally productive."

The master of the ancient outpost waved his hand and the surrounding space was transformed. The city disappeared, replaced by a small clearing in the middle of a dense forest. A board appeared next to him, and I found myself sitting at a real school desk. Exactly the same as those in the magic academy.

"In order to grasp the basics of spatial management, you first need to study the foundations of space itself. Understand what it consists of. How it works. What it interacts with. After we solve this issue, we will move on to the next one: matter management. You will have to learn to determine the structure, density, compressibility and expansion coefficients of any material you look at at a glance. Only after we can consolidate these two topics, will it be time to move directly to the creation of three-dimensional structures. It is dangerous to start crafting them any earlier: space does not like it when it is used thoughtlessly. When the laws embedded in the very basis of existence are violated. Do you understand what I mean?"

"That you can't create a deadly spear from ordinary earth," I nodded. "Because the body begins to fail."

"Not exactly, student. You can create a spear from earth. But you need to change the earth itself before that. Transform its structure. If you don't take care of this, there will be a rollback. Space will return all the unstructured energy back to the carrier. Moreover, the greater the discrepancy, the greater the rollback will be, up to and including the death of the summoner. Such cases are quite common among careless students."

"Transform the structure? You mean that the earth had to be compressed first?"

"If there are no other options," he confirmed. "But it is better to transform it using high temperature and changing the very structure of the molecular lattice of the earth."

"I don't understand..."

"That's precisely why you're here. To understand. I am unable to give you the material textbooks of the past, but I have the opportunity to embody them here and now. We will begin, perhaps, with the most important discipline of the ancients, from which we will push off all the time. Physics. Lesson one. What is physics and what is its place in this world..."

Chapter 11

"ARE YOU SAYING that after spending a whole week in the ancients' location, all you did was study physics?!"

I rarely saw my pupil dumbfounded, but today, as it turned out, was a unique case. The wise old schemer could not even imagine that someone would voluntarily agree to spend time that he physically did not have on some kind of study. Frankly, I thought the same for the first few days, but the more I immersed myself in the magical world of physics, the more I understood that humanity had lost a huge chunk of knowledge that for some reason had become unnecessary. The sixth-generation interactive neural network approached my training very sensibly: it understood that I would not be able to study all the material at once. Moreover, if we started from the very basics, then we would reach the topics that could really be useful to me after a few years, so it taught me only the most useful things. During the week that I spent visiting the ancients, I managed to understand the main thing: I'd have to spend a lot of time here over the next five to seven years. Physics turned out to be a boundless science, describing absolutely all phenomena in our world, even those that bear the mysterious concept of "magic." And I was going to figure it all out.

"I'm pretty sure I was speaking our common tongue. Yes, I was just studying," I tried to suppress a smile, but it was weak. Kimal Sarento's reaction was quite predictable, so it was funny. The location of the ancients had some special property of freezing the body. Inside, I did not need either rest or food. Only study, study and more study, because of which soon I even began to forget my own name! But wake me up in the middle of the night and ask what a molecular lattice is and how energy passes from one form to another and I would answer without hesitation. At the same time, I had no idea how all this would help me control space. And, to be honest, I did not understand the nature of this energy at all. We just hadn't gotten to that yet.

Kimal Sarento looked at me silently for a while, as if I were a traitor to humanity, and then quickly left the office, leaving me alone. Alia had told me in private that he had been restless all week. I had not returned to the city, I'd been uncontactable, and there had been no news of what was happening to me. In fact, everyone was worried, and my return turned out to be quite colorful: both wives expressed everything they thought about my long absence. Even the eternally calm Eleanore found a couple of minutes to meet with me one-on-one. The manager asked me not to disappear like that again, but the tone she used...Basically I had to repent and swear that this would not happen again. That I would always be in touch and, when I went to study again, I would definitely go outside at least once a day.

However, before the doors had time to close behind Kimal Sarento, they were open again. Looking at the guest, I frantically began to insert *Golden Dome of Protection* stone back into my magical field. Constant communication with the Inquisitor had forced me to temporarily turn into a light one, which was absolutely forbidden with this guest. The Interrogator stepped into my office.

"To what do I owe this great honor?" I asked, leaning back in my chair with relief. I made it! The Interrogator took the guest chair and stared at me with his black eyes for a while. Only after I activated my shield, showing that I did have it and that communicating with the coordinator of all the dark ones would not turn me into a spineless puppet, did he speak:

"Some problems have arisen. The Skron vessel learned of our plans and tried to stop us. Karina Fardi attacked One. I had to intervene and destroy her, but she achieved her goal: One has suffered irreparable damage. Despite the fact that it is almost impossible to destroy, at least the Skron vessel is definitely not capable of doing so, Karina Fardi managed to cause critical damage to the portal control system. Kerux has been left without a portal network. This is a problem that must be resolved as quickly as possible.

"Karina Fardi is dead?" I felt a shudder run through me. Could our world finally have found its long-overdue peace?

"No, she went to respawn, and we don't know where the location is. Skron carefully guards his vessel and constantly changes the respawn point. Right now we have no way to divert the resources to destroy it. This will require much more energy than fighting you."

"Is she that powerful?"

"Skron's vessel is already comparable in power to a third-orbital power. None of them, not even Zero, will be able to oppose it. It is developing at an unprecedented rate. A frightening rate. Already now, the time it can maintain conscious control is up to an hour and a half. When you battled it last, this value barely reached thirty minutes. Karina Fardi has become a force to be reckoned with. You have found a way to stop her, but at your current pace, this will take a few more months. Then the radius of the darkness created by Skron's vessel will increase to three hundred meters, and no crossbowman will be able to reach it."

"From my perspective, this is a problem for the dark ones. How am I or Hearth involved? If Fardi shows up outside the city walls, the Defender will send her back into the reincarnation cycle. If she simply shows up somewhere in the light lands, the commanders will deal with her. They are inert to the darkness, and Skron's vessel will not stand a single chance against them."

"The commanders cannot teleport. When they arrive at the place where Skron's vessel appeared, they will find only the remains of the dead."

"But the Inquisitor can teleport. Even if he can't personally engage in combat with Skron's vessel without risking losing excess energy, it won't take much effort to deliver the commander to whatever place the vessel appears. May the Light be with him and with the Inquisitor! Today I'll fly to the pope and hand him the intercom. As soon as Karina Fardi appears in the light lands, His Holiness will contact me, I'll teleport to the Citadel, take one or two commanders and deliver them to wherever Skron's vessel is raging. Protecting the lands from darkness is the main task of the Church of the Light. Let them do the work."

"By the time the information reaches the pope, we will have lost too much time."

"So I'll make dozens of communication devices and hand them to every bishop in the light lands. If necessary, I'll make hundreds, so that I can also issue one to the commander of the armies on each Wall. They contact the pope, he contacts me, I fly for the commander, and everyone enjoys the victory. The response time is ten minutes. Karina Fardi alone won't be able to do any serious harm in that short of a time frame."

"When Skron's vessel comes to the Bartolomeo Clan, the Citadel commanders will not stop it. They have no access to the lands of the dark ones."

"I believe that this is the problem of the respected Interrogator. The Skron vessel is a creation of the dark ones — not the light ones. And the dark ones must also answer for everything that the vessel does. If Karina Fardi attacks the Bartolomeo Clan, someone will have to help them. I think I even know precisely who. He's sitting in front of me right now, having a conversation, the purpose of which is completely lost to me. It has been clear for a long time that Karina is evil. Why are you suddenly so alarmed?"

"The portal network has been destroyed. The lands of the Kerux area are many orders of magnitude superior to the world of light. The territories of the clans are divided by rifts and ruins infested with the fog of Pharapho. Portals are the only way to travel. It has disappeared. You owe them help in restoring the portals."

"I owe them? Perhaps the esteemed Interrogator is mistaken in his words. Those who have been forced to use your services owe you. Those who voluntarily gave themselves into your slavery. I paid everything I owed, and even more. I went so far as to voluntarily give the keys to the Pharapho arena to the opposing factions. Have you thought about what will happen if these particles of the Light and Skron appear in this world at the same time? Personally, this worries me a lot, but who am I to interfere in the great affairs of Chaos? I have constantly had to make concessions, so I am not going to jump for free on your orders anymore. So the portal network is down? Great, there will be fewer guests in Hearth for some time. Send messengers to Zero, let him worry about restoring his brainchild."

"The portal network does not belong to the mechanoids. It is the creation of the geniuses of the ancients."

"The ancients?" The investigator managed to knock the ground out from under my feet. "How can that be? It's controlled by minotaurs."

"Servants of the ancient geniuses," confirmed the Interrogator. "Another of their creations. Approximately nine hundred years ago, a portal network was installed on all lands of the continent. In exchange for this, the ancient geniuses received immunity and the opportunity to conduct their own private affairs. However, now that the control circuit is broken, we will have to disturb the peace of these creatures again."

"So send messengers, what's the problem? Or, since you came to me, do you still have a problem with this point?"

"Yes, we do. The highest hierarch of geniuses has already designated the cost of restoration services. Chaos cannot agree to such demands. Today, war has been declared on the geniuses of the ancients."

I already understood perfectly well why the Interrogator had come to me. He wanted a certain Archduke Valevsky and his pupil to deliver the first blow in the war that had been declared. However, something did not add up, which I immediately pointed out:

"If the geniuses of the ancients are destroyed, the portal network will leave this world with them. Does Chaos really want this? What is the point of all these ventures you're undertaking?"

"We cannot allow this to happen, so it was decided to remove the functionality of portal management in favor of the new force of the second orbit. One was already previously in control of all movement, now it will perform this task consciously and officially. The geniuses of the ancients must leave this world, but leave behind a legacy. Your task will be to remove this legacy and during the formation of the second-orbital force, pass it on to One."

I didn't even want to comment. I was sure that if I started protesting, the Interrogator would come up with a hundred arguments for me to run right now to carry out this assignment, waving the flag and smiling happily. So I calmly returned to the papers that lay on the table, indicating that the meeting was over. The parties could not find common ground and remained solid in their positions.

"You will receive the coordinates of the place where, with a high degree of probability, there is a magic support stone, which will give you the ability to Heal from Pharapho's poison," the Interrogator said after a long pause. He was clearly not satisfied with my reaction, but he could do nothing about it. It was useless to put pressure on me. I was already completely crushed. All that was left was to negotiate, and, as expected, they threw me a gnawed bone from the master's table. Chaos didn't even see me as a dog anymore?

"With a high degree of probability? No, esteemed Interrogator. What you are asking is classified as 'impossible.' As the Inquisitor said, I believe. Therefore, if you need to destroy the geniuses of the ancients and take away the power that forms the portals before that, you must pay much more than some coordinates of some stone. If I really need it, I can get it into the Fog Arena, as the Inquisitor advised. Big deal, I'll suffer through forty waves. After going through it once, nothing can scare me much. What you want is several orders of magnitude more expensive than some stone, and I have quite weighty, yet reasonable demands. But before we continue, we need to clarify some details. My painful experience in communicating with the Inquisitor has shown me that everything needs to be clarified in advance. You want to remove the power that forms the portals. Will I be given instructions on how to do this, or will I have to figure everything out on my own?"

"We will give you a detailed sequence of steps, starting from how to obtain the power extractor and ending with how to transfer it to the carrying vessel."

"So I need not two, but three carriers?"

"More. Considering the fact that we no longer need the geniuses, we must siphon power not only to form the portals, but also to create minotaurs, the vessels, and much more that even the highest hierarch currently possesses. All this must be transferred to One."

"Which will make him the strongest of the three forces of the second orbit. Is Chaos ready for this? The strength given by the geniuses of the ancients, the Abyss and Pharapho is enough to start eyeing the first orbit."

"One will be warned that he cannot attempt such feats," the Interrogator answered again after a pause. "However, the risk still exists. It will need to be taken into account. But this point does not concern you. As soon as the third force appears in the second orbit and the world is restored to balance, your services will only be called upon in the most extreme cases."

"Like this one?" I grinned. The Interrogator didn't answer, but he didn't have to. The answer was clear.

"Okay, since I have my instructions, I can announce my price. In order to hire me for this crazy scheme, the esteemed Interrogator will transfer a complete list of all magic stones that currently exist on our planet to Hearth, along with full descriptions, limitations and requirements, if they exist. In addition to all methods of obtaining them — essentially all information regarding magic stones. I want a complete register. But that's not all. On top of that, I need the coordinates of all magic stones of exclusive status and higher, if there are any. One support stone will not do here, esteemed Interrogator. You want me to pull off another feat of madness? The price must be commensurate."

"Obtaining information about all the magical stones in this world will upset the balance," the Interrogator said, launching into his usual song and dance.

"Humans should have received a full list long ago. The fact that it does not exist is a huge omission that I plan to correct. It is needed, respected Investigator. It is desperately needed. As are all the places where stones grow. We do not need ordinary, magical and elite ones. Let them remain a place for ordinary seekers to find them. But we must know about all the exclusive stones that are freely available in the world."

"I need to think about it. Your demand is no less than that of the geniuses of the ancients."

"I'm in no hurry. The issue with the non-operational portals does not concern Hearth. As soon as you're ready…"

However, I didn't have time to finish: I was brazenly interrupted.

"We agree to your conditions, Archduke Valevsky! You will receive a guide to all the magic stones by the evening. As well as a map with all exclusive stones marked. Get ready for your trip — you don't have much time to pack."

Judging by the passion with which the Interrogator said these words, and also by the way he twitched before fervently assuring me that he had received the reference book, something had just happened somewhere. And it wasn't good. However, I was not allowed to ask what exactly influenced such a difficult decision. The representative of Chaos simply melted into thin air, teleporting to an address known only to him. Could it be that Karina Fardi had attacked One again? She should have been reborn. Strange.

The Interrogator's behavior was so out of keeping with his usual stoic visage that I didn't know how to react. Somewhere inside, I had an unpleasant feeling that I'd undersold myself by not asking for more, but it was too late — the verbal agreement had been reached. Selecting Kimal Sarento from my contact list, I mentally engaged the remote communication button:

"Tell me, my offended pupil, do you have any desire to take a nice stroll with me around our dear little planet and finish off a couple of extremely unpleasant beasts? Some that are capable of pumping your stone to the next important benchmark?"

"Too many uncertainties, my time-blind mentor. Who, when, how much? Give me more facts, then I'll decide whether it's worth wasting my precious time helping you. After all, the Interrogator came to see you, not me."

"You've heard?"

"No specifics. But the way the Inquisitor suddenly leapt up and flew off somewhere says a lot. The Interrogator has also left the city, I assume?"

"He also portaled away. The creatures of Chaos want to do what they didn't have the courage to do a thousand years ago. Finish off the geniuses of the ancients. Are you with me?"

"I hope you didn't sell yourself short."

"A complete list of all magic stones with descriptions, as well as locations for mining exclusive stones. All that exist in our world."

"A full list of magic stones? What did they demand from you? I need to know the precise conditions you agreed to!" Kimal Sarento's voice became tense. I had to retell our conversation, as well as explain the Interrogator's sudden agreement to my conditions.

"It's unlikely to be Fardi. Two forces wouldn't suddenly break down because of some girl. Even though she has become so strong. But the fact that the portals no longer work is bad. Very bad. For the dark ones, it's verging on disaster. Yes, my trouble-seeking mentor, I'm with you. I've long wanted to see with my own eyes the place of the conjunction, where all the forces appeared in our world. The place where humans finally lost. When are we going?"

"This evening. Before going to fight the geniuses, we need to get the extractor. The Interrogator promised to provide detailed instructions by this evening. So we wait."

We ended up waiting until the next day. The Interrogator only appeared in the morning. And he looked as if he'd been put through a meat grinder several times, pieced back together, then wrung out again, had several large chunks removed, and then from the remains, remolded into a new Interrogator. he had shrunk significantly and was now my height. I had not yet seen the Inquisitor, but I had no doubt that he looked no better.

The Interrogator entered my office again, sat down in the guest chair and, it seems to me, even breathed a sigh of relief. Although perhaps I was imagining things.

"The agreements are still in force," the Chaos creature declared, and a huge book materialized on my desk. "This is a reference book on all the magical stones of abilities, support, and enhancements that exist in our world. All four categories."

"I'll definitely check it out." I leafed through the book, but couldn't find a description of my *Praxis* on my first readthrough. I wanted to see what had been written about it in general reference books, but apparently I'd have to scour through to find it. There were a surprising variety of magic stones in our world.

"What about the map?" I asked, slamming the book shut. "I'll come back to it later."

"The Inquisitor will give it to you. He is waiting for you in the throne room. Hearing information of this caliber from me would be dangerous. The co-ordinates and names of all exclusive stones available for mining outside the rifts will appear on your map. This is what you asked for. There is a restriction that we cannot deviate from: this book cannot be used by anyone except the highest management of Hearth. The list of people who have access to it is limited. Currently, it includes Archduke Valevsky, both Archduchesses Valevsky, city manager Eleanore, the Archduke's pupil Kimal Sarento and Hearth's Defender. Other creatures are required to request access to the book only from us. You do not have the right to provide it yourself without our permission. Control over the execution of our order will be assigned to the protector of Hearth. The Defender will not be able to violate this order. Only humans have such freedom. There is a similar situation with the map. Only the aforementioned people have access to it. This is a mandatory requirement. We've already broken a lot of the rules of this world by bringing this reference book here."

"What about the instructions for obtaining the extractor?"

"Plans have changed once again. Last night was extremely tense and brought more unpleasantries: the conjunction point is temporarily inaccessible. If you go there now, you will die. Certainly and irrevocably. The place is now engulfed in pure Chaos, and will continue to be so for another three months."

"However, the dark ones cannot survive for that long without portals."

"You understand the situation correctly. Getting the extractor to the conjunction point was the easiest task. However, now the situation has changed, and you will have to extract it yourself."

"The Fog Arena," I sighed sadly, catching his drift.

"The Fog Arena. However, it's not that simple, Archduke. It's not that simple. I'm afraid you won't like the conditions for obtaining the extractor, but we simply have no other option. You must enter the arena without magic stones or armor. Just you and a regular spear with a steel tip."

"What for?" I asked, stunned.

"In order to get what you want, you need to increase the difficulty of the arena. Increase it significantly. It's not hard to pass forty waves, especially with your magic stones. But this will not give the Fog Stalker enough energy to form a power extractor. In addition to the waves themselves, there is also such a thing as difficulty. The state in which a person enters the arena. The fewer magic stones, amulets, rings, protection and other attributes that can make the passage easier, a person enters the arena with, the greater the reward he receives. The faster it grows. After the first wave, you can get a reward similar to what the Fog Stalker gives out on the fifteenth. And with each wave, this reward will only grow. This is one of the features of the arena. You do not need to pass through the entire thing — the extractor can be obtained on the twenty-fifth wave. Your task is to obtain it."

"With a single spear," I said sullenly.

"You haven't been paying attention, Archduke Valevsky. You are guaranteed to obtain the energy necessary for the extractor from the twenty-fifth wave of the increased difficulty Fog Arena. From just that one. Think about it, consult with your team and come to me. I will open the portal to the Fog Arena for you, after making sure that you have not taken anything with you that could reduce the difficulty. You have three hours to prepare. Your time has begun."

Chapter 12

"GREETINGS, HUMAN! You have chosen a strange method of traveling here."

"Does it make a difference how I enter the arena?"

"The standard paths differ significantly from the paths of Chaos. First of all, you will not have the opportunity to return to your world at your own will. You will be able to leave my arena only at the behest of a servant of Chaos."

I could only grin. The Interrogator, of course, forgot to mention this "small detail." How could I think that he would be any better than the Inquisitor? Didn't the interactive neural network say that these two creatures were echoes of the same entity? And clearly not the most honest fellow.

"I know why you were sent here, human. All that's left is to decide how you plan to get it. The extractor will become available if you complete the twenty-seventh wave. It will also be available to you after the twenty-fifth wave if you don't start receiving rewards. You need to choose."

"Whoever sent me here said that it would take twenty-five waves to get the extractor. Not twenty-seven."

"The Servant of Chaos has misjudged your capabilities, human. Yes, you have no armor, no magic stones, and no access to inventory, but you came to the arena with steel. This is more than enough to significantly reduce the difficulty of the arena."

"Since when did a simple hunk of steel become a dangerous weapon?" I asked sarcastically. "Does the esteemed Fog Stalker think I'll simply be able to throw it through my opponents?"

"You can make a weapon out of it. I know about the magic of the ancients, human."

"In that case, the respected Fog Stalker should know about such a thing as a rollback. Creating a spear from steel is not a problem. The problem is what will happen to the creator after the spear is destroyed. I will turn into a vegetable that any monster could devour."

"You don't need to create a spear, human. Crossbow bolts will do. They are steel in essence and will not cause recoil when destroyed."

"I have nothing to say to this wild assumption. Can the esteemed Fog Stalker remind me what kind of creatures appear in his arena? Are they ordinary humans who die from simple spear wound?

From what I recall, the arena is populated by the spawn of Pharapho and the Abyss. Tenacious, dangerous and quite difficult to destroy creatures. Even if I create crossbow bolts and make them pierce each monster that appears in the arena ten times, this will have little effect on the overall danger. Or am I mistaken?"

"No, you're not mistaken." The Fog Stalker thought for a moment and cast another glance at the meter-long cube of pure steel that I had dragged along with me. Which had proved quite a daunting task. Not only was it heavy, but I also had to make special notches to grip it properly.

"In that case, I want to return to the issue of twenty-seven waves. I came here without protection, without weapons, without magic, without enhancements or amulets. If we talk about difficulty, this must be the maximum level, and I should get the extractor not on the twenty-seventh, but on the twenty-fourth wave. Or does the respected Fog Stalker wish to cheat me? Maybe it makes sense to turn to an independent arbitrator? As far as I understand, even in this case, Chaos will evaluate everything impartially."

"Twenty-five waves, human. That is my final decision."

"Twenty-five? Even if I start earning for the extractor from the first wave?"

"You'll have to reach twenty-third wave." There was not a shred of emotion in the metallic voice. This creature did not care at all that someone wanted to go through his arena without armor, weapons, magic or amulets. So what? Another su-icidal maniac! How many of them had there been in the entire history of the arena? After all, the Fog Stalker had clearly come to us from some other world.

"In that case, what's the point of delaying the inevitable? Wave!"

I'd have to risk it. An emergency meeting of all Hearth leaders took place immediately after the In-quisitor left. Each idea we brainstormed was more hare-brained than the last, eventually culminating in the plan for me to leave Hearth, lock myself in the ancient outpost and refuse to leave for the next few years. Kimal Sarento immediately deciphered the Inquisitor's words: the initial difficulty of the arena does not depend on the items that a person can get upon passing each wave. In fact, the main thing I needed to do was somehow survive the first wave, get protection for myself and, moving slowly and surely, reach the required level to complete the task. After a long discussion, everyone agreed that this was the only reasonable way to complete the arena, since everything else would be blocked by the Inquisitor as a device that reduced the dif-ficulty of the arena.

"Max, what happens if you fall off of the edge?" Alia suddenly asked when we seemed to have fin-ished the meeting.

"I die. At one time, the Fog Stalker explained this to me in very plain words."

"And if the beasts fall off?"

"They also die. Before I pumped up my *Healing*

Aura, I had to throw them off, among other things. Into the nothingness in which the arena floats. The monsters did not return."

"Alia's speaking sense," said Kimal Sarento, gazing at the blushing girl with respect.

"Sense?" Unlike my pupil, I didn't immediately catch on. "Let's not tell riddles. Now is not the best time to lecture. Clearly and to the point: what exactly are you proposing?"

"Steel," Kimal Sarento and Alia said almost simultaneously. Alia looked at him and smiled, gesturing for him to develop his thought.

"If we are talking about how to increase the difficulty of the arena, then you don't need to take a weapon with you either," Kimal Sarento began, and a satisfied grin crept onto his face. "But who said that you need this weapon? Was it for nothing that you disappeared into the location of the ancients for a whole week? As has already been said, all you need to drag with you to the arena is steel. Lots of steel. Enough to guarantee it will last you through all the waves you encounter. This is what you will have to do, my mentor who knows how to manipulate the very fabric of space..."

My memories of the past evaporated — creatures began to emerge around me. I had to act and embody a product so familiar to me now, down to the smallest details: a table made of pure metal. Only now it had several minor details that made my creation perfect. Short legs, a thickened tabletop and a clear understanding that the table was made of steel, without any admixture of other materials. In order not to waste time on trifles, I immediately made four tables, placing them next to each other, and as soon as the arena monsters appeared and began to look in my direction, I set the structure in motion.

Alia was one hundred percent right: I didn't need to kill the creatures. I didn't need to show miracles of heroism. I didn't need to suffer. All I had to do was stand in the center of the arena and wield the flying tables, pushing the Fog Stalker's spawn over the edge of the platform. The monsters couldn't dodge, jump away, or avoid such a vile attack: the distance between us was too small. Besides, I had learned to wield flying objects well. Ever since the rift, when I had to operate a spear.

"This is a violation!" The Fog Stalker declared as soon as the first wave was over, essentially before it had even begun. My table weapon was working real miracles.

"A violation of what?" I asked, not even trying to hide my grin. "I came to the arena almost naked, with only a piece of unprocessed steel with me. Or does the respected Fog Stalker want to somehow influence my passage? It seems to me that this is exactly the sort of violation you are shouting about. If you have a rulebook that you can present to me, you are welcome to do so."

"You're not breaking the rules," he was forced to agree, but immediately added, "However, the rules for passing the arena will be changed. Arena spawns cannot be pushed off the platform."

"And these rules will come into effect starting

from the next run?" I asked just in case.

"That's right. You can't change the rules in the middle of the arena. But next time, human, you won't be able to use a technique so unbecoming of a real hero."

"In that case, dear Fog Stalker, where is my wave?"

All that can be said about the next twenty-two waves is that they happened. The Fog Stalker was having as much fun as he could. At some point, he stopped generating the usual Pharapho spawns, concentrating on the huge rift monsters, but it was of little help: the magic of the ancients did not require a fulcrum to push a body off the platform. No matter how huge and scary the monster was, it fell over the edge of the arena with the same ease as the most ordinary krona. And what pleased me most was that the stupid creatures did not even try to destroy the barrier. All their rapt attention was focused entirely on me, and they ignored the steel tables, considering them something insignificant. This allowed me to bring all four tables created in the first wave to the twenty-third. The last creature disappeared over the edge of the platform, and the Fog Stalker, somehow maintaining a calm tone of voice, proclaimed:

"The conditions for obtaining the extractor have been met. Your reward, human."

A small device appeared next to me. From a distance, it resembled a crossbow, but only from a distance. And only because it had a trigger mechanism. Where the bolts were supposed to fly out, there was something that looked like a watering can. Apparently, to scoop up as much power as possible from another creature and collect it in...Judging by what I saw, the extractor had no place to collect energy. In any case, I didn't see any container.

"In addition to the extractor itself, there should also be instructions," I said, having finished twisting the device. "I don't see it. Or a receiver where all this power will accumulate."

"You're asking questions without the right to do so," the Fog Stalker said, clearly offended. Usually he was willing to engage in any conversation.

"Alright, let's talk basics and specifics. Run it!"

The twenty-fourth wave was not much different from its predecessors. It was just a little more difficult to push the monsters off the edge, as they dug into the edge of the platform with their teeth and claws, not wanting to fall into the unknown. The tables were not suitable for the task — they were too big to work with near the edge. I did not want to check what would happen if the table flew off the edge of the platform. This wasn't a time to experiment with different ways of passing the arena. I had to create a long stick to shove the especially vivacious creatures off the ledge. The toothy face of the Fog Stalker grinned evilly when the last monster disappeared. Apparently, this behavior was due to the new tactics employed against my tables. But the Fog Stalker had not considered the possibility of a poking stick, and for his lack of foresight, he paid dearly: I passed the twenty-fourth wave.

"So, I need instructions on how to use this device, as well as a receiver where I can hold the power I've extracted. And I'll add up front that it will have to hold all the energy of a third-orbital being. The holding vessel must be able to withstand this."

"There is no receiver in the extractor. The carrying vessel is inserted into it," the Fog Stalker answered reluctantly. "Instructions on how to use this device will cost you another wave."

"Is the esteemed Fog Stalker joking?" I asked. "The next wave is the twenty-fifth! I should have been given an extractor for passing it alone. How is it that the instructions for the device are worth more than the device itself? Is the esteemed Fog Stalker trying to deceive me?"

"You weren't supposed to get the instructions, human. The servants of Chaos made it clear that I only needed to give you the device, without a description of how it works. Moreover, even if you pass the next wave, you won't be able to take the instructions from the arena. You will have the opportunity to read them, memorize them, write them down in your notebook, but not take them. Chaos forbade it."

"Why?"

"If I answer this question, you will have to pass not only the twenty-fifth wave, but also the twenty-sixth before receiving instructions. Are you prepared for this?"

"No, never mind. Alright, I hear what you said

about the instructions. What about the carrying vessel for the third-orbital power? How many waves do I need to pass through to get it?"

"Ten." The Fog Stalker had once again raised the bar sky high. "You will get what you seek on the thirty-fifth wave. Unlike the instructions, you will be able to take the vessel with you."

"Alright, I'll solve problems as they come. Let's see what's so unusual about these instructions that the servants of Chaos don't want me to see it. Wave!"

The twenty-fifth wave required some work. The Fog Stalker once again managed to adapt to my style and released small and nimble creatures that managed to dodge the tables. Some even got very close, but were impaled on my steel stick, which I used as a spear. Finally, the last creatures were thrown off, and somewhere deep in my soul I realized that I would not be able to cope with another ten waves. The large and heavy creatures would die, no doubt, but the small ones, which were the size of cats, or even ousels, would finish me off. I certainly wouldn't be able to brush them aside with a table.

"The instructions. Your time is not limited. You can study it as much as you like. You will not be able to take this document with you to the main world."

A translucent book appeared in front of me. My hand passed through it freely, and the Fog Stalker had to show me how to operate it — with hand gestures. The pages were thick enough, so I had no problems reading the information they contained. I did have some issues with understanding. Many of the terms were new to me. It seemed that the extractor was a creation of an alien world, which somehow ended up in ours. Someone had translated the instructions into human language, but had not adapted the terms. Or could not, since they were absent from our language.

Nevertheless, I managed to get the gist, and I couldn't say I was too happy about it. To be more precise, I sincerely considered breaking the extractor in half and never leaving the arena. Or somehow forcing the servants of Chaos to negotiate with the highest hierarch of the ancient geniuses. Because the mechanism that the Fog Stalker handed me had one unpleasant feature: it absorbed the life force of not only the creature against which it was directed, but also the wielder. Not all of it, only part, but it was life force energy that could not be restored over time. I carefully reread the document several times, but I still couldn't find any way to protect myself from the backlash. If I used it, it would definitely make me weaker. To the point that my dark mirror would disappear, and I would also not be able to use magic in the future. Even with my endless mana. To say nothing about my access to the status bar. All this would be siphoned into the battery.

"As it is, there's no way to protect against the extractor's radiation?"

"No." Surprisingly, the Fog Stalker gave me an

answer without requiring more waves in payment. Although he immediately explained his behavior: "You have some leftover credit after passing the previous wave, so we can discuss this point."

"How can I determine how much power the device will take from me?"

"There has been no practical experimentation in this area, so no one knows. Perhaps only your ability to use magic stones will disappear. Perhaps your dark mirror. Perhaps everything you have. Or nothing at all. This option cannot be discounted either. You are going to absorb the energy of the most powerful among the ancient geniuses, and this is quite a non-trivial job. In addition, immediately after absorbing one life force, you will have to remove the power of the Abyss and Pharapho. You don't think that they will be able to simply relinquish it on their own, do you?"

"So that means in either case, I'll be transformed into an ordinary human?"

"In an ideal scenario, yes. More realistically, you'll soon be transformed into a corpse. You'll be able to maintain your body in a stable condition for some time, but not long. My estimate is no more than twenty years."

"Years?" My voice trembled at the news. "Not minutes, days or weeks? Years? What do you mean by 'soon' then?"

"The human lifespan is too short to pay any real attention to. After using the extractor a few times, you will lose everything that makes you special, and you will also receive a permanent ban on life extension and healing magic. Any disease will be fatal for you — your body will be unable to fight back, even with outside support. But you will not die immediately. The extractor does not take away your life."

"Something you just said caught my ear — life extension. Does this information require payment?"

"You understand correctly, human. In order to obtain this information, you must pass through ten waves. From this one through to the thirty-fifth. Or you may pass forty waves in the standard arena."

"I don't need the mechanism, I just need to know how long and what the conditions are. Does one need to absorb the life force of other beings, like the ancient geniuses did? If prolonging one life requires the sacrifice of tens, or even hundreds of others, then let this lost knowledge remain lost."

"There is no limit on how long you can extend your life," the Fog Stalker responded after a pause. Clearly, he was weighing all the pros and cons. "The method of life extension that I can offer you is based on creating your own clone and transferring your consciousness into it. This technology was actively used by the ancients, but was withdrawn from circulation during the arrival of Chaos on the planet due to the risks involved. Immortal soldiers, capable of being reborn after each battle, could have a detrimental effect on the state of affairs in battles. Now there is no war and the planet is under Chaos' rule, so the ban on the technology has been lifted. Moreover, it was transferred to Skron to equalize his chances in the battle with the Light.”

“Converts,” I said. The mysteries of reincarnation that no one in this world knew anything about, but which everyone had encountered at least once.

“Correct. Converts are the true servants of Skron, who have given their souls in exchange for immortality. However, the current mechanism has one inconvenient feature: Skron is extremely sensitive to his brainchildren. As soon as one of them loses control over their body, Skron intercepts control over their consciousness. These converts are excluded from the respawn pool. It is impossible to transfer consciousness to a clone when said consciousness no longer exists. It has been burned out by the higher entity.”

“But the mechanism you can provide does not have this feature? Then I have another question: if I create a clone, use the extractor, and then reincarnate, will the new me still have these limitations?”

“Yes. The extractor works directly with the soul, not the body. There are no defensive mechanisms in this world that will protect against this process. None known to me, in any case. Your credit has run dry, human. If you wish to continue this conversation, you will have to pass through another wave.”

“Where I’ll be ground into dust,” I grinned. “You've already figured out how to get past my tables, right? No. Fog Stalker. I know my limit, I won't go any further. Take me back."

"As was stated, you can only return back at the behest of Chaos. At the moment, there has been no such request."

"So tell them I have the extractor. Let them open the passage."

"Giving out information for free is not my modus operandi, human. If you would like to convey this information, you will need to pay for it in energy. Your energy credit is currently at zero. Instead of leaving the arena, you chose to talk. That was your choice. The servants of Chaos will wait as long as necessary. They will not open the exit themselves. After all, no one knows how long it will take you to pass through the arena at this difficulty level."

"So that's how it is," I bared my teeth. I wanted to strangle the flying freak, but I knew perfectly well that I could not. In the arena, the Fog Stalker ruled supreme. "You know that Chaos won't let such betrayal go unnoticed, right?"

"You came here through the portal of Chaos. Everything obtained in the current arena is the property of Chaos. Regardless of whether you survive the next wave or not, the extractor will be given to its owner."

"Asshole," I muttered.

"Those who use unconventional methods of passing through should not be surprised that the arena will react accordingly. You did not break the rules, but the rules were not broken against you either. If you wish to leave the arena, you will have to pass the twenty-sixth wave."

"Well then..." I looked at the remains of the steel, and another crazy plan began to take shape in my mind. "If I must pass through, I must. You say that information about immortality is worth ten waves, up to and including the thirty-fifth? Tell me specifically what I will receive in exchange."

"Only information." My attitude seemed to make him tense up. "Any material items obtained in this arena will be given to Chaos."

"Will this information include a full list of all requirements? What devices and resources are needed, how to tie everything together and, most importantly, how to obtain and configure all the pieces?"

"Yes. The information will contain all necessary details. Everything that you need, aside from the devices themselves. You will even receive copies of the items so you know exactly what you are looking for. Are you ready to pass through ten waves, despite the claim that you've already reached your limit?"

"This limit was reached by an ordinary human, dear Fog Stalker. But do you see an ordinary human before you now? You shouldn't have made me angry. You really shouldn't have."

I said all this while crafting new items. Unfortunately, the tables wouldn't help anymore. They're useless against the small creatures. However, there was something that was guaranteed help, and I needed to create it. Half an hour passed before I was satisfied with the result. Three long steel rods, installed in the form of a tripod, united three meters above the arena. At the place where they met, I built a small platform, onto which I jumped. It was easier to observe the arena from here. But I didn't limit myself to one tripod — all four tables were destroyed and turned into a huge steel fine-mesh net. It hung over the arena, separating my platform from the arena floor. I spent the rest of the steel on another net, this time installing it vertically under the main net. I would use it to push the creatures off of the ledge.

"That is a violation!" the Fog Stalker practically cried when he understood what I was doing.

"Then call the referees!" I answered angrily. "Let them prove that what I'm doing is wrong. Otherwise, shut up and start throwing monsters at me. Let's see what you come up with now. Wave!"

Chapter 13

"YOU PASSED FORTY WAVES. What did you receive?" As soon as the last wave had subsided, the Inquisitor personally appeared in the fog arena.

"Two bouquets, a 'Say No to Tyranny' poster, and a flag that says 'Free Archduke Valevsky,' the Fog Stalker answered for me, handing me my prizes. After I'd received comprehensive information on achieving immortality, including copies of the blueprints for the mechanisms, I tried to have a little fun. Over the next four waves, from the thirty-sixth to the thirty-ninth, I received several answers to questions about the *Author* skill, as well as information on where the ancient geniuses were located, including a map of their main lair. Since Chaos had declared war on them, the immortality-hungry ancients would be ready for anything. They knew that the Inquisitor and Interrogator were capable of opening portals to any point on our planet, so it was highly probable that any attempts to break into the lair of the most powerful ancient would be futile. I needed an entry point from which two mages with level fifty stones (meaning myself and Kimal Sarento) could move forward without fear of traps. Of course, they could be formed right under our noses, but here I was relying on my *Author* abilities. After all, completing the current arena clearly demonstrated that I already had a good grasp on spatial manipulation.

I knew that as soon as I passed the fortieth wave, the servants of Chaos would appear and confiscate everything I'd received from the Fog Stalker. The cunning and powerful beings probably thought that I'd stock up on unique stones, weapons and defenses, so my requests for the last wave were, at first glance, the most irrational choices possible. At second and third glance, too. But I can say with certainty that they were worth it. The way the Interrogator's face elongated when he saw my loot was worth all the hardships I'd faced.

"For passing through forty waves of the arena on increased difficulty, you received an extractor and this?!" It seemed that the servant of Chaos would burst with anger. He glowered, grew in size, even pulled out his sword, as if he wanted to finish me off on the spot. But this no longer affected me. I truly hadn't received any other material objects.

"That is really all I received in the arena. I was

given the task of earning the extractor, and I fulfilled it. Then I got this, but I didn't have enough imagination for more. Hearth is now in such a position that we want for practically nothing, and anything we do need, we can earn ourselves."

"You wasted fifteen levels of the increased-difficulty arena?!" The Inquisitor seemed to have a stroke when he realized that we were not lying.

"Does the respected Inquisitor wish to accuse me of something?" I asked, raising one brow quizzically. It wasn't as eloquent as when Eleanore did it, of course, but it was still effective. "I received everything that I wished to receive. Flowers for my wives, a flag for my pupil and a poster for the throne hall. Is that not worthy of the last fifteen waves of the buffed-up Fog Stalker Arena?"

The Inquisitor did not respond, but a moment later I was standing in the throne hall with two beautiful bouquets in my arms. The poster and flag were lying not far off — the Chaos creatures had found no further use for my "prizes." They paid no heed to the fact that the huge poster and massive flagpole were crafted from sellar mined from the ninetieth level of the rift. And who in their right mind would miss that detail?

According to the Fog Stalker, sellar was the strongest material on the planet. Mithril didn't even come close. A blade made of sellar could slice through mithril armor like paper, while a blade made of mithril couldn't make a scratch on sellar. The notebook already contained full instructions on how to process sellar, and what pleased me most was that this metal significantly reduced the influence of darkness. I had to rack my brains to come up with a way to outwit the creatures of Chaos, and judging by the fact that the poster and the flag were still with me, my little prank had been a success.

Now I just had to be careful not to let my grin give me away.

"If you think we're going to hang this somewhere, you're sorely mistaken. Eleanor and I will think about how else we can use it." Soon Kimal Sarento appeared in the hall and walked over to my pile of winnings. He made no mention of the fact that I had passed through forty waves of an increased-difficulty arena, received everything I needed and, in fact, was quite heroic in the process. Although how could he think of any of these things — as soon as I found myself back in reality, the notebooks had synchronized and a new entry had appeared on the "Kimal Sarento" page:

As soon as I leave the arena, I need you to run to the throne room immediately and pick up two items that will be there. A poster and a flag with a huge flagpole. This is important! Details later, in private meeting.

I had to give Kimal Sarento his due — he acted with lightning speed. Seeing the notebook flicker, he, of course, immediately opened it, saw huge chunks of new information, but immediately noticed the changes to his own description. It took him a minute to find my entry, get his bearings and get to the goal.

"Are you kidding me? I passed through forty waves in the Fog Arena to get them!" I said in faux-offense, biting my lip so as to not break into a grin and give myself away.

"You were only asked to go through twenty-five. The fact that you decided to be a hero is your own problem, my restless mentor. Let's go, we'll return all your stones and discuss where to put this nightmare. One option is to hang it over your bed. Your wives will be so happy..."

We were in my office in a matter of minutes. Kimal Sarento tried not to let on how difficult it was to stay upright. The immaterial backpack freed you from the bulk, but not the weight. I still shudder to recall the state I was in when I carried that steel cube. I was rooted to the spot. I hadn't lost all my mobility, my arms and legs still twitched, but I could not move even a millimeter. With immense difficulty, the servants had dragged the steel to the throne, where I hid it in my backpack, then the Interrogator carried me to the Fog Arena, where I had unloaded my burden.

"Tell me," Kimal Sarento unloaded the flagpole and poster from his inventory and sighed with relief.

"You can read it in your notebook. It's all there," I couldn't help myself. There was a lot to tell, but my innate mischievousness kept me from ignoring his remark.

"I'll most certainly comb through it later. I want to hear everything first-hand. With the details that are not in the book."

I could have resisted further, but I didn't see the point. We needed a decision, not a demonstration of my arrogance. Since I'd had the sensible idea to invite Eleanore and my wives.

While everyone was getting ready, I got dressed in my mithril and stuck my magic stones back in. It was hard to even describe in words how much I had missed them. I'd gotten so used to them that it seemed like I'd torn out a whole layer of my own essence when I got rid of the magic octahedrons.

Soon the girls showed up, and I began to tell them of my heroism, paying special attention to the Fog Stalker's words and the newfound knowledge that I would soon have to transform back into an ordinary human.

"Tell me, my mentor, who knows how to find trouble where there is none, are you absolutely sure that the extractor will eat up your power?"

"The full set of instructions has been copied into the notebook. In fact, you and Eleanore have full access, you can study it yourselves. And the idea that I'll lose all my magic abilities didn't come fro me. The Fog Stalker said as much. Although he did say that there were no precedents for this so he can't promise a specific result. There is a non-zero chance that absolutely nothing will happen to me. But somehow that's hard to believe."

"Is there an option to refuse the path to the ancient geniuses?" Alia, per usual, was trying to solve problems instead of bemoaning the injustices of our world.

"On this point, I'm afraid, we have no choice.

There are very few people on this planet who could stand up to a third-orbital power. And, coincidentally, they're all in this room right now."

"You've forgotten the empresses," Eleanore reminded me. "They also have stones and mithril armor."

"With all due respect, I don't have much faith in them. Naira and Alia can handle themselves, they've got the right character. You've spent a quarter of your life in the rifts. I don't need to say anything about myself or my pupil here, but our empresses are incapable of such feats, I'm afraid. And they have a different duty right now. They need to raise up the empire."

"Alright, let's say you're right and there are no other options — Max must attack the ancient geniuses. Who said he has to be the one to operate the extractor? We could craft another suit of mithril armor, stick it on an ordinary human with nothing to lose, and teleport him to the necessary location. I don't think Max would suffer any consequences for this."

"It won't work," Eleanore said, tearing herself away from the notebook. "Only people with certain access may use the extractor. Access is granted by the Chaos creatures. We all know that they want to punish Max, so they will only give access to him."

"Let's say he's not the only one with access," Kimal Sarento said, also leafing through the instructions page by page. "'All participants in the extraction process.' Now the only question is, how do we convince our esteemed guests that an ordinary human must take part in the process? And ensure that they survive until the moment we need them? If I understand the specifics of the magic of the ancients, it's oriented around spatial manipulation. My resourceful mentor has obtained a map of the ancient locations, of course, and has even determined the most convenient point to portal to, but we'll still have to fight our way through the hordes. An ordinary human would not survive. We need a doomed soldier."

"Who you will outfit with mithril armor and level-fifty magic stones?" Eleanore scoffed. "A human with nothing to lose? Not the brightest idea."

"I don't have any others."

"But I do." The air shimmered, and the Inquisitor appeared in the office. Good thing I was sitting — his voice once again crushed me. Naira squeaked somewhere nearby, and to the Inquisitor's approving nod, Kimal Sarento carried the unconscious girl out of the office. Finally, I pulled out *Golden Dome of Protection* and sighed with relief. His mere presence made me tense up. Kimal Sarento returned to the office, and the Inquisitor began to explain his idea:

"We have figured out what you actually received from the arena, Archduke Valevsky. I admit you were clever. Obtaining what you did while ensuring we wouldn't confiscate it was a strong move. And all within the rules — we have no right to punish either you or the Fog Stalker. However, we should not have been surprised. You are a known violator of the established rules. However, there is one thing we still are fully within our rights to do: send you to the geniuses of the ancients right now. You have been granted access to the extractor."

The nasty little device that would turn me into a stranger appeared on the table in front of me.

"You have an hour to get ready," the Inquisitor said and turned around, wanting to leave the office through the door. Everyone was silent, not knowing what to say, but surprisingly, I found some words.

"So the respected Inquisitor wants to break his word to the pope? I suppose that somewhere in the throne room the respected Interrogator is now composing a fiery speech about why the dark ones must remain without the main source of their value."

"What are you talking about?" The Inquisitor stopped and looked over at me quizzically.

"About the fact that you, esteemed Inquisitor, promised the pope and the Temple of Skron or leader of the dark ones, that they will ascend the throne after One, that each of them will receive a piece of this power. The pope will receive a piece of the Light, the misty servants — a piece of Skron. In order to get all this, you need to pass through forty waves. In my current state, I can still accomplish this, even if the Fog Stalker has more tricks up his sleeve. If I go now to the geniuses of the ancients and use the extractor, then I will no longer be capable of passing through forty waves.

The promises that were given to the pope and the Temple of Skron will remain unfulfilled. Whose fault will it be? Certainly not mine — I was left with no choice."

The Inquisitor's silence was filled with more meaning than all the words in this world. Although this silence was paired with a glaring look. The Chaos being was angry again, but could not find anyone to blame but himself. After all, it was they who had declared to both the light and dark that they would return the lost relics to them. Going back on all the promises they made, just because they had a distaste for one particular archduke? For beings of this caliber, this was akin to a death sentence. Who would trust them after that?

"You have twenty-four hours to pass the arena," he finally said.

"Twenty-four hours? Esteemed Inquisitor, you are clearly unaware of the fact that it is impossible to pass through the entire Fog Arena three times in the span of a day. I'll have to spend the first run getting that stone that will allow me to cure Pharapho's poison."

"You were given a map with all the stones!" the servant of Chaos barked.

"On which there are more than a thousand magic stones. How long will it take to find and compare stones and their descriptions in the huge tome that we received? Everything takes time, esteemed Inquisitor. By the way, in what form will I receive the relics? Have you thought about what will happen to me when I take a piece of Skron in my hands? Or the Light? Will I immediately burst into flame, or will I have time to scream in pain before dying?"

"The relics will be in the carriers," the Inquisitor replied, but I didn't like the pause that preceded it.

"And, presumably, the Fog Stalker knows this? Forty waves will be enough to obtain both the relic and the battery?"

"You'll need to pass through the arena at a higher difficulty level."

"Again?! My trick won't work again — the Fog Stalker has clearly stated that he is going to change the rules. The creatures that spawn in the arena will have to be killed, not thrown off the platform. I was lucky this time, I won't be so lucky again."

"So you'll need to get two carriers before you go after the relics."

"I only have three arena keys, esteemed Inquisitor. The math doesn't add up. Or will you send me at your own expense?"

"We have exhausted our ability to send creatures to the arena. We can make our next attempt in a year. You will have to go to the fog-filled lands of Pharapho and obtain new keys to the arena. You will be given twenty-four hours to do this."

"A day for the keys, a day for the arena. Does the esteemed Inquisitor not know of any other time periods? I am not a mechanoid who can work without rest. If you haven't noticed, I just happened to return from the reinforced arena, after almost dying, I'm in a state of extreme exhaustion and I need to recover. Moreover, we haven't even touched on the important topic of the extractor. Why do you want to destroy me? You know that I've seen the instructions, right? Why should I act on the side of Chaos if I will die as a result? This is your war with the geniuses of the ancients, not mine. I am not your warrior, not your debtor. I am a simple head of an autonomous city, but the esteemed Inquisitor seeks to destroy me with frightening regularity."

"Ordinary humans are in no state to use the extractor. Yes, we are aware of the side-effects of using this mechanism, but we have no other choice at this point. There aren't many in our world who can withstand the aura of the highest hierarch of the ancient geniuses. And almost all of them are in this room right now. If not you then who? Should I assign this task to your pregnant wives?"

"Let's say that I do it," Kimal Sarento said, reminding the Inquisitor of his existence. "As I understand it, we are all set to accompany my truth-speaking mentor. He cannot handle the army of ancients awaiting us on his own. Have you officially declared open war? With all the associated consequences?"

"Yes, it is official. The geniuses of the ancients are preparing for an invasion," said the Inquisitor. "It will not help them. This force will be wiped off the face of the planet. No one has the right to give us an ultimatum."

The phrase was meant to be ambiguous. The Inquisitor made it clear that he would not tolerate disobedience on our part. However, Kimal Sarento did not stop.

"If they are preparing for an invasion, then we need to go at least together. By the way, why should my young mentor use the extractor? What will happen if we dress an ordinary mage in mithril armor? Will he be struck by the aura of the supreme hierarch?"

"The mithril armor would help preserve their sanity," the servant of Chaos was forced to agree.

"In that case, access to the extractor should be given to all those who go to the lands of the ancients. What if something happens to someone and they can't use the mechanism? I think it's necessary to foresee all options. After all, the servants of Chaos need results, not a failure, right? It would be stupid to fail the mission if for some reason my nimble mentor and I lose consciousness, and the person who goes with us can't use the extractor."

"There is a grain of logic in your words. You will go to the lands of the ancient geniuses together, and access to the device will be given to both of you. We must reduce the risks."

"I repeat: they are waiting for us there. Two mages against creatures with spatial magic would not produce the best odds in our favor. The more people go there, the more likely we are to destroy them and get what we want. We just need to..."

"Enough!" the Inquisitor suddenly roared, and a deathly silence fell over the office. It was hard to talk when you were under the pressure of the most powerful being in this world. "The time for talking is over. We are tired of playing along and pretending that we are ready to make concessions. You forget who you are dealing with. We are not peasants or your subjects. We are Chaos! In all its splendor and unity."

Apparently, we'd managed to hook the Inquisitor after all. Space shimmered and his dark counterpart was embodied next to him. But, unlike the previous cases, this time the Interrogator did not stop the Inquisitor.

On the contrary, he glanced at each of those present and stopped at me. The option of what to do came instantly: before the dark one had time to open his mouth, *Golden Dome of Protection* was already in my magical field.

"Now I speak directly to you, Archduke, and it is in your interests to listen to me carefully. I will not repeat myself. If you ask even one question, if you disagree with anything or start asserting your rights, I will talk to other residents of Hearth. And I will start, perhaps, with those who are in this office. Do you wish this to happen? This was a question, Archduke, I need an answer."

"No, I don't want you to turn my loved ones into Skron's puppets," I said. The Inquisitor's aura was still very present, and the pressure from the Interrogator had been added to it. Both sides of the same entity had suddenly decided to demonstrate their strength, and I wasn't ready for it. No one was. Judging by the stunned eyes of Alia, Eleanore, and even Kimal Sarento, they didn't understand this sharp change in mood and atmosphere.

"Excellent. I always knew we could negotiate with you, Archduke," the Interrogator said, unable to hold back his sarcasm. "The global situation is difficult, and we do not have time to waste. Because the balance is broken, a new entity has recently wanted to penetrate this world. Chaos had to spend too much energy to stop the invasion. But the path has already been trodden — until we have access to all our forces, we are not able to hide the planet from others. Therefore, we must act decisively and quickly, without looking back at the consequences. The main destabilizing factor now is you, Archduke. Your interference in established laws forces us to make mistakes that our enemies use. You have acquired too much power, which is unacceptable for an ordinary person. It must be taken away and given to someone worthy. To someone who will restore stability to the defense and allow us to concentrate on blocking the planet and preventing its destruction. We are talking about One. Therefore, you will be the one using the extractor. Not Kimal Sarento. Although we will also provide him with access to the mechanism. Now you will go for the keys to the Fog Arena, you will be given a day to do this. Then you must go through four arenas, by which time you will be given a stone to block the poison. We do not wish to wait. You will be given a day to go through four arenas. No more. Then, in three days, you must destroy the geniuses of the ancients and obtain their power. By this time, Pharapho and the Abyss will have prepared their part. One has already accelerated his pace, he will be at the point in a week. By this time, the chaos level at the breakout point will have decreased to a sufficient level to conduct the ceremony of forming the power of the second orbit. Calm will return to the planet, and you will return to Hearth to live out your last days. Nod if you understand my words."

I had to strain myself to nod. Chaos had finally decided that I was a little too rowdy and needed to be relieved of all my strength. But he intended to do it in such a way that my death would also be useful. I wonder if they'd order me to dance too?

"Your eyes reflect the emotions that rage in your chest. We know that you will not obey and will try to do everything your way. In a way that we don't need. So we will insure ourselves."

The Interrogator waved his hand, and dark hoops appeared around the necks of Alia and Eleanore. Something similar to those that were put on mages to block magic.

"You have a choice, Archduke Valevsky. Either you do everything we order and do it the way we want, and then only you will die, or you can play your own card and try to deceive us. In that case, not only you will die, but also everyone dear to you. All three of your women and all three children they bear will be destroyed. And in such a way that before their death they will curse the moment when they first met you — your women will die slowly and painfully. We can guarantee you this with full responsibility. So choose, Archduke, either you will die alone, leaving behind three heirs, or the entire Valevsky line will die. But someone is sure to die. Such is the will of Chaos."

Chapter 14

TWO STEEL SPEARS formed before I had time to think about them. My subconscious took over control of my body and acted clearly and confidently. It demanded one thing: to punish and kill the bastards that had threatened my loved ones. Before the spears had time to appear, they were already flying at the heads of the Interrogator and the Inquisitor. It was too late to think, scare or try to negotiate. Chaos had made its move. Now it was my turn. A loud blow was heard, after which sparks and shreds of molten steel sprayed in all directions, turning into dust near the floor due to the destroyed spell. The spears that could fight Skron or the Light were powerless against the creatures of Chaos. They did not even flinch. Perhaps they pressed them down with their aura so that no one in the office could move. But none of this mattered for spatial magic. Where one spear could not cope, the second would easily pierce through. Or the tenth. Maybe even the hundredth. After all, even water can destroy stone.

The spears appeared in the air again, only to crumble into fine steel dust a moment later. Then again. And again. I sent spear after spear so fast that a new one began to form even before the previous one hit its target. But the result was always the same: bright sparks and scraps of steel flying in all directions. In my anger, I used the stone from under the Interrogator's feet for the spears. Even if it didn't kill, at least they would fall down, relieving the pressure. But that didn't work either: the creature of Chaos simply hung in the air, as if it weighed nothing at all.

"It's all useless, Archduke Valevsky," the Interrogator declared. There was no hint of anger or resentment for my actions in his voice. Just a dry statement of facts. "You are too weak to pose any danger to us. A thousand years ago, we were able to defeat those who wielded spatial magic at an absolute level. Those who were able to lift mountains and bring them down on the heads of their enemies with just the power of thought. Now we will turn a blind eye to your reckless behavior. We understand that you are upset and that emotions are speaking in you. They will soon subside, and you will be able to think rationally. If not you, then your loved ones will help with this. Your fate is predetermined, Archduke. You will die. If you do everything as we say, we will grant you the right to live until the birth of your official children. The children that your wives bear, despite the fact that we did not coordinate your marriage with Mother Alia. We will give you the opportunity to hug your children, to see their first smile. If you give into your emotions or try to cheat the system, everyone dear to you will die. If you have decided that we will not be able to fulfill our plan without your help, we will have to disappoint you: the Citadel commanders or the named servants of the Temple of Skron, starting with Six, will do for our purposes. If necessary, we will sacrifice them too. They will consider it an honor to die in the name of Chaos. But we do not want to waste valuable resources. Why would we, when we have you? One man who flew too high and forgot his place. You have twenty-four hours to get four keys to the Fog Arena. If you fail, delay, or try to cheat, Alia and her child will die. We'll start with her. So that no foolish desires to save your women arise, we will take them now. They will be freed after you have completed our task. Or they will begin to die. Slowly and painfully, cursing the day they met you. Your twenty-four hours have begun, Archduke."

The pressure disappeared, and with it the Interrogator, the Inquisitor, Alia and Eleanore. Only Kimal Sarento and I remained, silently looking into each other's eyes. Frankly, I didn't know what to do. My anger had evaporated, and panic began to creep in its place. All-consuming, voluminous, tightening the chest and forcing me to scream from my own powerlessness.

"We can't contact the girls," Kimal Sarento said. "The connection is blocked. I believe they are unconscious in some secret location within Chaos. I think Eleanore would have found a way to communicate the coordinates through the notebook."

Silence fell over the office again. I couldn't reply — I think I'd forgotten how to talk. Crazy thoughts flashed through my head, one stranger than the next, but none of them led to any logical result. Steel, created before Chaos came to this world, was powerless against these all-powerful freaks. It was the only weapon that could harm them in any way. Magic, the resources from the rifts, the fog of Pharapho and everything else were creations of Chaos. These objects were useless against their creators.

"Max, are you going to sit there wallowing or are we going to get down to business?" Kimal Sarento hadn't called me by name for a long time. There was none of the usual sarcasm in his voice now.

"They took them!" I managed to squeeze out this great feat of eloquence and deep meaning. "Those freaks took my wives!"

"Moreover, they will start killing them if you continue to sit still, moaning about your difficult fate. As long as they are not dead, we can fight. Or have you already started to consider yourself a corpse? It is still too early. It seems to me that you have missed one important detail: you were promised to keep your life until the birth of your children. All children, mind you."

"Are you serious?" I had to force myself not to scream. My emotions were pouring out, and Kimal Sarento was the perfect person to unleash my anger on.

"Alright, you're incapable of rational thought right now, so let me think for the both of us. I gleaned the key information from our less-than-simple little meeting: the Chaos creatures are extremely sensitive to their promises. So much so that they're willing to spend two precious days allowing you to get the fragments of Skron and the Light. They promised to keep you alive until your children are born. Alia and Eleanore are due in two months, but our precious Naira has only just begun her difficult journey to becoming a mother. Considering her progress, you have at least five months for Alia to become pregnant again. By the time Naira's child is born, Alia will be pregnant again, and the creatures of Chaos will have no choice but to extend your life for another nine months. Then Naira's time will come, and your death will be postponed for another nine months. It so happens that you, my lucky mentor, are the only person in this world who has two official wives. And we must definitely take advantage of this. I don't think the girls will object. During this time, we will figure out what to do next. Maybe One will go crazy and we will have a real chance to bargain for another thirty or forty years for you. Moaning and groaning is all well and good, of course, but those who do so usually do not live to old age. The only thing you need to do is carry out the orders of the creatures of Chaos in such a way that they have no chance to claim failure. I believe it is time to place your pride and thirst for justice into a deep hole and act in a way that will allow you to survive. Or decide that you will not give in to the Interrogator's threats. Go to the throne room, tell them so, and die. I believe that after death you will not particularly care what happens to your women and unborn children. Death is like that. There is no emotion. There is nothing at all."

"What's the point of life without magic? If I do everything Chaos wants, I won't even become an ordinary human — I'll end up at the very bottom!"

"The very bottom of what? The human food chain? Remember, my forgetful mentor, who you are. You are the Archduke of an autonomous city. The fact that your magic will disappear is not such a big deal. So what, you will return to the state you were in a year ago. You didn't have magic a year ago, did you? That's what I'm saying. However, let me ask you another question: what is the point of death, even with magic? Dying is easy, living is hard. Besides, it's still unclear what exactly we will lose."

"We?"

"Naturally. Instead of heroically sucking out the power of the highest hierarch of the ancient geniuses in one person, sacrificing all our energy, we will divide this process into two. Yes, something will vanish, we will lose something, but clearly not everything, as Chaos intends. The drawings you brought include one rather fascinating little mechanism. As soon as we get sick, we will immediately create clones and transfer consciousness into them. The situation is, of course, critical, but not fatal."

"Those bastards must be destroyed!"

"Do you hear yourself, my vengeful mentor?" Kimal Sarento's usual good spirits had returned. Having come up with a way to deceive the system, he became inspired. Even the smirk returned to its usual place. "You were in the location of the ancients. The interactive neural network clearly explained to you that there is no way to destroy the creatures of Chaos. You checked, and from what I understand, you gave it your all. The results are lying on the floor in the form of dust. Chaos is capable of destroying other gods that invade our world. Can't it find a way to resist a person? No, my warlike mentor, we will not win by force. Only by cunning."

Kimal Sarento fell silent, allowing me to consider his words. Gradually, my emotions subsided, returning common sense. My compromise-loving student was right: cunning would help us survive. Both me and my wives. But I did not want to agree with that. More and more, I was inclined to think that the ancients were right to destroy the planet. Better this way than to live in eternal slavery. No matter how you look at it, both the light and the dark are in slavery. Of Skron, Light, and, as a result, Chaos. The balance must be upset, but how can I do that? I am not able to destroy Pharapho or the Abyss. These entities are of a different order. I will not even mention Skron and Light. I will die on the threshold of their lair. By the way, where is it? Actually, it doesn't matter — I won't be able to upset the balance, and after One becomes a new second-orbital force in a week, the world will acquire the stability that will allow Chaos to distract almost all forces from blocking the bomb."

Damn it! No matter how I looked at it, I only had two options. Either die now, and then I really wouldn't care about what happens to my loved ones, or resort to trickery, as Kimal Sarento suggested. I didn't even consider the first option — I wouldn't resort to such cowardice, meanness and betrayal. So, there was only one option left. One that made me feel the lowest of the low, like a huge pile of shit. My gaze stopped again on my student, and the pieces of the mosaic came together: as long as we were alive, we could fight. Corpses don't fight.

A portal, flickering with a bloody light, appeared next to me.

"I'm going to Black Mountain. It's easiest to get the arena key fragments there. Tell the Inquisitor that you'll need a stone to block Pharapho's poison. Since they promised it, let them work for it."

There was no point in threatening the creatures of Chaos, even though I wanted to. Like, if something happens to my girls or children, then I...But everything stopped after those words. I didn't have a single reasonable statement, except for emotions. Emotions were a weakness. I couldn't show them. One thing was clear: very soon, I'd make the sixth-generation interactive neural network cry from my tediousness. I would learn everything I could about the ancients and their weapons. If I couldn't get access to the ancient bomb, then I would create it from scratch. Physics versus Chaos. Let's see who would win...

It took me only a couple of hours to collect the required number of keys. The spawn of Pharapho, not used to meeting resistance near the head boss' lair, did not think about safety at all. Soldiers, sergeants, even a couple of majors — a huge army of creatures crawled towards me, capable of sweeping away any living creature. However, right now I was barely even conscious. I was an angry and irritated archduke, who had been pressed against the wall by the creatures of Chaos. I wanted to rage and destroy, and the fog monsters were the ones who suffered my wrath. I also discovered what could be obtained from the majors. The huge jelly-like substance tried to grab me and drag me inside to digest, but my mithril glove was faster: one blow, and the creature went back to its creator, leaving me its essence and a stone that allowed me to form a cell for a development crystal at any arbitrary point in the model. I couldn't even imagine how much such a thing could cost — if the dark ones were ready to give up their entire fortune for crystals, then they would agree to a life of indentured servitude for the chance to form a cell anywhere they pleased.

However, I did not return home right away.

Light knew what the future would hold. I needed to take precautions. Make sure that Hearth always had a stack of Fog Stalker keys on hand. This would give me bargaining chips that would allow me to get rid of any unpleasant conditions or stipulations in future negotiations, even if the irreparable happens and I am gone. Unless, of course, I managed to blow up this planet — then no one will need the keys. Now this was my number one goal, and everything else was a trifle not worth wasting time on.

"I have the keys." I returned to Hearth twenty hours after the Inquisitor gave me the ultimatum. I had four keys to the Fog Arena, and I didn't tell anyone that at that moment Kimal Sarento was taking twenty-five additional keys to the arena to the treasury. The creatures of Chaos probably knew this perfectly well without my words. But they preferred to pretend that it didn't concern them right now. Instead, the Inquisitor made a deft move, throwing me a small octagon flickering with a red light:

"A support stone for *Heal.* You can use it to block Pharapho's poison. Integrate it into the magic field and proceed to the next stage. Your twenty-four hours have passed. You must complete four arenas of forty waves, obtain two batteries and two relics."

"Give the girls back. I do whatever you want. The way you want it. No need to keep pregnant women unconscious."

I didn't like that I couldn't contact any of the

three of them. I felt uneasy: I remembered what Alia had become when she was kidnapped by Dark Magister Elor. If it weren't for my strange grandfather, who never decided which side he ultimately was on, I would now have one less wife.

"They are conscious, Archduke. Their life, health and pregnancy are not in danger. The place where they are placed is shielded, so they cannot be contacted. As soon as One becomes a second-orbital power, you will get them back. Not a moment before. Your twenty-four hours are ticking, Archduke. Do not waste time in vain."

Once again, I was unable to gain any leverage with the representative of Chaos. Unless I acted like a child: fell to the ground and started throwing a tantrum, demanding candy. I think that would amuse everyone a lot.

I completed my runs through the Fog Arena in some kind of comatose state, so there was not much I could say about it. My body moved on its own, healed, attacked, but my mind was somewhere else. And not in any specific place, it just dissolved into the void. My emotions, desires, and aspirations had all vanished. I did the work like a mechanism: precisely, harmoniously, but soullessly. The only problem I had was communicating to the arena master that the particles of the first-orbit forces should be placed in the batteries I had received, and not just dumped on the platform. I had no doubts about what would happen in this case: I would die. And it didn't matter whose relic it was, dark or light. For an ordinary human, either would be deadly. The Fog Stalker resisted, declaring that he was not going to work for free, and that I did not have enough energy to pay for the placement of relics in the vessels. I did not want to argue, so I simply left the arena without starting any of the waves, approached the Inquisitor and explained the situation to him. He disappeared for a moment to return and inform him that there would be no more problems with the placement of relics.

I had to duck back into the treasury for another key, soon I had two sparkling metal cylinders in my hands. They vibrated, as if the power inside was yearning to break out. Even holding these objects in my hands was difficult, so I threw them into my immaterial inventory to prevent irreparable things from happening. What if the lid flew open at the most inopportune moment? What did I know about these storage devices? Absolutely nothing.

"The Temple of Skron and the Citadel representatives are aware that you have obtained the relics." The Inquisitor met me personally in my office after my final run through the arena. The Chaos creatures decided to keep their finger on the pulse, not allowing me to rest even for a minute. I had not yet completed one of their tasks, when I was immediately given another:

"Now you must go to the mechanoids and take the stabilization system from them. Without it, everything further will be useless. Considering that Zero is unlikely to give up the system without a fight, you are given three days to complete this task. You can take assistants with you, but you are capable of completing this task alone. Your time has begun, Archduke. You can begin."

The Inquisitor didn't mention that the containers with the relics should be left in Hearth. I knew it was petty, but I needed to relieve my anger somehow. Instead of handing the batteries over to the servants, I left them in my immaterial inventory. The servants of darkness and light would wait for me in the Hearth, nothing would happen to them. Moreover, the dark ones wouldn't be able to come see me anyway, as the portals were still inactive. And, as far as I could tell, they would remain inactive for at least a week.

"You know, my self-pitying mentor, I understand your condition, but you shouldn't go to the mechanoids in such a state." Kimal Sarento appeared to me a few minutes after the Inquisitor disappeared. He looked cheerful. While I was running around the arena, spending three or four hours on each run, he was kicking his legs back, napping and preparing for battle. His perfectly geometrically manicured beard was more infuriating than even the Chaos creatures. How much time had he spent on it? Apparently, no less than I spent on all four arenas!

"As if I have a choice!" I replied angrily.

"There is always a choice!" The man said pointedly. "The question is, are you ready to commit to this choice? You have been given three days, so go to your room now and take a bath. I have already ordered a servant to draw you one. Then you rest, eat, and when you have regained your strength, we can begin the task."

"The longer I rest, the longer my wives will suffer."

"I don't think they're suffering. They are probably sitting in some high tower, like princesses from a fairytale, playing cards with dragons and waiting for a mysterious knight to save them. The only difference is that we already know who the knight is, and the dragon is unlikely to be sitting in the same tower with them. The Chaos creatures think too highly of themselves to be careless with their prisoners. They still have to return them later. So nothing will happen to our ladies, even if you rest a little. Trust your wise, old apprentice."

I was in such a strange state that it was easier to obey than to explain to Kimal Sarento why now was not the time to rest. However, as soon as I pulled off my mithril armor and climbed into a hot bath, a clear understanding came: Kimal Sarento was right. This was exactly what I had been missing for so long. My oppressive thoughts melted away, my brain cleared, and soon I had a clearer perception of reality, and could think soundly and rationally. Initially, I thought that Chaos had won the war, so further resistance was useless, but after a pause and rest, I realized that we had lost only one battle. An important, fateful one, but just a battle, not the war. All I needed was to gather my strength, consider my strategy for the upcoming battles and implement it.

I fell asleep as soon as my head hit the pillow. I was not woken, but allowed to sleep as long as my body required. When I opened my eyes and called the servants, it turned out that I had been lying in bed for more than fourteen hours. My clean mithril armor was already waiting for me by the bed, and when I put it on, I felt like a completely different person.

"Now I see that you are ready," Kimal Sarento was beaming again. It seemed the lines in his beard had become even straighter than before.

"Thank you," I said sincerely, and I was surprised by this impulse. For the first time in my entire communication with Kimal Sarento, I had a sincere desire to thank him. Even after he had saved my life, dragging me home for three days after the battle with the lithoids, such an impulse did not arise.

"'Thank yous' won't help us get to the mechanoids," said Kimal Sarento. "It is my understanding that we're not going there to negotiate. So there's no point in holding back. Come on, don't keep us in suspense, my indecisive mentor. The sooner we start, the sooner we buff these magic stones, the sooner we see the geniuses of the ancients. Don't forget, our girls are still sitting in their high tower, awaiting their prince on a white horse. Here's what I was thinking: Zero is essentially a workhorse. We'll ride him!"

Chapter 15

"I WASN'T QUITE PREPARED for this," said Kimal Sarento, putting his elbow forward in a vain attempt to block the flurry of snow beating in his face. The mechanoids had settled in the very north of the continent, hidden among the high mountains. Even in the dead of summer, there was likely snow cover here, but now, on the cusp of winter, a blizzard raged in a terrifying demonstration of nature's power. If any ordinary human had ended up here, he would have simply frozen to death, and no amount of warm robes would have saved him. At least, that's how it seemed to me. We were protected by mithril armor, which managed to block out the cold. But the wind gusted us around like a rag on a flagpole, and the snow beating at our faces (although it didn't reach our faces, as the mithril armor blocked it as well) managed to significantly obscure our vision. At a distance of several meters, absolutely nothing was visible behind the veil of white.

"If the map those Chaos freaks gave us is to be believed, we're here," I said, spinning around several times in search of any hint of the mechanoids.

"Something tells me this isn't quite right," Kimal Sarento said, tired of fighting through the snow storm. He stopped and turned to me. "Tell me, my witless mentor, was there any other number in the coordinates you received? For example, the altitude or, perhaps, depth?"

"You think it's under the ground?'

"Where else? It's a bit deserted here, as you can see. And stop calling the guests in Hearth's palace 'freaks.' You'll have to live in peace and harmony with them for a long time to come, so ruining your relationship with a casual slip of the tongue is not the wisest idea. I won't give you lessons in humility, of course, but I will not let you ruin my future either. We are not going to destroy a third-orbital power so that you can accidentally call the Inquisitor a freak to his face and have your head blown off for it. Just call them 'guests.'"

He had a point, but I chose to ignore him for now. I was really worried about the question of where the mechanoids were hiding? The coordinates that those freaks — that our guests had given us contained no additional location parameters. The latitude and longitude were precise — we were right on top of Zero, but neither he nor his henchmen were anywhere in sight.

"Shall we try to break through downwards?" I suggested, pulling out my katars. Cutting out chunks of rock and throwing them aside would be easier than maneuvering inside this terrible storm, even though our bodily enhancements also allowed us to somehow withstand this inclement weather, albeit barely. An ordinary person, I repeat, would be flash frozen and then torn to pieces.

"I would suggest returning to Hearth and clarifying the coordinates," Kimal Sarento was more skeptical about the situation. He didn't seem too keen on the idea of becoming a miner.

"I know exactly what he'll say, I can picture it now: 'We gave you the correct coordinates. Search for it.' You need to dig, my lazy apprentice."

"Alright then, let's dig," Kimal Sarento begrudgingly agreed and activated his own katars. The storm had packed the snow so tightly that it had turned into stone. After making a few cuts and pulling out the first block of snow, I was about to throw it aside, but my pupil stopped me.

"Give it here," he said. At first I didn't understand what he was talking about, and then when I did, I jumped up and started looking around again. The block I'd cut wasn't snow at all. It was metal.

"I have a theory." Kimal Sarento took the block, assessed it and, so as not to waste, hid it in his immaterial inventory. Metal was too valuable a resource in our world, even unknown metal. It could be melted down and used for something useful. Especially in Hearth, where our mechanical defender lives. I am sure he will be able to use not only this piece, but all those that we cut out. I had my own theory, too. Before my wise student could tell me about his theory, I told him about mine:

"The dark pyramid that everyone considers to be the Temple of Skron is the brainchild of Zero. Considering the size of the pyramid, we can draw certain conclusions that the higher-ranking mech-anoids have a fairly large physique. Our palace guests were not mistaken in sending us to this mountain. It's just that this entire mountain is Zero."

"You know, I'm already getting bored. Before, you were looking me straight in my face and de-manding revelations, now you have started to churn out these revelations one after another. Yes, my clever mentor, this mountain is Zero, in all its glory. A huge mechanoid of gigantic dimensions. I suppose the wind is also its creation. It wants to blow us off its belly. So you are right: we must dig. I don't really want to search for natural openings to get inside."

Breaking through the metal skin of the Zero was not so easy: we had to go several dozen meters deep, that's how thick it was. Remarkably, as soon as we hid in the depths of the Zero, the wind im-mediately stopped. Kimal Sarento and I dug next to each other, hiding the cut chunks of metal in our immaterial backpacks, so we got a pretty good pace going. We did not have to waste time throwing away the extracted rock. The width of our borehole was small, just enough for two people to sit in it.

While at first, this wasn't an issue, a few meters deep we began to feel uneasy. The window of light above us kept getting smaller and smaller until it would fit into a needle's eye. The narrow walls pressed in on us, causing an acute attack of claustrophobia. Despite the fact that I'd never had that phobia before. I had to take several breaks just to acclimatize and not go mad.

"Wait!" Kimal Sarento commanded as he plunged my vyrma blade into the metal once again. Zero's skin gave way to the vyrma, but with significant resistance. Now it slipped into the metal quite easily, as if there was an empty void beneath us. Kimal Sarento pulled the blade out, and light struck through the tiny hole. As we dug our way down, we knew that Zero would arrange a meeting for us wherever we broke through. Since no fire, poison, water, or any other substance for killing particularly nimble folk such as ourselves rushed in through the hole, they apparently had no time to organize a welcome party, so we would apparently be met with mechanoids. They were in no hurry to make themselves known, preparing to greet us within Zero's depths.

"Ready?" Kimal Sarento asked, looking up at me. I nodded and he activated his second katar and stuck both through the floor. I did the same on my side of the borehole. "On the count of three. One! Two! Cut!"

I had no way to test the effect of darkness on the mechanoids, so I couldn't guarantee that the level fifteen dark mirror would be able to handle them. Besides, I had a man with me who hadn't yet managed to acclimatize to that level. So our only defense was the level fifty *Golden Dome of Protection,* as well as the mithril armor. Zero's skin cracked under our feet and caved inward. But my student and I remained in the mine, clinging to the notches we'd cut in the walls. What if we had cut through to a bottomless well and we'd be falling for hours? We had no experience of being inside giant mechanoids, so we had to rely solely on our own logic. And it told us that before leaping blindly into something, we needed to study that something first.

A loud bang rang out a second later. If our eyes were to be believed, the ceiling of the room was about five meters tall. It looked like a corridor — a long, tall, wide intestinal tract stretching off somewhere in the distance in both directions. On the downside, the corridor was filled with all sorts of mechanoids. They ranged from tiny and awkward to equally as tiny, but elegant in design. *Analyze* offered little help in assessing the situation. These creatures were unknown. *Golden Dome of Protection* began to spark. They had noticed us and, with astounding precision for a living creature, began to send little metallic fireballs at us. Exactly the same ones that one of the foggy servants of the Temple of Skron used when he wanted to finish me off. However, the matter was not limited to just metal blanks that exploded upon contact with the protective dome. The mechanoids started shooting at us with rather strange crossbows. Tiny metal projectiles flew out of small tubes at such a speed that I couldn't track them. If I hadn't pumped up *Golden Dome of Protection* to level fifty, perhaps our adventure would have ended right now. Because even with *Praxis* and my crazy mana regeneration, my blue bar began to drop steadily to zero. The damage that the mechanoids brought down on us would have knocked anyone down. I think even the Inquisitor and the Interrogator would have been in trouble.

"Okay, now it's our turn," Kimal Sarento grinned and extended his hand towards the mechanoids. Lightning flashed and there was a sharp smell of ozone. The mithril armor even switched over to its internal air supply system. But all our minor difficulties were nothing compared to what his chain lightning had turned the mechanoids into. A lifeless crater of smoldering metal remains had formed beneath us. The flow of shells and metal fireballs sharply decreased: the ones on the edges couldn't reach, and there was no one left to shoot from below.

"Going down!" Kimal Sarento said, and without waiting for a response, flung himself down through the opening. A moment later, I was flying after him, twisting around midair and sending a *Dark Thorn* deep into the corridor.'

You destroyed 15 small mechanoids with a Level 50 *Dark Thorn*.

Dark Thorn gains +0.015% of the XP required to reach Level 51.

Fifteen thousandths for fifteen small mechanoids. I didn't need an academic degree to calculate the number of mechanical creatures needed to upgrade the stone. A thousand mechanoids would give me one percent, a hundred thousand to a whole level. A hundred thousand mechanoids...I couldn't even imagine where I'd find so many! These weren't like the lithoids, an endless river of rock. These were mechanisms. I doubted there were that many in the whole mountain.

"Right or left?" asked Kimal Sarento after once again filling the space with his *Chain Lightning*. While I was aiming at the next enemy, preparing to cast, he had already destroyed all the mechanoids in a decent radius, grabbing all the experience for himself.

"Down, I would assume," I replied. "The structure of the mechanoids was not part of my mandatory training, but logic dictates that vital centers are unlikely to be located near the skin. I personally have no desire to run along the corridors and look for a passageway We are not here to commit genocide against the mechanoids. We will take the stabilization system and leave."

"We just need to figure out where it might be." Kimal Sarento climbed onto the remains of the mechanoids and looked down the hallway. "You start cutting out a hole, I'll go hunting for now."

"There are different kinds of hunts, my power-hungry pupil," I said. "By destroying mechanoids from afar, you upgrade your stone, but you bring absolutely no good to Hearth. No essences, no additional devices, nothing at all. As *Devour* has shown, there is no loot left from the charred remains. So my cunning and lazy pupil will have to dig. As for me, I will take up the hunt in order to benefit Hearth."

The look he shot me could have frozen me on the spot, but surprisingly, he didn't argue. Shaking his head as if to say, 'Who have I gotten into business with?' he leaned over and began to cut another hole in the floor. I used *Dash* at the maximum distance available to me and found myself somewhere in the depths of the wave of mechanoids pressing on us. Kimal Sarento was fifty meters behind, so I turned on the twenty-meter dark aura of level twenty-five without hesitation, waiting to see how the mechanoids would react.

The result thrilled me: the metal creatures froze in place and began to tremble slightly, as if all their parts had begun to jam up. After hitting the one closest to me, I received the essence of a small mechanoid, as well as a bunch of useful gadgets directly into my inventory. *Devour,* hungry for loot, sucked the mechanoid dry, leaving only a metal hull. Grinning, I rushed forward, thrusting my mithril gloves into two of the trembling chunks of metal at once. A momentary pause, and another blow. And another. Another...

"I'm pretty much done over here, my easily distracted mentor," Kimal Sarento said in my ear, distracting me from the harvest. I came out of my trance and I found myself standing at the far edge of the corridor, about half a kilometer from the hole my student was making. Between us stretched a whole field of dead mechanoids. It seemed there were at least a thousand of them. If not more. I had gotten so carried away by my wave of metallic carnage that I forgot about guarding Kimal Sarento. An army of mechanoids was closing in on him from the other side of the corridor, and even from such a great distance, flashes of lightning were visible. He had completed his part of the job and after giving me a moment to enjoy myself, was reminding me that he still existed.

"Did you level up?" I asked, returning to Kimal Sarento with a few *Dashes*. My ousel was already carefully holstered within my mithril suit.

"Fifty six," he nodded, releasing two lightning bolts at once. One into the corridor, the other into the bore hole. "And it looks like the action is going to get more intense as we descend. The deeper we go, the stronger and more capable the mechanoids are. Since you are so eager for prey, I grant you the right to go down first."

Peering into the hole, I saw the charred remains of new mechanoids. The protective dome immediately began to spark: Zero's defenders on this level were even more accurate and deadly than the ones above. But this didn't stop me, of course. Fortunately, the room was barely over five meters tall. Jumping down, I reflexively activated my dark mirror. It wouldn't broadcast through the ceiling, as I already knew, and my student was unlikely to follow me immediately. He'd probably run along the upper corridor, clearing it of mechanical creatures. Getting level fifty-seven *Chain Lightning* was excellent motivation.

The mid-sized mechanoids died just as readily as their smaller brethren. I couldn't help but shoot the closest ones to check the amount of experience I was getting.

You destroyed 8 medium mechanoids with Level 50 *Dark Thorn*.
***Dark Thorn* gains +0.08% of the XP required to reach Level 51.**

I received ten times more experience than from the smaller ones. Or, translated into the common tongue, only ten thousand medium mechanoids are needed for the magic stone to reach level fifty-one. The entire floor was strewn with burnt pieces of iron: while I was busy getting loot from above, Kimal Sarento was actively leveling up. This wasn't a problem. There almost seemed to be more mid-sized mechanoids than small ones, so there would be enough loot and experience to go around.

The second level of Zero's bowel also resembled a corridor. Choosing a side, I set forth filling my inventory with various devices, resources and essences. The names of many items were unfamiliar to me, but I had no doubt that our Defender would be able to find the perfect use for them. As an option, he would pump himself up to the next level, turning Hearth into an impregnable fortress, even against third-order forces. Those mysterious watermen could come to the walls of my city and, after encountering our defenses, would leave with nothing. Wasn't that a good reason to spend a little time collecting?

Soon, Kimal Sarento jumped down from above. Unlike me, he didn't care about the well-being of Hearth, focusing only on himself. He took the other side of the corridor in his mad dash to get to level fifty-seven as quickly as possible. But was I going to allow him to do that?

"We need a new hole! Let's keep going down!"

"Has anyone ever told you you're a terrible commander, my spoil-sport mentor?"

"Yes, my careless student always strives to have the last word," I quipped back. "We have no idea how many levels there are and where they lead. Our only hope for success is that the coordinates of the guests from Chaos are correct and that we're standing directly above Zero's power source. And you know we only have two days left to complete our task. So don't get distracted — you'll upgrade your stone as we go down. So dig, my prized apprentice, dig!"

Once again, Kimal Sarento shook his head, regretting the moment when he foolishly agreed to go with me on this expedition, and I once again rushed into the throng. The Inquisitor was right in claiming that I could handle this mission on my own: the mechanical creatures could do nothing to counter the dark aura. They froze and began to tremble, regardless of their rank.

"I suggest we take a break and portal somewhere," I said when I returned about thirty minutes later. Kimal Sarento had long ago finished the next hole and was currently wreaking havoc on the mechanoid population. Eventually, the corridor was completely blocked by charred mechanoids. The floor below looked just the same — only scraps. They appeared to be around the same size as the ones on the floor above.

"A pause?" Kimal Sarento frowned, not understanding why. "Where are you going? Didn't you just say that we only have a few days left?"

"I've had a thought. We'll need to test the extractor before we use it against the highest hierarch of the ancient geniuses in any case, right? So why don't I go through the Fog Arena now and get another battery to siphon some of the power from Zero? We won't take all of it, I suspect they'll catch on and we'll be in trouble, but a little, the tiniest fraction...Our guests from Chaos gave the go-ahead for us to do absolutely anything we want with the creatures of the third orbit. So why not weaken the mechanoids?"

"Spend an arena pass for a simple battery? No, my mentor who can generate interesting ideas, you will not go to the Fog Stalker. However, I like the idea, and I know one place where these batteries are currently in active operation."

"The location of the ancient geniuses?" I frowned. This option never even occurred to me.

"The very same. We're going to see them in three days anyway, so why not portal there now?"

"Maybe because I don't have a battery for the highest hierarch? I'll go to the arena for them as soon as we return from the mechanoids."

"What do we need the batteries for now? No, my slow-witted mentor, you don't understand. We'll use the battery you get in the arena against the highest hierarch. I'm talking about something else — we'll show up in the ancients' lair, kill a couple of them, and take their loot. The Fog Stalker said that the batteries are a means of trade for the ancient geniuses. That means they have a lot in stock, and we'll go in there in style and take a couple for ourselves. And it will give us a chance to see how they fight."

"In that case, we'll have to portal to a different location than the potential invasion spot," I said. "They'll throw all their forces into repelling our attack. Next time we come back, it'll be far more dangerous."

"But don't forget, we won't be back for a whole three days. All that time they'll be waiting, nervous, not sleeping. If they sleep at all. A demoralized enemy is a defeated enemy. The question is: will you be able to return to this very point? I have no desire to dig through Zero's hull again."

"Not just here, but a level lower," I said, jumping down to the third floor and looking around. Finally, a noticeable difference from the upper levels: the corridor had become narrower. If that trend continued, then there were only ten floors left to our goal. I didn't want to think that there are almost a hundred levels here, like in a standard rift. It would take too much time to dig through.

Kimal Sarento jumped down after me and

without further ado began to cut a hole to the next level. He was captivated by the idea of visiting the geniuses of the ancients, but this plan would require a little preparation. Zero was certainly capable of shifting around his outer levels. Maybe even the inner ones. But logic dictated that this gigantic construction was incapable of changing the vital parts of its body. He was too huge and inert. So we needed to go down to the fifth, ideally to the sixth level and ignore the loot for now. This was only to Kimal Sarento's advantage. Having motioned for me to dig, the cunning beetle began to systematically destroy the mechanoids. On the third, then on the fourth, fifth and sixth levels. All I managed to do during this time was use *Analyze* a couple of times to understand what we were dealing with. There were also mid-sized mechanoids on the fourth level, but the ones on five and six were much bigger. Not just in name, but in appearance and means of killing. Large mechanoids used a whole bunch of weapons against us: metal shells, fireballs, poison, streams of fire, acid. *Golden Dome of Protection* puffed, steadily eating up my mana, but blocked everything. I didn't want to let attacks through to the mithril armor. It would protect me, of course, but I wasn't sure it would be able to absorb the momentum of the blows.

"Enough!" I sat down on the floor of level six and started fiddling with the teleportation command phrase. I needed a point not far from the lair of the ancient geniuses, away from our future penetration point, but not too far from the center. Because it would be a bad idea to waste time running around, searching for the ancient geniuses. There was too little time left to finish things with Zero.

"Ready! Let's go!" A red-flickering portal appeared next to me, and Kimal Sarento was the first to dive inside. I followed him and, as soon as the outlines in the space around me unblurred, I squinted from the bright light. There was a second sun hanging in the air, dispersing the autumn gloom. Kimal Sarento stood nearby, covering his eyes with his hand, and not far from us, a meter above the ground, a man was hanging in the air, sitting in the lotus position. The light was emanating from somewhere in side him, penetrating through his clothes. There was no hair on the sun-man's head, his clothes resembled the robe of the servants of the Light, and, most pleasingly, our appearance did not attract his attention. *Analyze* suggested that we were dealing with a genius of the ancients, and not some embodiment of the Light.

"Seen enough?" I heard Kimal Sarento's voice in my intercom. "Two more on the right, one on the left. This one is yours, I'll take care of the rest. We need to get the battery — there it is, hanging on his belt. And don't forget to pierce his chest. I want to know what can be extracted from the geniuses of the ancients. On the count of three. One, two...Here we go!"

Chapter 16

SOME MIGHT SAY we acted like dumb brutes. That there was no point in such unmotivated aggression. That I first should have spoken to the glowing ancient geniuses, and only then make rash decisions. What if we could calmly come to an agreement and get the battery without any unnecessary violence? Maybe I could find allies in these creatures, and together we could counter our Chaos "guests." There had been many paths we could have gone down, but we chose the aggressive course of action not because we were overcome by madness or because we were simply bad guys. Our rational became clear once my eyes adjusted to the light and I saw not just the floating humans, but everything surrounding them. After that, there was no way to stop Kimal Sarento.

I should probably start with the setting: we

were in the middle of a huge, flat area housing a collection of shallow pools separated by wide stone paths. Most of the pools were empty, but those over which the ancient geniuses hung were full. The idea to attack came as soon as Kimal Sarento and I saw what they contained: a burgundy liquid in which the remains of human bodies floated. Thin vortices of energy were drawn out of the pools, uniting the glowing people with their eerie bath. If I understood correctly, we were witnessing the process by which they extended their lives. And these were clearly the more privileged class, because in the distance, ordinary people milled about, emitting no light. Either slaves or a lower class of ancient geniuses whose plight it was to serve their elder brothers. No, they definitely weren't servants. I don't think most people would trust servants with a knife. Before Kimal Sarento finished his count of three, one of these assistants had slashed the throat of a bound captive (an ordinary human, if I remember correctly) with a knife and threw him into the pool. The tank was being filled for another procedure.

"Here we go!"

Kimal Sarento finished his count and we were off toward our individual goals. I didn't want to try any fancy experiments, so I used my trusted *Dash* to fly towards the nearest floating human lantern. But I never reached my target. The impact against the unseen barrier came as such an unpleasant and painful surprise that I actually blacked out for a few seconds. It happened so quickly and the blow was so powerful that neither my mithril armor nor *Golden Dome of Protection* could save me. However, I landed on my feet: I came to my senses in the air and managed to regroup. I was thrown into an empty pool, so I was fortunate enough not to be bathed in the blood of their unfortunate victims. As I landed, I jumped and used *Dash* again. I couldn't leave my opponent waiting for long. The blow had affected not only me, but also the human lantern. He was born off to one side, tearing off the ribbons of energy from the blood-filled pool. There was an explosion, but I had no time for such minor details. My opponent had lost his ability to levitate, falling hard inside an empty pool. Following the explosion, screams, a strange hissing, and the humming and crackling of my student's *Chain Lightning* were heard, but I again dismissed all this as unnecessary information. *Dash* delivered me to my goal.

The human lantern had not yet been extinguished. As I got closer, I saw where the light was emanating from. In his chest, in the spot where a heart normally should be, there was something else — something extraordinary and bright. He sat up and opened his eyes, staring at me through strange holes of light. Not the Light that filled the eyes of the highest hierarchs of the church, but some unnatural, lifeless and blinding. Although, judging by the fact that the genius was clearly looking at me, he was not blind. A hand stretched out in my direction, but I couldn't let this bastard use spatial magic. Two *Dark Thorns* crashed into his barrier, completely shredding it. In any case, that was the plan. When the darkness evaporated, the stunned, yet stubbornly whole man was sitting squarely in the pool and looking at me with varying shades of shock. His eyes didn't say much but the rest of his face was expressive enough. He didn't understand how I'd managed to inflict so much damage on him, while I couldn't understand how a level fifty magic stone, which had begun its march toward level fifty one, couldn't take down his shield. According to all my existing theories, only creatures of Chaos could block magic of this level. Everyone else should have thrown in the towel and died.

However, the human lantern had no intention of dying. His state of shock passed quickly enough, and his hand extended toward me again. Growling in frustration, I once again cast a double-strike with *Dark Thorn*. The radius of his shield was too large to try to break through with the mithril glove. A second, third and fourth volley of dark thorns followed the first, and by the fifth I finally remembered my main weapon and activated my level thirty-five ousel. The highest creature available to me. Actually, this was the final chord: my opponent's defense easily dealt with the magical attack, but was useless against a dark beast of this level. When the darkness dissipated, the remains of the ancient genius, which had lost their glow, appeared before me. He had been completely torn apart. The protective dome was still in place, meaning that it wasn't the ancient himself generating it, but one of the many devices lying next to the body. I stretched my hand towards the dome and felt the tension: the defense resisted the mithril glove! I managed to penetrate only a palm's length in before my hand was repelled. The technology that the ancient geniuses used could resist the flesh of Pharapho, a second-orbital being! How was this even possible?

Alright, if it could block mithril, what about vyrma? I unsheathed my katars and thrust them into the dome. Nope! Vyrma was also useless. Enraged, I activated my steel spear and stuck it in. Again, it didn't work. The spear crumbled and fell to the ground, and a wave of revulsion passed through me. No, this wouldn't do! I was a spatial mage, Skron damn it! What did I need this protective dome for? Sure, I couldn't destroy it, but who said I had to? It's not like I don't have other things to do!

"If you're finished, I could use some help, my great and powerful mentor," Kimal Sarento said over the intercom. Judging by the tension in his voice, he wasn't doing so well either. The geniuses of the ancients had invented some crazy mechanism that was capable of blocking any physical or magical damage, only letting through aura.

"Drag them towards me," I responded, deactivating the dark aura.

"Have you finished yours off?"

"Yes, but there's a problem with the loot. I can't reach the body."

"The dark aura worked?"

"Where would we be without it? Magical and physical attacks are both completely ineffective. Mithril won't pierce through the defensive dome, and level fifty magic only stuns them, and just for a couple of moments. Only a dark mirror reflecting a level thirty-five ousel worked."

"I've had a similar situation. I finished off the assistants, but these human fireflies are driving me crazy. I manage to break through the defense, but it they're recovering at an astonishing speed. If I was only up against one of them, I'd be fine. But I can't handle three at once. Jump so I can see where you are now. I'm heading toward you. Try not to hit me with the aura. I'm not too fond of the experience."

I jumped up and launched *Dark Thorn* into the air so that Kimal Sarento would see exactly where the battle had taken me. As I landed, I opened the *Author* skill and began to scroll through the list of standard phrases. I needed a small plate to form directly under the device creating the protective field. It had to be located smack dab in the center, right? A few seconds to adjust the size, select ordinary earth as the source of the material, give the plate the ability to fly and finally activate it. At the command of my hand, the protective dome flew into the air and returned to the ground a few meters to the right, granting access to the body. Or rather, what was left of the body.

Devour only sighed sadly, declaring that he had nothing to gain here. I grabbed his belt, on which several devices hung, but at that moment I was distracted. Kimal Sarento flew past my pool at great speed, screaming:

"Turn it on!"

His panic was justified: he was being tailed by three fireflies at a distance of a mere ten meters. Their arms were stretched out towards Kimal Sarento, and the way the ground was transforming under him indicated the active use of spatial magic. The ancients did not want to destroy him, only to detain and study him. They were probably interested to discover what miraculous beings had come to pay them a visit. The tiles under my feet also began to move, losing their density and turning into a viscous substance. They had seen me, assessed me and decided to take me in for inspection as well. Once Kimal Sarento was out of range, I reduced my aura radius to twenty meters, just in case, and struck the enemy. Never fear, Valevsky was on the job!

Three corpses fell to the ground, and the tiles beneath me regained their solidity. I had to rip my legs out, freeing myself, and use my previously tested method of moving their protective dome generator to the side again. Unfortunately, it only worked with one: two geniuses had their generators integrated into their belts, not hanging in material space. I told Kimal Sarento he could come back.

"We need to break through the dome. Can you do it?"

Instead of answering, my student, who was scared of the ancient geniuses, stretched out his hand towards the generators and activated *Chain Lightning.* It took several minutes and two vials of mana before the protection disappeared with a loud bang. But the generators themselves were also destroyed by the powerful flow of Kimal Sarento's magic. As was everything under the dome. We couldn't hope to extract anything from the bodies this way. Not a feasible option.

"Is this a switch?" Kimal Sarento picked up the burnt generator and turned it over in his hands. Several switches of unknown purpose were found on the burnt mechanism. Most of them were located on the front side, where the screen had once been, but there was a small and separate button on the side of the device. It was located under a cover that prevented it from accidentally being pressed, so it must be very important. I had to spend some time developing a clamp for the generator and a small control "finger" with which I could pry back the cover and press the button. Approaching the two intact geniuses, I began to manipulate the space, trying to turn off the protective field.

It took me a while to press the button — my lack of experience with such delicate devices was painfully evident. But as soon as I pressed and released the button, the shield vanished as if it had never existed. I did the same with the second dome, excited by my new acquisitions. I conducted an experiment: hanging the generator on my belt, I deactivated *Golden Dome of Protection* and switched on the ancient device. Unfortunately, I did not get any results — the generator refused to turn on. Neither with my hands, nor with the help of spatial magic. We were doing something wrong. Either the device was turned on in some special way, or it was tightly tied to its previous owner. In any case, this mechanism needs to be taken to our Defender. He'd figure it out.

"It seems to me, my mentor, who is so enraptured by his study of ancient technologies, that we need to get out of here quickly. I don't like the looks of that bright light rapidly approaching from the direction of the lair"

"Let's go. Back to Hearth." I waved my hand, forming a portal home, and jumped out of the pool to see the approaching armada with my own eyes. But there was none. Yes, a glowing point of light was rapidly approaching us, but it wasn't exactly dazzling. Just a small group of people eager to see with their own eyes the chaos we had caused.

"There is no need to do that, my thoughtful mentor," Kimal Sarento correctly understood my confusion.

"If we don't check, we'll never know. I'll be there in a couple of hours. Give the devices to the Defender, let him figure out how they can be used. Go now."

Kimal Sarento merely sighed, but submitted. Despite all his might, he was useless in this battle. In fact, everyone was useless in this battle. Except, as it became clear, the highest hierarchs of Skron and the Light. Only my darkness or the commanders' light could penetrate their defenses.

The portal collapsed and I turned up the radius of my aura to the maximum and prepared to meet the geniuses of the ancients. They were approaching with great speed — in my estimation, about twenty seconds to contact. There were many options for how these creatures would act. They could attack me right away. They could run up and, hidden by their domes, try to figure out what was going on. They could take the bodies and drag them away without bothering to sort things out. They could simply run past, led by a goal known only to them. As I said, there were many options, so I decided to cut off most of them by hovering above the pools a few meters. The design that I used in the Fog Arena came in handy — a tripod joined to a small platform. I did not know how to fly, as the geniuses did.

They noticed me. They slowed their approach significantly. Now I could make out the individuals in the group: five ancient geniuses emitting light accompanied by several dozen ordinary people. This entire procession stopped about fifty meters from me, finally allowing me to use *Analyze* on those without an inner light. I expected anything, but not that these were also ancient geniuses. And without any additional parameters like "restricted" or "lower," or anything like that. Ancient geniuses. Just like their light-bearing kin. However, I immediately noticed another difference between these two groups: the glowing ones flew on their own, while the light-deprived ones were on a small platform. They had to use "crutches" to move at great speed. It was a fascinating little device. I needed to make a similar model for myself. I could steer the spears, right? Why not the platforms as well? Or even make them universal remote so that they could on their own. This would solve the problem of transportation in the light lands. It looked like I'd have to go to the Fog Arena again to study this issue. I was sure I'd be told again that the creatures of Chaos didn't like this method of transportation.

"Greetings to the ancient geniuses!" I shouted, still waiting for an attack that didn't come. The space around me began to change, but so far I hadn't noticed anything mortally dangerous. Big deal, the bars were growing, forming something that looked like a cage. What, like I couldn't get out of a cage? The ancient geniuses considered it unnecessary to answer, and continued to form the cage. It was formed surprisingly quickly: just ten seconds and a fence about fifty meters high of seemingly impenetrable bars grew around me. They didn't make a roof — apparently, none of the ancient geniuses had ever flown that high. Naive...If they knew how I'd climbed the Black Mountain and met Pharapho, they certainly wouldn't have overlooked this escape route.

Finally, the structure was finished and the glowing geniuses of the ancients flew right up to the cage. The ordinary ones started running around, pulling the remains of their relatives out of the pools. Kimal Sarento had destroyed all the non-glowing geniuses, but he couldn't do anything with those that had protective shields. All four of the glowing ones, by the way, were lying not far from me inside the cage. So it wouldn't be possible to take them for now. Nevertheless, the others noticed the bodies. They started exchanging glances, as if communicating. They likely used some sort of communication device similar to the one installed in my armor.

"Apparently, you didn't hear me, so I'll repeat myself: Greetings, geniuses of the ancients! I come in peace!"

Surprisingly, again no response. Evidently, because I was in a cage, there was no need to be afraid of me, it was probably possible to talk, but the geniuses of the ancients did not want to make contact. Were they really so upset by the fact that four of their relatives were lying not far from me, having lost their glow? Well, there is nothing to be upset about, the rest would join them soon. The first attack was due to the element of surprise and the fact that the opponents were absorbing living souls. Now I had a rough idea of what to expect, and only my desire to talk postponed their death. But they refused to make contact. Which was very strange.

However, I wasn't giving up that easily. The enhanced geniuses with glowing chests were clearly some local bigwigs. There were too few of them in comparison to their simple counterparts. These five clearly knew what they were doing: as soon as the walls of my cage formed, they began to shrink the confines, reducing my room to maneuver. The stone beneath me also began to move: they softened, turning into a viscous substance. My tripod was clearly not prepared for such a turn of events, so it began to tilt, threatening to throw me off. However, I was still determined to find common ground, despite this troubling behavior.

"I am a human, just like you! I propose we cooperate! I need your help!"

Once again, I failed to get an answer. The tripod tilted at a dangerous angle, so I had to act. Realizing that we wouldn't come to an agreement, I reduced the radius of my aura so as not to hit two or three ordinary ancient geniuses standing at a distance. When the leg of my pedestal finally sank into the ground and I began to fall, I had to turn on my aura. I landed on a solid surface — the magic abruptly cut out and the material returned to its original state. There was no more light. The five fireflies had been torn apart by the level thirty-five dark aura. Despite all their technology, they had not been prepared for this.

The simple geniuses also got their share, following the others into death. Because I was falling forward, I miscalculated the distance, and instead of two or three, only one remained alive. Judging by his gaze, the concepts of horror and fear were not foreign to these creatures, especially after I destroyed the walls of my prison with two blows from my vyrma blade. Approaching the creature in whose chest the light had recently burned, I expected to stumble upon a protective aura, but, surprisingly, it was not there! I got to the body and once again confirmed that *Devour* could only collect information from exploded corpses. However, if I had attacked right away, I could well have gotten some valuable thing. Damn it! Why didn't I check to see if the shield was there first?

Who I'd really wanted to speak with was one of the glowing geniuses, but I couldn't throw away the opportunity to communicate with a simple one. He didn't even try to run — he stood there, eyes wide and fixed on the bodies of his brethren, and he continued to stand there, even when I came closer. Now he was clearly in no condition to communicate. Grinning, I formed a portal to Hearth and began to throw the vestiges of their bodies inside. Both the elders (that's how I started referring to them) and the simple ones. First of all, I needed to figure out if there were any differences between them and humans, and also find the light source in the chests of the elders. What were these miniature suns?

No one else was in a hurry to come see us, so I approached the surviving genius of the ancients, who was still in an extreme state of stunned shock, hugged him by the shoulders as if he were a relative, after which I forgot about any kinship and threw him into the portal, hoping he wouldn't suffer much from the rough handling. There were many in Hearth who were capable of making even a mute talk. The Evil Engineer, for example, who flatly refused to return his human name and continued going by the name given to him by the Church of the Light. And it was his right, who was

I to protest? As long as he continued doing his job.

"Tell me, my mentor who loves to get his grubby hands on everything he can, what is this?" I heard Kimal Sarento say in my ear. He was awaiting my arrival and did not expect to see corpses come through the portal, nor the live specimen that followed.

"Examine the corpses, interrogate the living one and find out what is going on here. Special priority assigned to understanding the difference between the glowing and ordinary creatures and what other types exist. I tried to establish contact, but I did not succeed. Apparently, the ancients have some special way of communicating, it may be that they don't know how to vocalize at all. If he cannot talk aloud, make him write. Although who am I to tell you? My wise apprentice knows very well how to squeeze information out of someone who is unwilling or unable to talk."

"You know that you can't completely absorb Zero," Kimal Sarento warned. He knew perfectly well why I hadn't returned to Hearth after delivering the loot. I was going to return to Zero, switch on my aura, and continue my descent. Whether he liked it or not, he would only slow me down. The Chaos guests were right — I could complete this task on my own.

"I'm not going to absorb it completely. I'm using the smallest storage device, I have a lot of them now. I need information, so get to work getting it. And another thing: it's also very important to figure out what kind of place this is. The five fireflies that came to protect their fellows didn't have protective domes. Only those who hung in the air and absorbed other people's power had them. I suspect that this location carries some value to the geniuses, so they'll rush to protect it. Maybe even the supreme hierarch himself. This is how we'll get our hands on him. It'll be easier than winding our way through their lair and searching for him. So get me that information, my pupil, who can make even the impossible happen. I'll deal with the rest. I still have a day and a half left to get the stabilization system, so I'm going. I'll make it. I can't afford to make any mistakes."

Chapter 17

"AND YET I INSIST — Zero's power must be divided among us," Kimal Sarento said. He was on his fifth hour of nagging. My persistent pupil categorically refused to accept the fact that I would have to absorb the power of the main mechanoid alone. He demanded that we divide the responsibility, the testing process, and in general, I still had to deal with the highest hierarch of the geniuses of the ancients, so it was no place to be greedy now. At first I joked, then ignored him, but gradually my irritation began to accumulate. I wanted to block off the communication, or even portal back to Hearth and hit him with the dark aura. I'd never seen him so persistent before.

Now, instead of snapping back, I punched another mechanoid, absorbing its contents. Small, medium, large, massive, elite — I encountered all varieties of mechanoids inside Zero, but after a certain point, they could do nothing to oppose me. They all turned into statues under the dark aura, allowing me not only to calmly cut a passage to the lower level, but also to walk along the corridor, collecting their mechanical contents. I didn't spend too much time on this — about twenty minutes per level — but even that was enough to fill my inventory fairly quickly. There were many mechanoids, and they all sought to protect their master. Which only worked to my advantage: I did not have to run along the corridors, looking for another target to absorb. Eventually, my seemingly bottomless inventory was full. Our Defender, whom Kimal Sarento had already given the chunks of Zero's hull, had howled with avarice and came to see my apprentice personally to demand more. It was the most superior building material the mechanical creatures had ever made. I had to cut out a huge piece of the partition and jump back to Hearth with it, unloading all the loot from the small, medium and large mechanoids at the same time. I probably shouldn't have done that: our Defender was completely overwhelmed. He jumped around the loot, wrung his hands, made strange sounds and squealed incessantly about how all this needed to be immediately put to use. There were a lot of projects scheduled to fortify Hearth's defenses that were constantly being postponed due to lack of materials. Now he'd be able to create something incredible. Something like no mechanoid had ever created before...

In short, the Defender sent me off to slaughter its relatives, motivating me by saying 'there's no such thing as too much loot.' So I ran around the level for twenty minutes, loading myself up with all sorts of different devices, the names of which were unknown to me. Soon, however, the trouble I had expected much earlier finally arrived. The elite mechanoids that I met on level twenty of Zero didn't feel so great in the deadly aura of the level thirty-five ousel, but they could still move, and even tried to attack, sending projectiles at me. They still died at the hand of the mithril glove, still gave up their resources, but I knew full well that another three or four levels down and the ousel would be rendered useless. When I had to resort to magic to advance, no matter how much I might wish the opposite, I'd have to call Kimal Sarento, who was still buzzing in my ear, for backup. Because without him I would never reach my goal. As if hearing my thoughts, the persistent student struck up the same familiar tune again:

"So what do you say, my heroically inclined mentor, will you take me with you?"

There were no living mechanoids nearby, so I had nothing to take my anger out on. Instead of answering, I activated a portal back to Hearth. I needed to clear my inventory out again, and I'd take him back with me.

"Took you long enough," Kimal Sarento said. He was waiting for me in the throne room, shamelessly sprawled across my throne. The proximity of the Inquisitor and the Interrogator did not bother the man — it was only six months ago that these creatures could be feared. Now, when they are as tied to Hearth as Hearth was to them, and they were a force we could negotiate with. Or try, at least, as the Chaos guests were still the same authoritarian bastards as they always had been.

"You have seventeen seven hours left, Archduke," the Inquisitor reminded me. He clearly didn't like the fact that I had to keep returning to the city to empty my full inventory. I was wasting time instead of completing their particularly important task. I didn't pay him any attention. As soon as my task was complete, I'd be sent to the Fog Arena for a new round of batteries. For the highest hierarch of the ancient geniuses, as well as the Abyss and Pharapho. I had to transport their power somehow, didn't I? I wondered if our guests would demand that I provide them with my own supplies or send me into the Fog Arena again. The second option would be ideal for me, but experience dictated that the former was more likely.

"What about the prisoner? Did you get him to talk?"

"Well..." Kimal Sarento hesitated, which was unusual in itself. "Not yet, but the Evil Engineer and Viscount Kurpatsky are working on it. The steel cage prevents the ancient from using magic, so he is completely at our mercy."

"The steel cage blocks spatial magic?" This was surprising. "What nonsense is that? Steel does not affect the magic of the ancients."

"A magic that our prisoner and his kin never

possessed," explained Kimal Sarento. "It's good to use your head sometimes, my slow-witted mentor, I recommend it. And logic shows that the geniuses of the ancients cannot use the magic they developed, for they entered into an alliance with Chaos and have become a part of it. Of course, you can ask our esteemed guests about how this alliance was concluded, but I'm not sure that we'll be willing to pay the price for this answer. If you think about it, the Fog Stalker cannot grant you knowledge about the ancients, for he understands little about them. Everything that is accessible to this strange echo of Pharapho belongs to Chaos. So if our prisoner has any relation to the ancients, then only by name."

"That still doesn't explain why our prisoner remains silent."

"He's silent for the simple reason that he cannot speak. He lacks the knowledge and experience — he was never taught. He can moan. He can scream. But he can't speak intelligibly."

"Then how do they communicate?"

"Through mental speech — telepathically. We haven't been able to communicate with him at all. We have many theories and are working through them all now. We handed him paper and writing utensils and are teaching him to write. It turns out that the ancients didn't do this either. Slowly but surely, we are moving closer to finding answers."

"We'll get these answers if we move just as slowly *after* I siphon the power from the highest hierarch of the geniuses."

"That path has its associated risks as well," Kimal Sarento said. "But it's better to do it this way than not at all. Answer me this, my hard-headed mentor: why did you suddenly give in to my nagging? The aura stopped working, and now you need cover?"

All I could do was grin and nod, marveling at his insight.

"To be honest, I thought it would happen much sooner. According to my calculations, you should have called me a couple of hours ago. Is Zero really that huge? Or did my greedy mentor decide to thoroughly plunder the poor mechanoids?"

"What about the devices? Have you learned anything from them?" I asked, ignoring his questions. Entering into a polemic with him would be stupid and short-sighted. That was his domain, and he'd wipe the floor with me if I tried to compete.

"No need to rush, my insatiable mentor! I am not Eleanore with her ability to be everywhere at once. The devices were given to the Defender, no results yet."

A message abruptly appeared before our eyes:

"There will be no results. The devices are not subject to study: this technology is unknown to me. The principle of operation, how to switch it on, the power supply — it's all too non-standard and confusing. By all indications, a system like this should not work, and yet it does. More time is needed. Ten to twenty years, no less."

"Time won't help here, only communication with the sixth-generation interactive neural network," Kimal Sarento responded to the message. "Most likely, this device came to geniuses from the time when Chaos had not yet visited our planet. If so, then there's only one place we'll be able to find these answers. I believe that even the geniuses themselves cannot explain how it works. They use it, but do not understand why it works."

"We've made contact!" One of the guards said as he ran into the throne room. "The prisoner communicated with us!"

"Is that so?" Kimal Sarento looked at me in bewilderment, as if he hoped to find an answer there, but, finding nothing, looked back at the guard. "How did you teach him to read and write so quickly?"

"Not reading and writing! We're communicating through drawings!"

This news was so captivating that I decided to go see the prisoner for myself. Zero wasn't going anywhere. This huge mechanical carcass was unlikely to sprout legs and walk on its own, and seventeen hours was enough to dig down at least to level one hundred, if I worked in earnest.

The two most protected spots in Hearth, the treasury and the prison, were located not far from each other. The cell where our prisoner was placed hardly resembled a cage — the steel bars were hidden behind stone. Nevertheless, it was an ideal place to block any mage in the world. The genius was enthusiastically drawing with a pencil, sitting

at a small table. He was doing surprisingly well —
I recognized the glowing figures at once. The Evil
Engineer was sitting nearby, periodically poking
his finger at this or that detail. The prisoner
seemed to understand — he took another sheet of
paper and immediately drew a new sketch explaining the final idea. One of the guards handed me
several already finished pictures depicting the hierarchy of the geniuses of the ancients. At the top
was a single leader, which made sense. The highest hierarch of the geniuses of the ancients. On the
second tier there were twenty glowing beings, almost half of which were crossed out. Nine out of
twenty, to be precise. It was not difficult to guess
what these crosses meant: in this way our prisoner
let it be known that Kimal Sarento and I had managed to finish off almost half of the second tier of
the geniuses of the ancients. Below was the third
caste, and here I had to strain to understand the
meaning embedded here. The prisoner had drawn
ten simple beings, circled them, then drew ten
more next to them, outlined the previous circle
and new members with a second circle, then ten
more beings and a third circle, and, as a final
chord, four figures outside all the circles. I couldn't
make heads or tails of the scribbles, but Kimal
Sarento, who was hovering over my shoulder,
helped elucidate.

"Ten in the first circle. Ten tens, or a hundred,
in the second. Ten hundreds, or a thousand, in the
third. The four outside the circles are four thousand. Maybe not the most accurate count, but a

good way to give an estimate."

"We need to find out how the protective domes are activated and why the ones that showed up later didn't have them. This is an important issue," I said, deciding to shift some of the responsibility from our mechanoid to the prisoner.

"May I?" Kimal Sarento took a sheet of paper and several pencils from the guard and rather clumsily depicted a radiant genius of the ancients, surrounding it with a protective dome. The same creature appeared nearby, only without a dome. Having meticulously assessed his creation, Kimal Sarento handed it to the prisoner, poking the dome of one and its absence in the other several times. Moreover, my cunning mentor extracted one of the mechanisms that refused to turn on, causing another attack of bewilderment in the prisoner. There was no other explanation for his wide-eyed gape.

We didn't receive a response immediately. The prisoner needed some time to explain the way the location with the pools worked. If one were to translate his images into words, it might sound like this: the field with the pools was one of the most important places of the geniuses of the ancients. This was where the life extension process happened for the luminous ones. Those who remembered a time before the coming of Chaos. Of course, some of this was our assumptions, but I believe this is what the prisoner wanted to tell us. They did, in fact, use this field to absorb the energy of living creatures, thus extending their lives. But at the moment of absorption, the creatures become extremely vulnerable, so those who go to the field are given protective devices, which were the barrier generators able to counter both magical and physical damage. Where the geniuses had gotten these devices from, the prisoner did not know, but he indicated that they were very limited in number, they were personally configured by the highest hierarch, and were passed from hand to hand to the next luminous relative. Actually, his was why the process was only carried out in small groups. The prisoner had been born recently — the task of the third caste was to serve the higher comrades, if necessary, giving them everything, including their lives, if there was a shortage of victims. These victims were supplied by the man-made creations of the geniuses of the ancients: the minotaurs. Our prisoner did not even formalize them as a separate caste and clearly did not consider them living beings, but rather independently operating automatons whose duty it was to deliver crowds of victims to their masters. And they did not particularly care whether they were people or any other living creatures — life force could even be drawn from the mechanoids. The main thing was to know how to do it. The life force passed into the batteries, which the geniuses then used or traded.

The prisoner could have told us much more, but time was running out. One thing was clear: without the higher hierarch, these devices were useless. All my dreams of being able to fight the

Chaos guests on equal ground once again went out the window.

"Time to go," I said to Kimal Sarento, who was still enthusiastically drawing pictures. "Or would you rather stay here and keep chatting with our prisoner?"

"You, my mighty mentor, know exactly how to push my buttons. Yes, it's time. Give me a minute — I'll write down a few topics that need to be clarified. I'm not that excited about the news that the lair of the ancients is guarded by an army of minotaurs. We must find out as much as possible about this. Especially where they are allowed to go, where they are not. And don't smirk like that, my mentor, who is eager to destroy all enemies single-handedly. A hundred meters is not so much for an experienced fighter with a crossbow. Your level fifty *Golden Dome of Protection* will save you from a hundred shots, of course, but what will you do with the hundred-and-first? Hoping for luck is the last thing you should do. We are getting enmired in a difficult situation and I'd like to insure myself a little. That's all, these are my questions. Evil Engineer, be sure to shake the answers out of the prisoner."

I formed a portal right there in the cell, stunning the prisoner once again. He knew for himself that magic didn't work inside the cell (he probably tried it), so he clearly did not dream of seeing a flagrant refute of his entire world order.

"After you," I pointed to the shimmering veil. He just grinned and dissolved in the maroon swirl.

I had no right to waste time letting Kimal Sarento play with the elite mechanoids. Unlike me, my pupil did not have level fifty protection, so he had to rely only on mithril armor. Which, as practice showed, was not the most reliable means of preserving someone's life. I managed to do it in time: the surrounding space barely had time to rematerialize before a whole sheaf of sparks flew up around me and Kimal Sarento from *Golden Dome of Protection* being struck by the mechanoid attacks. The dark aura wouldn't stop the elite members of Zero's children, but it did slow them down significantly, allowing me to not only dig passages to the lower floors, but also to hunt for huge mechanisms. Now, without the aura, the elite showed everything they were capable of. In fact, they fully justified their name, forcing me to use a mana elixir for almost the first time in the last few months. The protective dome was eating up too much mana, and *Praxis* was not able to restore it in time.

However, the attack of the elite mechanoids did not last long. Within a minute, a lifeless void had formed around us. Satisfied, Kimal Sarento, standing under my protection, destroyed the creatures by the dozens, if not hundreds, continuing to strengthen his magic stone, until finally I heard a gleeful cry. *Chain Lightning* had reached level fifty-seven. The highest-level magic stone in the world.

This went on for five levels. I cut holes as Kimal Sarento mowed down mechanoids, and Zero was enraged at his helplessness. That must have been the explanation for the furious vibration that started a few more levels down, right? I didn't think that Zero's insides were so worn out that they could shake the whole body. No, this was the fury of a being with no way to stop us.

"Next one's ready!" I cut a hole to the level below and, without waiting for a response, jumped through. I had *Dark Thorn* at the ready to demonstrate how unwise it was to get too close, but to my surprise, *Golden Dome of Protection* didn't immediately start sparking. The confined space I'd fallen into was devoid of both mechanoids and light — in fact, it was completely empty, aside from a cube about my height standing in the middle of the room, emitting a low hum. Soon Kimal Sarento jumped down and immediately grimaced: the hum set his teeth on edge and sent his internal organs on a winding path, tumbling into one another. Being near the cube was extremely unnerving, and with each second this negative feeling only increased.

"I assume this is what we came for?" Kimal Sarento said, compelling me to use *Analyze*. I didn't have the wherewithal to remember that any unknown object must be studied first.

Zero. Mechanoid.

The list of parameters that flashed before me was so long that it made my eyes water. It turned out that Zero itself was a small point inside a huge cube, surrounded by a hundred different devices, the outer layer of which was the very stabilization system for which we had come all this way. Kimal Sarento approached the hole and looked up. We had cut holes strictly under each other, exactly under the coordinates that the Chaos guests had given me. I believe that if we had moved even two or three meters in either direction, we never would have made it to this room. There were no doors, the walls were probably a hundred meters wide, plus the entire level could have been flooded with molten iron. That might be the reason why it was so hot. If it weren't for the mithril armor absorbing all the heat, we would have long ago lost consciousness.

"I don't like your pensive attitude, my sluggish mentor. Have we reached the goal? Or do we need to dig further?"

"No, this is it." I took the extractor out of the immaterial inventory and inserted one of the batteries. The devices fit together perfectly, as if they were made for each other. I aimed the extractor nozzle at the cube to be the first to try out this miracle machine, but suddenly Kimal Sarento stood between me and Zero.

"I think you're forgetting something, my hapless mentor," he said, nodding at the extractor. "My turn first."

"Only press it once," I reminded him and reluctantly handed the extractor to Kimal Sarento. Indeed, we had agreed on this, so it was stupid to argue now. "Just take a little. We don't want to accidentally kill him."

"Naturally, my overly fussy mentor," he said, grinning. "It's still too early to write me off as a suicide. Alright, I approach the cube, press the button, and..."

What happened next can only be described as an "oopsie." As soon as Kimal Sarento activated the extractor, an invisible force smeared me across the wall next to which I was standing. It pressed against me so hard that I couldn't breathe. Kimal Sarento himself remained in place, but his frozen figure showed that something out of the ordinary was happening. A thick beam of energy flew out of the cube and dug into the wide opening of the extractor. A moment passed, then a second, then a third, but the stream of energy didn't end. It flowed and flowed, although Kimal Sarento should have removed his finger from the button a hundred times already. But he didn't! He didn't move at all, continuing to absorb Zero, sucking the life force out of him. I wanted to scream, but the pressure that was generated in this room did not allow it. Realizing that every second counted, I focused my gaze on Kimal Sarento and used *Dash*. Or rather, I tried — I was jerked forward, but then immediately pressed back into the wall. The force of pressure was much greater than the power of my magic. The hum shook the room and an otherworldly shriek rang out, for some reason in the voice of Kimal Sarento. But I could not do anything about it: I was locked in place.

I can't say how long this went on, but at some

point I lost consciousness from lack of oxygen. I couldn't breathe, even with all my strength. When I finally opened my eyes, there was absolute darkness all around. The Gourfan light crystal wouldn't work. There was no light coming through the hole we had cut either: where the lanterns had once flickered, there was also pitch darkness. The hum was gone. As was the rumbling. Even the heat seemed less oppressive. There were no sounds at all, except for a strange, barely audible crackle of lightning. But perhaps it was the noise in my ears after everything I had been through. It was hard to move, but after three *Heals* my body began to feel much better. I even managed to get to my feet and touch my helmet to turn on the light.

The cube hadn't gone anywhere. It was still standing in the center of the room and was still identified as "Zero." Kimal Sarento was lying face down not far from the cube, still clutching the extractor in his hands. That same crackling sound I'd heard a moment ago was coming from the battery. Part of Zero's power had been transferred. He couldn't have taken all of it, right? Since the cube was still identifiable as the head of the mechanoids, that meant we hadn't killed the third-orbital power, right? And there was no message. Three *Heals* went to Kimal Sarento, but they didn't achieved any visible effect: the man hadn't regained consciousness. However, he was alive — *Analyze* was clear about that. Suppressing the urge to rush to him and shake him awake, I approached the cube. It was time to fulfill the task of the guests from Chaos and get this unfortunate stabilization system, so that later I could ask the same Inquisitor why the extractor had such a strange trigger mechanism. The timer showed that I had only thirty minutes left to return to Hearth, victorious.

Unfortunately, that wasn't the last blunder of the day. As soon as I touched the cube, a huge canvas of messages appeared before my eyes.

Stabilization system obtained
Blocking system obtained
Cooling system obtained...

The hundreds of mechanisms that made up the Zero's shell moved from the real world into my immaterial inventory. But the most important thing was not these messages, but what followed. A small round piece of iron fell to the floor, rolled over and froze, emitting black smoke. And, as if someone had been waiting for this very moment, a new message appeared:

The mechanoids have left this world.

Left the world? Did Kimal Sarento completely absorb the mechanoids, unable to cut the extractor off in time? I slowly turned my gaze to him, afraid to even breathe. It looked as if we'd have one less powerful mage left in the world...

Chapter 18

"YOU MUST GO to the Abyss and Pharapho, hand them the empty batteries and pick them up in exactly twenty-four hours. You have one hour to travel to the second-orbital forces. Proceed."

I didn't even want to ask if our Chaos guests would pay for the essences needed to get to the Abyss. Right now I was preoccupied with a much more important question: what happened to Kimal Sarento? He still hadn't regained consciousness, even after I delivered him to Hearth. Without my wives, I felt as if I had no arms, and now Kimal Sarento had deigned to collapse into unconsciousness. *Heals* drained into him as if into a bottomless well. It seemed that I cast it more than a hundred times, to no avail. The extractor and the damned battery holding the power of the Zero went into my inventory, although I wanted to throw them far away. I knew that the exodus of the mechanoids would cause many problems, so I did not even think that Kimal Sarento would even think of doing something like this. And now I had to reap the fruits of our stupidity — who asked us to absorb the main mechanoid? After all, it would have been enough to attack him and take away the stabilization system...It was greed, bare-faced greed...

But the problems weren't limited to Kimal Sarento alone. While I was laying out the essences around the Abyssal triangle, a message from Hearth's Defender appeared before my eyes:

"The exodus of the mechanoids did not pass by unnoticed. In three days I will switch off. During this time I will create a description of all the developments. Maybe you will be able to implement them, despite the fact that all the systems have shut down. In addition, I need to create an access list and give it to Viscount Kurpatsky. Who, where and when has access. This is vital to keep Hearth functioning normally after I am gone."

"You are not dependent on Zero!" I said, taken aback. "Pharapho gave you to me! What do you mean, after you're gone?"

"I also thought that the outcome of the mechanoids would not affect me, but the situation is what it is. I have a countdown timer. As soon as it ends, so will I."

"Wait, what do you mean, the systems are shutting down?"

"Hearth has no defenses anymore, master. No

barriers, no force field, no alert system for unwanted guests. Nothing is operational. Hearth has become an ordinary city, just like all the others in this world. Destroying the mechanoids has destroyed all their creations."

"Is there any way to turn them back on?"

"Not by any existing methods known to me. All the information on the developments that I will transfer to paper media will be functionally meaningless. You will not find any use for it — the power of the mechanisms was tied to the Zero. As soon as it was gone, the energy that powered the devices went with it."

"What about One? He's also a mechanoid! Will he switch off too?"

"Yes, but much later than me. After all, he is a self-sufficient structure that has left Zero's subordination. I believe he has a month or two. During this time, you will have to make him a second-orbital power. Otherwise, he will switch off, and then no force will bring him back to life. I will switch off. It turns out that talking also takes energy. I have just reduced my lifespan by two hours. I must be economical with my remaining resources and efficient in arranging my affairs. The paperwork containing all defense developments and access information will be in the treasury."

The Defender switched off, leaving me in a state of complete despair. Things weren't just bad — this was a complete disaster, and I had no idea how to improve the situation even a little. On pure autopilot, I opened a portal to the Abyss and gave it the battery. Reaching Pharapho was easy — the portal opened directly onto the ledge on Black Mountain. When I returned to Hearth, a countdown timer appeared before my eyes. In twenty-four hours, I would have to pick up the filled batteries and begin the next phase — the destruction of the ancient geniuses. And I would probably do it alone. Because my stupid student, who had decided to sacrifice himself, was still lying unconscious.

However, I was wrong. Pale and looking like a corpse, Kimal Sarento was sitting in my office. The man looked terrible, as if he had aged twenty years at once. Gray hair and wrinkles had appeared out of nowhere, although there had been nothing like that before my trips to the Abyss and Pharapho. It seemed that the life force was draining from him and he could do nothing to stop it. Even the eternal smile with which he greeted everyone seemed forced and looked more like a grimace painted over a flesh-covered skull.

"Do I look that bad?" Kimal Sarento asked in a strange voice.

"More like awful," I said. "What happened in Zero's inner chamber?"

"A lot happened. First of all, the extractor cannot be switched off by one's own will. It will switch off by itself when it has sucked out all the power or when the battery is filled to the brim. Unfortunately for me, the geniuses of the ancients carried around batteries with such a large volume that all the energy of the third-orbital power could easily fit into it. I couldn't turn the battery off until all of Zero was inside."

"You were screaming."

"It was painful. The process of extracting great power is not the easiest procedure, as it turns out. I couldn't help it."

"What did it take from you?"

"That's the second part of the story. My status bar has disappeared. My health has plummeted. I've lost thirty, maybe forty years off of my life. My body aged sharply, as if the extractor had taken not only my strength, but also the life gained by destroying the lithoids. The ones whose life force have allowed me to survive after the exodus of the offworlders."

"Just your status bar? Do you still have magic?"

"I need to check." Kimal Sarento extended his hand toward the wall, closed his eyes and cast *Lightning Strike.* The sharp smell of ozone filled the air and the wall shook from the powerful impact, causing a flurry of servants rushed in to extinguish the shelf that had caught fire.

Once they left, I continued our unhappy conversation:

"Magic's still intact. I just have to use it the old-fashioned way, like when I didn't have a status bar. It's inconvenient, of course, but I don't see anything critically wrong."

"So, minus health, minus status bar, what else?"

"As if that's not enough?" he chuckled bitterly.

"I think we made the right decision, testing it on me. I had more abilities to lose. Now, before going to the geniuses of the ancients, I can safely say that you cannot go alone. The human body will not withstand the work of the extractor. You will lose consciousness and will not be able to complete the task. Conclusion: you need an escort."

"That is precisely why you will go with him," the space that had become the Inquisitor said. Our Chaos guest clearly demonstrated who the real master of Hearth was. "The human body can withstand the absorption of power without losing all of its abilities and skills. This is an important clarification, we will think about how to use it in the future. However, we will not provide anyone else with access to the extractor. The two of you are enough to complete this task. Destroy the geniuses of the ancients, hand over the filled accumulators to One, and return to Hearth, where you await the birth of your official children. Chaos keeps its word. The Archduke will not die immediately."

I really wanted to send the Inquisitor back to the Chaos he had crawled out of, but I held back. No ordinary human could do that. An archduke needs to think about his city and its people. So I struck up my familiar refrain:

"Bring my girls back. We need their support. You want this mission to be completed without incident, right? You can see Kimal Sarento's condition — he's barely alive. The two of us can't get this thing done without serious consequences. We need help. Or we'll just stumble over something trivial and everything will collapse at the very last moment. Is that what you want?"

"We will think about this issue and make a decision soon," the Inquisitor avoided answering. "Get ready — in thirty-seven minutes the Abyss will give back its battery. In forty-five, Pharapho will follow suit. Then you will immediately go to the geniuses of the ancients. One is already approaching the breakthrough point, he cannot stay there for long. It is dangerous. You do not have time to warm up, you need to get to work."

The Inquisitor disappeared just as instantly as he had appeared, clearly pleased with himself. Doing something nasty brings joy to the heart. I supposed that was the motto by which all Chaos vessels live.

"Well, I have a little less than an hour to try to get back on my feet," grinned the aged Kimal Sarento. "What about our Defender?"

"Scheduled to shut down in three days. Hearth will be left defenseless."

"Not good. Phantoms, spies and illegal inhabitants of all stripes will slip through the cracks. You'll have to shake down the sixth generation neural network to recreate the defense system through improvised materials."

"Me? Not us? What, you're writing yourself off so soon?"

"Perhaps you haven't noticed, my conclusion-jumping mentor, that I'm not exactly in tip-top shape? Your *Heal* can't do much for me now, I'm afraid. A gust of wind may do me in. So only warm compresses, baths and complete isolation will allow me to last a little longer than a few years. And what more can I ask for? I've lived long enough. Let's go to the geniuses of the ancients together."

"I won't let you use the extractor again! It will kill you!"

"Let's cross that bridge when we come to it, okay? In any case, you have the device, and it's up to you to decide who will use it. I..."

Kimal Sarento was interrupted by the office door opening. Naira stood on the threshold, out of breath. A few seconds later, Alia and Eleanore appeared behind her. It was harder for these two to run, but they didn't lag far behind. The throne room was not that far from my office.

"Max!" Alia immediately threw herself around my neck. Naira hesitated for a second, but then joined in. A moment later, the girls burst into tears, like children after being told a frightening fairytale. Only Eleanore stood back, observing. Approaching Kimal Sarento, she stared at him for a long time, then asked:

"How much time do you have?"

"A little. A year, maybe two. Let's not do this, I don't see the point. It's what it is. It can't be changed now, and to be honest, if I could do it again, I wouldn't change a thing. Hearth has its own problems to deal with, and I have no idea how you're going to get out of all this. The mechanoids have left our world, and in three days the Defender will disappear. With all that entails."

Eleanore sighed heavily and looked at me. My

wives, who previously had nerves of steel, had finally gone soft. I'd never seen them so tearful. I whispered sweet nonsense to them and they worked together to tell me how they had fared in the complete nothingness, where there was neither up nor down. How they had been floating in this nothingness, unable to talk to anyone. The Chaos creatures had kept them all separate from one another.

"We'll think of something," Eleanore said, not permitting herself the same weakness as my wives did. The true countess that my manager was would give a head start to any archduchess who received this title during her life. People like Eleanore were not broken by minor troubles. Eight years in the rifts did not pass so easily.

However, as much as I wanted to prolong the happy moment with two beautiful girls clinging to my sides, I had to tear myself away. There was too little time left before I teleported to the Abyss and Pharapho, so we had to go over all the details. Which, in fact, Kimal Sarento and Eleanore were already doing, drawing circles, diagrams and tables. Soon Alia and Naira joined them. Surprisingly, both my wives understood what their older comrades were drawing, while for me these scribbles remained just scribbles, clothed in numbers and familiar names. The intricacies of city management eluded me, and it was stupid to dive in right now. I moved away, not wishing to interfere, and when I jumped into the Abyss, it seemed that no one noticed my departure. They were all otherwise occupied. The white seraph noticeably was noticeably weaker: he looked dried up, as if the Abyss had drained all his power.

"The Abyss is handing over the filled battery." A sparkling energy container hung in the air in front of me. "Our side of the agreement is fulfilled, the Abyss expects Chaos to fulfil its obligations as well."

"I'll pass it on. I have a few questions. May I receive answers?"

"Depends on what questions, depends on how much you are willing to pay for them," the white seraph said too quickly. The Abyss needed energy, and the essences of the rift creatures were the easiest to digest.

"The mechanoids have left our world. However, I have one of their race left in the city — one that Pharapho gifted me. My mechanoid said that in three days it will disappear. However, I do not want to lose this power. Question: how can I keep our Defender alive and functioning?"

I didn't waste time on small fry and immediately rolled out two Rift Master essences.

"If the mechanoids have left the world, then nothing will save your Defender," explained the white seraph, not taking his eyes off my essences.

"Even if you transfer it to some other force?"

"Impossible. It wouldn't know what to do with this creature."

"The mechanoids were destroyed while using the extractor. Can it help somehow?"

"You transferred Zero's energy into a battery?"

The news was so surprising that the white seraph even looked up from the coveted essences.

"I think we're speaking the same language. Yes, Zero's power was taken and placed in the battery. Question: if this power is transferred to One, will the mechanoids remain in this world?"

"The power will return, which will allow them to function. But in order for your Defender to remain alive, you'll need One's good will. He must initiate the transfer of part of his energy. Without this, the mechanoid will not survive."

"He has a little less than three days left. If the power transfer occurs after that, will it be possible to resurrect him?"

"It is possible to return life to the mechanism, but it will be a different consciousness. If you wish to keep this particular individual, you must hurry. And, I repeat, the consent of One and some action on his part will be required. This is my full answer, human."

"Go ahead, you earned it." I unclenched my palm, and the two essences evaporated, migrating into the greedy paws of the servant of the Abyss. "Another question. Does the Abyss know anything about the technology of the ancient geniuses that creates a protective dome? The ancient geniuses use it when absorbing other people's lives."

"No," the white seraph answered after a pause. "We know what you're talking about, but we can't explain the principle of operation behind these mechanisms."

"Okay, what about information on how to turn

them on? The highest hierarch of the ancient geniuses does this somehow, right?"

"The activation trigger is individually tailored for each device and depends on the parameters of the person, its structure, the mechanism itself and the way it is fed. It is impossible to give you a single formula."

"But is it possible to tune one of these devices to me?" I pulled one of the devices out of my immaterial inventory, praising myself for my foresight. "I can't turn it on. Can the Abyss help with this?"

"It will cost you a lot, human," the white seraph said this phrase too quickly again, forcing me to smirk. You can solve almost any problem, if you had the means to pay.

"Will that be enough?' I formed a container in front of me and dumped several hundred essences I had collected from my last rift into it. There was nothing particularly valuable there, but the very fact of having essences of level thirty, forty, and even several dozen at level fifty might loosen the white seraph's tongue. At the same time, I checked one thing that I should have checked a long time ago: the magic of the ancients works perfectly in the Abyss.

"That's enough for one device," the white seraph replied, and the container instantly emptied. It seemed to me that the creation of the Abyss even became a little denser. I had provided it with a good boost of energy. "The setup will take some time," the white seraph warned, taking the device.

"I have fifteen minutes. Will that be enough?"

"Plenty. Stand still, human. The binding process can be painful — you need to transfer part of your essence to the device. Only then will it protect you."

The Abyss vessel was right: it was painful. But for a person who had reached the fifty-ninth level of the rift, the sensation was akin to a light prickling. The white seraph did not work for long — ten minutes later he handed me the ancient device. I took the mechanism and froze — something had changed in it. It remained just as cold and lifeless, but somehow I could feel it. I understood how to turn it on, how to turn it off, how to increase the radius and, most importantly, how to transfer part of my mana so that a protective dome would form around me. The switch that I used to deactivate the device was not required: the mechanism worked through mental commands. Which was extremely convenient: I couldn't always rely on hand gestures.

"What will happen to people who fall inside the field?"

"They will die. This is not a dome in the literal sense of the word. Not a shell. The device forms a sphere filled with you and the energy tuned to you. Any living being placed in the sphere without prior tuning will be destroyed instantly and irrevocably."

"I need to set up a few more devices for other people. Can I learn how to set them up?"

"No. To do this, you will need several additional devices that are used by the highest hierarch of the ancient geniuses. By the way, you can get them in the Fog Arena. Return with them, and we will be able to teach you how to tune. The fee for this, as you understand, will be significantly higher than for tuning to you."

"Okay, another question: can I bring one more person here?"

"You can, but they will die. Without a stone blocking the influence of the Abyss, it is impossible to survive here. Just like too near Pharapho, the Light, Skron or Chaos. The forces of the second orbit and above generate too powerful energy fields for a person to safely survive within them. If someone needs to get to the Abyss, they must go your way. Through the rift."

This wasn't the happiest news. I had planned to give the transport triangle to Kimal Sarento and send him here to obtain his own absolute protection. However, the rift option didn't suit us: in his current state, he would hardly survive even to level two. And this despite the fact that he was fully adapted to level ten!

I had to go back. More precisely, open a portal to Phrapho, where a creature similar to the Fog Stalker also handed me a filled storage device. At the same time, this copy of the Fog Stalker looked as dried up as the white seraph. Apparently, the missing life force had taken a toll on the Abyss, Pharapho, and all their spawn. However, no one dared to refuse Chaos: all agreements had been agreed upon, payment had been received. I wondered what Chaos bribed both second-orbital forces with so that they agreed to such madness.

"Now the next phase." The Inquisitor was already waiting for me in the throne room. The flickering red veil of my portal had barely disappeared when the guest from Chaos had already arrived to reveal his next will. "One will be near the conjunction point in twelve hours. You must finish with the geniuses of the ancients in that time. One cannot remain near the conjunction point for too long. Proceed!"

"Twelve hours?! I'll spend all that time just finding the highest hierarch! Before, you gave me three days for this task!"

"You destroyed nine out of twenty governors in a matter of minutes before. We thought that it would take you longer to deal with them, but reality presented a pleasant surprise."

"What do the governors have to do with it? There's an army of minotaurs! What should I do with them?"

"Ignore them. Destroy them. You are free to do as you wish. You have eleven hours and fifty-nine minutes to find the supreme hierarch of the ancient geniuses and use the extractor against him. What you do with those who protect or hide him is of no particular concern to us. The result is important, not how you got there. You are wasting your time, Archduke. If you do not show up at the conjunction site in twelve hours to begin the final phase of the project, everyone you care about will die."

"There is no need to anger our dear guests. Let's go, we don't have a lot of time," Kimal Sarento said as he approached me. He could no longer move without aid, so he used crutches. Real wooden ones. How had he procured a pair so quickly?

"You stay here. I can handle the geniuses of the ancients myself. This time I'm certain."

"I would like to tell you what you can handle on your own, my heroic mentor, but there are ladies here. You are not going anywhere without me. Unlike you, young man, I know exactly what will happen when you use the extractor, so I will not let you anywhere near it. You have been promised a long and fulfilling life, let's not waste it on useless heroism and self-sacrifice, okay?"

"Using the extractor a second time will kill you!"

"It will make me weaker," Kimal Sarento disagreed. "It will knock off a few more decades. But it certainly won't kill me. Let's stop this useless argument. Everything has already been decided, Maximilian Valevsky. Take me to the head of the ancient geniuses and step aside. I'll take care of the rest. Any questions? Great. Open the portal. We have eleven hours left and who knows how many minutes. You wouldn't believe it, but I'm actually feeling too lazy to count. Yes, open the portal right back to those damned pools. I'm sure the head of the ancients will be waiting for us there."

Chapter 19

"I COULD BE WRONG, but somehow this place doesn't look much like a field with swimming pools," Kimal Sarento noted, examining the surrounding area.

"I have a bad feeling about that place," I said. "Something tells me that they will be waiting for us there. And not the leader of the ancient geniuses himself, but the entire army of minotaurs, led by the remaining governors. It was one thing when they wanted to catch us, another when they want to kill us. I have no desire to fight those who can control space. That's why I opened a portal here, to a point I'd predetermined a little earlier."

"We only have twelve hours," Kimal Sarento reminded me. "Aren't you afraid of making a mistake? Everyone you love will die."

"I always knew you'd make a great motivational speaker," I grinned and formed a small steel platform. "Get on, I'll take care of your transportation. I assume you can't move yourself?"

"Why not? I can walk. Not as quickly as I'd like, but I still can. Are you sure you could lift me?"

"Since when does a spatial mage need to do physical labor? I stole this little trick from the second group of ancient geniuses who showed up at the showdown. The governors flew themselves, but the simple ones used crutches like these. I'm not sure I formed the sentence correctly, but it made the spear fly, and I think it will make this thing fly too."

I moved my hand, causing the created platform to rise into the air and hang in place. It seemed to work: the platform did not fall, no effort was required to maintain it in this state. Could I really have created an adequate magical sentence on my own? Yes, I was a spatial mage!

But reality once again taught me not to count my chickens before they hatch. Kimal Sarento hopped over to my platform on his crutches, turned his back to it and sat down. The platform, unable to bear the additional weight, collapsed to the floor, dragging the powerless mage along with it.

"It seems you forgot to take something into account," Kimal Sarento croaked, trying to rise.

"Stay there. It will be easier to build it that way," I said, blushing. I was ashamed to admit it, but I hadn't thought about the extra weight. After making a few changes to my proposal, I waved my hand again, and the platform rose into the air again. This time, along with my student, who grabbed onto it with both hands, afraid of falling.

"I've got one question: can we add some amenities to this wonderful transportation system? I'd like some handles to hold on to, a back to lean on, maybe even a footrest. As-is, I'm afraid to breathe, lest I fall off. Come, my ever-hasty mentor, let's make a few changes. I won't fly on this. Better on crutches than on this."

Snorting with displeasure, I began to amend the phrase. The geniuses of the ancients spared no thought for comfort. They calmly settled on flat platforms, not demanding unnecessary amenities. In his desire to make his life more comfortable, he was higher-maintenance than some girls. This doesn't work for him, that needs to be changed, and I really should approach my duties with more care and responsibility. As a result, I got some semblance of a chair: a back, armrests, even a footrest had to be made. When my creation once again soared into the air, Kimal Sarento grinned — now he was pleased. Nevertheless, he still managed to find something negative to say:

"I suppose I'm not able to steer it remotely?"

"Your task is to destroy everything that stands in our way. I'll steer."

"Then why are we still here? The main hall, as far as I remember the blueprint of the lair, is a little further. Onward, my control-freak mentor! The supreme hierarch of the ancients awaits!"

The lair of the ancient geniuses resembled a

huge estate. Rooms, corridors, high ceilings and, what immediately attracted my attention, unusual devices and pieces of furniture. Strict lines, sharp angles, none of the delicate curls typical of our palaces. Moreover, there was surprisingly little wood here — mainly metal, glass and some hard material that replaced wood. Kimal Sarento flew next to me and meaningfully grunted, asking to drag him over to this or that piece of furniture or device. All the items he took a particular liking to were sequestered away into his immaterial inventory.

"We need to figure out what they are and how to replicate them," he explained to my silent question. "Don't you think that the geniuses of the ancients understand style? Personally, I like this interior much more than anything you can see in classical palaces or even Hearth. Such severity, minimalism and above all, practicality. Nothing superfluous — everything is functional. However, I have a question: where are the masters of this place? We've been here for fifteen minutes, and no one has taken care of us yet."

"Maybe because they don't know we're here?" I suggested. 'Everyone rushed to the pools, leaving the lair unguarded. And who in their right mind would think of attacking space mages? The Inquisitor and the Interrogator don't have the right to do this on their own."

Pushing another door, I opened a passage into a huge room that served as the local throne room. Seeing out what was inside, I froze, fighting the urge to vomit.

"Hmm...Strong. Drag me to the right pile," asked Kimal Sarento. He was not at all fazed by the towering pile of gutted minotaurs. The blood from the portal guardians flowed into special grooves and disappeared somewhere under the hall. I was afraid to imagine how many bodies were in one pile — at least fifty or sixty. There were eight piles in the hall, all equidistant from one another forming a regular octagon, in the center of which stood an empty throne. Finally, a departure from the minimalism of the rest of the facility — the snow-white throne seemed to be carved from a single piece of bone from some animal that had an unprecedented number of curly horns.

"They were killed about an hour ago," said Kimal Sarento after completing his examination of the minotaurs. "Apparently, the supreme hierarch needed some borrowed power. As I said, he personally went to the field with the pools. I could be wrong, but there is a non-zero probability that there is no one in this huge house at all. Maybe some servants who do not have access to the central rooms. What do we do next, my risky and mistaken mentor? Jump in to pay them a visit?"

"After what we've learned?' I raised an eloquent eyebrow. "The head of the ancient geniuses pumped himself up to the eyeballs with power. They've set a trap and are just waiting for us to appear. An hour ago, he was still here. Around this time, the Abyss and Pharapho began transferring their power to the batteries. Don't you think that's too many coincidences?"

"Are you trying to say that the ancient geniuses somehow received information about what was going on?" Kimal Sarento frowned.

"That's what it looks like. They knew not only that we would show up, but also the approximate time of our arrival. Someone leaked the information to them. The question is, who?"

"Then the next question: how? I remind you that the portals are still down."

"The portals tied to One are down," I corrected him. "I don't think the ancient geniuses would limit themselves and transfer all functionality to a mechanoid. The portal network of the dark ones is broken, but clearly not the portals themselves."

"Not many are privy to Chaos' plans," said Kimal Sarento. "I'll rule out us five first — it's unlikely that any of the girls working for the geniuses of the ancients. As far as I know, you did not pass on information to them. Neither did I. That leaves Chaos itself, as well as the great trinity: the Abyss, Pharapho and One. The Dark Pyramid cannot be discounted either."

"The Abyss and Pharapho won't conspire with a third-orbital power. They're not on the same level. We wouldn't conspire with ants, would we? Chaos is unlikely to tell about its plans to those it has declared war on. That leaves One, but, Light tear me apart, I can't even imagine a reason why it would do that. Its only desire is to become a second-orbital force. Why would it suddenly put a spoke in our wheels?"

"I don't think it's him," Kimal Sarento said

thoughtfully again, looking closely at something. "Pull me up to the throne, please, and lower me a little."

"Did you see something?" I did as he asked and stood next to him, trying to figure out what detail Kimal Sarento had noticed.

"Either our esteemed leader of the ancient geniuses is a woman with a small shoe size, or a certain lady has recently visited here."

Kimal Sarento nodded towards the floor next to the throne, where the bloody footprints of a woman's shoe were clearly visible.

"Karina Fardi," I said, and my insides went cold. The bitch wore some pretty specific boots. I'd had to study them more than once during training, lying on the ground, unable to get up, so I could say with a high degree of certainty that this print belonged to her.

"I think we know precisely who sold us out to the ancient geniuses. That was why the local leader was so concerned about pumping energy — he was preparing for battle. As for where our — I won't call her a 'girl' anymore — got the information about the plans, we can only guess. And, as it seems to me, there is a completely reasonable explanation even for this. One."

"What does he have to do with it? Why would he suddenly leak information if he himself is interested in implementing the plan?"

"I suppose when it's a matter of life and death, there's not much to choose from. For some reason, Fardi can't kill One, but I suppose she can hurt him.”

"Even if so, it does not explain the fact that she is in league with the geniuses of the ancients. And is it really her?”

"It's actually quite easy to check,” Kimal Sarento chuckled. “You just have to go to the field with the blood pools to see this strange collaboration with your own eyes.”

"I have a better idea.” I unfolded the map of the lair of the ancient geniuses once more. “If this is the local throne room, then right below us there is a large room with only one entrance. Which, as you can easily see, is located right under the throne. I suggest we go down. Where all this blood flows. If I am right and this room is somehow connected to the power center of the ancients, then the supreme hierarch will rush to us in a second to protect his value. This is where we will catch him.”

"Sensible,” agreed Kimal Sarento. “I just wouldn't touch the throne. I don't like how unnaturally white it is.”

"Got it, I'll get to work now.” Kimal Sarento's hint was clear as day. Checking the map, I activated the katars and began to cut a hole in the floor, large enough for our flying chair to fit through. The stones reinforced with metal pins fell down, clearing the passage, and I leaned over the hole, activating the light crystal. Before climbing into any unknown place, it needed to be studied first.

"Great Light!” I blurted out when I realized

what I was seeing. This was not some artifact that absorbed blood and filled the geniuses of the ancients with borrowed power. Judging by the few grooves I had cut, that was exactly what the snow-white throne that Kimal Sarento had disliked so much was doing. Down below, in the room where the only road led under the throne, there was a warehouse. My eyes ran wild when I tried to count the shelves, but I couldn't do anything: I lost count at fifty, and that wasn't even a third of the total. The shelves consisted of seven or eight shelves, each of which contained ten to thirty ancient books. The devices with glass screens.

"Would you like to pull me a little closer too, my lazy mentor?" Kimal Sarento's voice was offended. The man was infuriated by my helplessness and dependence on my will. Pulling him closer, I showed him the contents of the room. Unlike me, the former chancellor of the magic academy knew how to keep his emotions close to his chest.

"If I understand correctly, your three dictionaries should be somewhere around here," Kimal Sarento approached the process of studying the warehouse from a practical point of view. "But to be honest, we don't have time to look for them among this mess. I don't think the supreme hierarch will show up here if you jump down. The contents of this place are, of course, priceless, but not so priceless that we should rush headlong into a trap."

"This is the history of humans before Chaos

appeared on the planet," I whispered. "A description of their technologies, their way of life."

"Or a vast library of fiction," Kimal Sarento said calmly. "Fairy tales, poems, fables. Myths and legends of an ancient world that has been dead for a thousand years. Do not idolize the ancients, my stunned mentor. After all, they were the ones who made the mistake of bringing Chaos into our world. They were the ones who died trying to fight it. What we learn from these undoubtedly priceless books will not be of much use to us. Except, I repeat, the three reference books for the *Author* skill, which we are now unlikely to find."

"I'll try anyway," I said, unable to control the desire to grab this entire library into my immaterial backpack. Reason told me it was impossible, but greed, multiplied by the desire to become stronger, managed to drown out its voice. Jumping down, I took the first book I came across. Amazingly, there was no lock — the book turned on without a problem. My heart started pounding when I read the title: *Physics. Beginner's Level.* Physics! The very science that the sixth-generation interactive neural network was so eager to impart to me! Next to physics were "astronomy," "geometry," "algebra," and a dozen more textbooks intended for the beginner level. If all this were given to my wives eager to teach their children...Hearth would become the center of not only power, but also education! The center of civilization, engaged in the process of enlightenment. After a thousand years, humanity would be able to regain its former knowledge! It would become great again! And what pleased me most was that my wives were not limited by time. Before the servants of Chaos finished me off, I needed to build a device to create clones. The ruling class of Hearth would live forever! They would become the wisest people in this world. They would be able to understand the knowledge of the ancients and, perhaps, come up with a way to banish Chaos from our planet! It was worth risking everything and staying alive.

"Are you sure this is what you should be doing right now?" Kimal Sarento leaned over the hole, watching as I furiously hid the ancient books in my immaterial inventory. In ten minutes I managed to clear three shelves, and I was not going to stop there. Yes, it was getting harder and harder to walk with each passing moment. Despite the fact that each book individually weighed little, in huge quantities they could make even me tense up. But I was not going to give up — even if I would not be able to steal everything at once, I was obliged to steal everything I could from the geniuses of the ancients.

"At least two or three trips," I answered, emptying the fourth shelf. There was no time to sort through everything that fell into my greedy hands. The main thing was to fill the backpack so I could jump back to Hearth and dump everything into the treasury. Eleanore and my wives would figure out what to do with it.

"One, and I wouldn't recommend even that," insisted Kimal Sarento. "You need to set your priorities straight, my greedy mentor. If we fail to find the head of the ancient geniuses, if half an hour is not enough to destroy him, then all your current actions will be in vain. There will be no one to use these devices: Chaos will destroy everyone in Hearth. When we complete the task and finish off this force, the entire library will be in your hands. You will be able to portal here and calmly, without rushing, take everything back that you wish."

There were many things I wanted to tell him, but reason prevailed over greed. No matter how you look at it, Kimal Sarento was right: if I managed to destroy the geniuses of the ancients, their entire library would become mine. If not, then neither I nor my loved ones would need the books anymore. Nevertheless, I did not unload the devices back. The portal to Hearth opened in a matter of moments. Finding myself in the main hall, I was surprised to note the absence of the Inquisitor and the Interrogator. As far as I understood, it was not within their normal reception hours, and besides, the dark ones could not get to the Interrogator, so their absence seemed rather strange. Nevertheless, these thoughts did not stop me from urgently unloading the inventory right in the middle of the hall to save time. Eleanore would then drag everything to the treasury.

All in all, it took me no more than a minute — unloading the books turned out to be much easier than stuffing them into my immaterial inventory. It took some more time to form a portal to the main hall of the lair of the ancient geniuses. And then...then I needed more time. Not to portal somewhere or do something. It took time to comprehend what I saw. Next to the snow-white throne of the main genius of the ancients stood an angry Inquisitor and Interrogator. Naturally, they were angry at me: as soon as I found myself in the lair of the ancients again, two swords were aimed at me.

"Where were you?!" The Interrogator seemed to have put all the anger he had been so skillfully hiding all the time into his thunderous roar. It crushed me — I don't even remember how I ended up on the floor, completely flattened by the power of Chaos.

"I have eleven hours to complete the task," I wheezed, confused by the unexpected visit.

"You don't have time!" The pressure increased. In some ways it began to resemble the same pressure that had arisen when absorbing Zero. Except that I could still breathe. Talking was no longer an option. This suited the interrogator more than well. He was never a big fan of what I had to say. Without lowering his sword, he continued:

"The supreme hierarch of the ancient geniuses found a way to contact the Skron vessel and establish cooperation. He decided that if the Skron vessel is made with a second-orbital power, it will protect the ancient geniuses and keep them alive! We cannot allow this!"

I was glad I couldn't answer. Because I wouldn't be able to censor myself. I wanted to tell Karina Fardi, the geniuses of the ancients and the guests from Chaos themselves exactly what I thought of them, but if I blurted anything like that out, my adventures would come to an abrupt end on the spot. The Chaos creature's mood was too deadly to argue.

Gradually the pressure eased. Somewhere to the side, Kimal Sarento began to cough — he had suffered much more than me. Still, my weakened body was not yet ready for such stress.

"Skron's vessel attacked the First. Karina Fardi knows about our plans!"

"So send your commanders into battle!" I said angrily, trying to find the strength to get to my feet. "What does this have to do with me? Our original agreement did not include fighting the Skron vessel! She will finish me off with her aura as soon as she sees me!"

"We grant you temporary protection from her aura," the Interrogator said reluctantly. "The commanders and digital servants of the Temple of Skron are already near the breakthrough point. Right now, they are fighting against the vessel of Skron and the supreme hierarch of the geniuses of the ancients, but the battle is not going in their favor. If the vessel of Skron finally wins, all our plans will collapse. We do not have a spare candidate suitable for the role of becoming a second-orbital force."

The servants of Chaos once again admitted their own impotence against the forces of our world. For some reason, they were not only unable to contact them, but also unable to influence them. And not only them, but also anyone who had gained sufficient strength. Chaos could not stop Karina Fardi on their own. Why this was, and why they required crutches in the form of commanders, digital and nimble archdukes was unclear, but such was reality.

"I have eleven hours to take the power of the supreme hierarch of the ancient geniuses. This is the task you have set me. The fact that the rules of the game have changed during the process is your problem. Do you want me to join the fight? No problem — let's negotiate. If we win and One gets his power, Chaos will spare my life and that of my loved ones. Hearth will be untouchable as long as it abides by the rules of our world. My life in exchange for the life and power of One. It seems to me that this is a worthy exchange."

"You will die!" The Interrogator's sword stopped a few millimeters from my neck, cutting through the mithril armor. As if it wasn't there. My neck was scorched — the darkness from the Interrogator's sword was hotter than fire. But I couldn't get away: you can't run very far lying on the floor. Finally, the creature of Chaos showed its true power, turning on the aura to maximum. Or close to the max. Now I couldn't even breathe.

"We're wasting time," the Inquisitor, surprisingly, played the voice of reason. "If we kill him now, the outcome of the battle will be predetermined. Archduke Valevsky and Count Sarento are those unknown quantities that can tip the scales in our favor. The balance must be maintained.

That is our mission."

"He's setting conditions for us!" the angry Interrogator turned towards his fellow, slightly easing the pressure.

"He's trying to survive. Like any other mortal with too few years to live."

"If we agree to his terms, he will build a cloning machine and become immortal!"

"If we don't agree, we'll have to spend the next thousand years trying to hold the peace together. It's already tottering on the brink because the Abyss and Pharapho have been so weakened, and the mechanoids have left. If another invader shows up on the planet, we won't be able to do anything about it. The world will collapse, and we will go along with it. Is that what you want? Finishing off the Archduke is no problem. The problem is how we'll sort out the difficulties later. We don't have anyone to replace One, as you rightly said. I don't want to see Skron's Vessel even as a force in the third orbit, let alone the second."

"Are you suggesting that we give in? Once again bow our heads before a common man?"

Instead of answering, the Inquisitor took a step back, suggesting that the Interrogator solve this problem on his own. Despite my position, I could not help but be struck by the oddities of the creatures of Chaos. It seemed that they were always playing the madman and the sane one, and they would switch roles frequently, according to the circumstances.

"Very well, Archduke!" The Interrogator understood perfectly well that every second we delayed would just cause more problems down the line. Somewhere there was a battle going on, and the forces on the side of Chaos were losing. "If One becomes a second-orbital power, you will live. Hearth will become an independent city not only legally, but also *de facto.* Are these conditions acceptable to you?"

The pressure disappeared completely, and again the muffled wheeze of Kimal Sarento was heard nearby. This was who had to suffer because I decided to argue with the creatures of Chaos. No matter — he would endure.

"Works for me. There is one condition I need to bring up right away: I need protection, not just for me, but also Kimal Sarento. The dark aura will do nothing against the Skron vessel and the head of the ancient geniuses. We will have to work with magic. He is the best mage on the planet. I need him."

I found the strength to sit up, and a pendant with such a black stone that it seemed to absorb all the light that fell on it jingled in front of me. A similar pendant fell not far from Kimal Sarento. Unfortunately, he no longer had the strength to even sit up.

"You must leave immediately!" The Interrogator waved his hand, forming a portal. "Only one commander and Two are left alive. They could die at any moment."

"Can you stand up?" I rolled over to Kimal Sarento. He looked terrible. *Heal,* quite predictably, did nothing for him.

"As if we have a choice?" His voice was as hoarse as a crow's.

"There is always a choice. You can die here and now. Or you can stumble around for a bit longer."

"Hurry!" The Interrogator urged us. Apparently, the defenders were not faring well.

"I like the second option better," Kimal Sarento put on a gaunt, monstrous grin. "Will you help me? I'm feeling a bit too lazy to get up myself right now."

I hung the amulet around my neck, and then with great difficulty rose to my feet. It's funny, but *Heal* didn't really work on me either. It was as if the aura of Chaos had sucked all the power out of my magic, turning it into a useless piece of trash. Gathering my remaining strength, I accomplished a feat: I managed to lift Kimal Sarento, hanging the amulet on him in the process. He was swaying like tall grass and couldn't stand on his own. I had to constantly support him. For some reason, I didn't think about forming another flying throne to replace the one that had collapsed. It was easier by hand.

"Time! The battle is almost lost!" The Interrogator clearly wanted to hit us with magic again, but his last brain cell told him that after that we simply wouldn't recover from the blow.

"You could have made the portal closer," I muttered discontentedly, taking a step towards the shimmering circle.

"Wait," Kimal Sarento whispered. "Give me the

extractor right away so I don't have to mess around with it on the battlefield."

"I don't think it will work on Chaos creatures," I answered angrily, glaring at the Interrogator. He remained silent, gesturing towards the portal. Nevertheless, Kimal Sarento's plan was reasonable: if there was a battle near the conjunction point, we simply physically may not have time to get the extractor and charge it with the battery. This had to be done in advance.

And once again I had to perform a heroic feat: maintaining an upright position and supporting the weight of Kimal Sarento, I embodied two devices in my hands, uniting them with one deft movement. I had to give the weapon to my pupil — I simply did not have enough hands for everything. The three steps to the portal felt like one of the Evil Engineer's training sessions. Sweat had not poured into my eyes for a long time. I did not even take the last step, I simply fell forward, dragging Kimal Sarento with me. Space lost all hard outlines for a few moments, before solidifying into the strangest place I had ever seen in my life. The world around us lost all colors, except for various gradations of gray. Everything was gray: stones, grass, sky, clouds. Even the huge portal arch, probably about ten meters, created from massive stones. However, the grayness was not limited to the surrounding world: my hands had also changed color. Turning my head, I saw a gray Kimal Sarento. He had looked creepy before, but now he resembled a living corpse.

And the coloring wasn't an acute issue — a little ways off, a battle between four creatures was unfolding, fighting against the backdrop of a once black, but now also gray pyramid that had fallen on its side (I never thought that a pyramid could be sideways like that). On one side were the commander of the Church of the Light, striking with a sword blazing with gray fire, and a misty servant of the Temple of Skron, wielding ancient fireballs. Also gray. On the other side were two creatures. They could be called people, but they had not been considered human for a long time. Karina Fardi, who had entered the active phase of unity with Skron, and some pot-bellied man hanging in the air in a lotus pose. Karina wielded dark lightning, the head of the ancient geniuses attacked with everything. I saw a demonstration of the term "full spatial control" before me: the earth itself rose up against the warriors of Chaos. Spikes, boulders, other pointy structures, God knows what else, never stopped testing the opponents' defense for strength. And this defense did not look strong at all. The bleeding cleric and the limping mechanoid showed how effective the ancient's attacks had been.

Even in the heat of battle, Karina Fardi noticed us instantly. The space between us was torn apart by the sound of her malicious shriek:

"Valevsky! I knew you'd show up! The Chaos creatures were certain to send their favorite little lapdog here. It's time to send you back where you came from!"

"Don't go anywhere," I said, flinging Kimal Sarento to the ground and taking a few hasty steps forward. If the Chaos creatures (who were still nowhere in sight) were to be believed, we would be protected against Skron's aura, so our main task was to defend ourselves against all our adversaries' normal attacks. I didn't dare use the magic of the ancients — it would be a silly move against the highest hierarch of their order. What if he could suddenly seize control of my ability and block me from accessing it? I wouldn't want to make such a flagrant misstep.

I was forced to rely on the tried-and-true level-fifty *Golden Dome of Protection*. It proved its worth immediately, as soon as I was engulfed in Fardi's black lightning. She didn't launch into any long-winded monologues, or hesitate for even a moment, but went straight for the attack. *Reflect Damage* worked perfectly and her black lightning was thrown back at her. It didn't do any damage, which disappointed me, but at least it distracted Fardi from the rest of the battle.

"You're dead, Valevsky!" she cried and turned her full attention to me. I didn't even have time to flinch before she was by my side. The dome blocked direct access to my body, but she didn't need it — all she had to do was get close. She held something small and sparkling in her hand, which she immediately thrust toward my chest. At this point, my muscles finally received the signal from my brain and my body sprung into action. My mind turned off and I began perceiving the surroundings with my body, like in the Evil Engineer's trainings. Fardi was always stronger than me. Both then and now. Everything that I gained went to dexterity and accuracy. Despite her speed and strength, I was able to grab her wrist and tug her sharply to the side. Inertia was a harsh mistress, even for a vessel of Skron. Fardi flew past me and cried out when I jerked her back the other direction and flung her a few meters away. Before she had the chance to land, another level-fifty *Dark Thorn* was flying toward her. Level fifty and some tenths, to be precise. Almost fifty-one! The weapon I had used against the ancient geniuses also worked against Fardi — she was pushed back another few meters. The tears in her clothing showed that at least some of tha damage was getting past her shield, but Fardi didn't show it. Landing on her feet, she leapt up to attack again, but at that moment a stone spike materialized beneath me, throwing me into the air. If not for my defense dome, it would have pierced through me, and I wasn't sure the mithril armor would have done much. The head hierarch of the geniuses had also fixed his sights on me. He didn't like the how I had treated his minions.

"You came here in vain, Valevsky!" Fardi said, still thirsty for blood. "I could become a second-orbital force and forget all about you, like the wretched little vermin you are. But you limped here on your last legs, like an obedient dog. Well then, a dog's death for a dog like you! Today you will know the wrath of Skron and the ancients!"

"A lot of talk, not a lot of action," Kimal Sarento wheezed through the intercom. "Tell me, my heroic mentor, can you get them all in one place? Within hand-holding distance, if possible."

"Do you really think now's the time for sarcasm?" I rolled out from under the boulder that had appeared above my head and sent *Dark Thorn* towards the head genius. The blow did not damage him, while the commander and the temple servant were thrown aside.

"Actually, I'm quite serious. I need Fardi and the ancient one close to each other. We won't get a second chance. And as close as possible. Keep in mind, I don't have much strength. The most I can give you is a minute. Then I'll switch off, and you'll be left to your own devices. Don't jump, attack! Remember what you did to the Wave boss!"

Kimal Sarento's words managed to set my mind straight. Indeed, for some reason I'd been doing nothing but defending myself for the last few seconds. Even Fardi had returned to the commander. Once again, I rose into the air from behind a stone spike that had grown under my feet, and stretched out my arms towards the combatants. It was my turn to attack.

A stone block appeared above my head again, but now I was even glad of it: it would serve as a source. Ten stone tables with their legs pointing inward appeared around the combatants. I understood perfectly well that someone who could easily control space was not afraid of any physical barrier, but I did not need to imprison him. Kimal

Sarento needed me to gather everyone in one place, that was what I would do.

I brought my hands together, clasping my palms tightly. My tables immediately rushed forward, repeating my movements. The legs prevented the victims from moving aside, and no one thought of jumping to avoid the attack. Yes, there were downsides: I caught the commander and the temple servant as well, but they'd have to be considered collateral. Fardi leaned against the table, trying to stop it, but began to slide along the ground, leaving two deep furrows. Now I was stronger. The tables slammed together and, as I predicted, collapsed at the same moment — the supreme hierarch of the geniuses of the ancients did not like my attack. I collapsed to the ground. The simultaneous destruction of ten stone tables turned me inside out. Circles danced before my eyes, but I was still able to see the result of my actions: all four ended up in one place. More precisely, the head of the ancient geniuses remained in place, all the rest were smeared on his defense shield. The tables disappeared, Fardi even turned her head to the side to find me and finish me off, but this was her last action as Skron's vessel.

For Kimal Sarento seized this moment to use the extractor.

I was pressed into the ground, but because I was far enough away from Kimal Sarento, the pressure was an order of magnitude weaker this time. His shrill scream filled the space again, and all I could do was clench my fists in frustration.

Kimal Sarento knew what he was doing. He knew what would happen if he used the extractor again. Nevertheless, he went for it, because for some reason he wanted to leave me whole and healthy. So that I could live a little longer than before the birth of my children.

The pressure disappeared after a minute, and the surrounding space sank into a frightening silence, diluted by the hum of a filled battery. I rose to my feet and, ignoring the loot dropped by the geniuses and the fact that the message about their exodus had not yet arrived, ran up to Kimal Sarento. He was changing right before my eyes: his body was drying up, gradually turning into a mummy. Something similar had happened to Meram and, as I was told, to the Dark Elor, the former mentor of Karina Fardi. The exodus of the offworlders had returned them to their true age, and the body could not bear such treatment.

Suddenly, my student's chest split open like an overripe watermelon, and a whole scattering of magical stones spilled out into the light. Both gold and red. The body rejected the foreign objects, turning Kimal Sarento back into a human. It was a terrifying and repulsive sight — ribs turned outward, a shriveled heart that beat once every ten seconds. I could do nothing to help my student *Heal* once again proved useless. All I could do was watch as one of my closest and most trusted friends died. Finally, his heart twitched one last time and froze.

Kimal Sarento, the former chancellor of the

magical academy of the Zarak Empire, the most powerful mage in our world, my apprentice, a cunning fox capable of finding an advantage for himself in any situation, even a losing one, finally died.

The coughing that came from the four figures brought me back to reality. *Dash* carried me to the bodies, where I found Karina Fardi kneeling. Clearing her throat and looking up at me with a dull gaze, Fardi laughed. The maniacal laugh of a madwoman. Though there was nothing human in her eyes anymore. There was no reason there. The creature that the once beautiful girl had become evoked nothing but disgust. She drooled, laughed hysterically, pointing its fingers in all directions, eyes rolling madly, unable to concentrate on one thing. The extractor had taken her power, cutting off contact with Skron, but before escaping, the power of the first orbit had burned out the mind of its vessel.

I didn't even want to dirty my hands with her. All I did was mentally activate the ancients' defenses. Karina got inside the dome, twitched a few times, and Fardi's life ended. I didn't even feel relieved that I had finally avenged my family. Quite the opposite — I felt dissatisfied. It wasn't me who killed Karina Fardi, it was Skron. The elder Fardi was finished off by fire. It turns out that the only one I really got vengeance on was the Duke of Odoevsky's assistant. I finished him off with my own hands, all the others...Eh...

The dome on the supreme hierarch of the ancient geniuses was still in place. Using the old proven method, I managed to turn it off, and as soon as I touched the body of the pot-bellied man, the anticipated message appeared before my eyes: **The geniuses of the ancients have left this world.**

I probably should have taken the weapons and armor from all four of the dead, but the apathy that had set in prevented that. Kimal Sarento was dead, I would no longer be able to hear his eternal taunts or the mentoring tone when I failed at something. I would not be able to see his satisfied grin. Something in my chest tightened, and I even had to use *Heal* to return my body to a normal state. I'd never thought that in a year, this man and I would become so close.

But I wasn't even allowed my moment of grief. The Interrogator's cry rang out:

"Do not delay, Archduke! You must fulfill what you came here for! Space is ready for the birth of a new force!"

Raising my head, I didn't immediately understand where he was shouting from. It turned out that both echoes of Chaos were standing a hundred meters away from me. Where the world had regained its colors. Neither the Inquisitor nor the Interrogator could enter the gray area. Or they didn't want to, so as not to disrupt the process.

By the way, what was this process? I had not yet been given instructions for this stage. The Interrogator realized this himself, because he continued to yell:

"There is an altar near the portal! One is already lying on it, dead. He died only twenty minutes ago, so you still have time to revive him! First, place the stabilization system around him, linking it to the body. Then activate the batteries with the powers of the Abyss, Pharapho and the highest hierarch of the geniuses of the ancients and stick their spikes into One! This will be enough to start the process! Hurry, time is running out!"

The instructions were quite clear, except that I didn't know how to activate the battery. But the Interrogator came to the rescue here too, shouting out how to turn one end of the buzzing device so that a sharp pin would come out. Clear enough.

I turned toward the portal and slowly trudged over to the shimmering grey shroud. All my emotions were gone. All that remained was continuing to do the work that would keep me and my remaining loved ones alive. But not Kimal Sarento. He was already dead. All that was left of One was a metal ball full of torn wire. He was lying on a large flat stone ten meters from the portal. I found it difficult to stand here: an unknown aura was pressing on my brain, sweeping away all thoughts. I wanted to lie down, rest and forget this whole nightmare. But I could not afford such luxury. I had a family that I must protect. Even at the cost of my own life. Just like Kimal Sarento did, taking the full force of the extractor on himself.

I laid out the stabilization system on the altar and lowered the contact spikes onto the lifeless ball that had been gone for a full twenty minutes.

All around there were dead people, but for some reason, this was the one that would be revived. Why? Because he was beneficial to Chaos. Because he would do whatever they told him. Was that really what our planet needed? And did I really want to live in a world ruled by Chaos? What good would that bring me? Me, my family, all of humanity? Slowly turning towards the stone where the mangled body of the aged Kimal Sarento lay, I hung there for a while, trying to catch the elusive thought.

One was supposed to become the second-orbital power. He was a mechanoid and was quite capable of absorbing all the power granted by other beings. But Karina Fardi also dreamed of becoming this power. This means that the human body was quite capable of withstanding the energy. Kimal Sarento had only been dead for five minutes. According to the Interrogator, he could be brought back. Tear him away from the Light he had been striving for all his hundred and fifty years. What risks did this bring? The threat of death. For me and my loved ones. Not a low price. What could I get out of it? A second-orbital power with a mind of its own. That would fight Chaos. That would come up with a way to detonate this stupid bomb of the ancients, turning the entire world into ruins and destroying Chaos. Was it worth my life? The lives of all my loved ones?

Definitely!

"Come back and finish the process!" the Interrogator's cry reached me at the very moment when

I was lifting Kimal Sarento's body into my arms. He was so dessicated that he weighed almost nothing. Just in case, I grabbed all the stones and went back to the altar. I needed to act as quickly as possible before the creatures of Chaos realized what was happening and interfered with the process. The metal ball fell to the ground, and I laid Kimal Sarento in its place. The first battery appeared in my hand, and it was at that moment that the Interrogator realized what I was about to do.

"No!"

The thunderous scream should have pressed me into the ground, but the distance between us was large enough that only echoes of the pressure reached me. The pin of the battery containing the power of the Abyss extended, and without thinking twice, I pressed it into the torn chest of Kimal Sarento.

The device blinked red, beeped and suddenly lit up green. Taking this as a good sign, I repeated the operation, only this time with the Pharapho battery.

The pressure increased — I had to fight for every movement. Wheezing something inarticulate, I bent down for the extractor that I had dragged along with Kimal Sarento and tore out the battery with the power of the four we had just destroyed. And stuck it into my former student!

It became almost impossible to stand — the weight of the entire world fell on me. Damn it all — I had to make it!

The battery with the power of the Zero almost

fell out of my hands when activated. The device seemed to weigh almost a hundred kilograms. Hold on! Activate and plug in!

That was it! All four drives...

No! Not all! In addition to the standard four, I had two vessels with the power of Skron and the Light! If I was going to be killed anyway, I didn't need to worry about Chaos fulfilling its obligations to the Citadel and the Temple of Skron!

I took the last two accumulators out of the immaterial inventory. While I was activating them, I managed to turn around — the Interrogator and the Inquisitor were running towards me. They didn't teleport, they ran. Like ordinary beings, deprived of any power. However, they were too late. The distance between us was shrinking at a monstrous speed, but still not enough to stop me. I drove both activated batteries into Kimal Sarento's body at the same time, after which I collapsed to the ground. That was all I could muster. My strength left me. Already lying down, I heard a click — the last battery had turned green as well.

"Die!" the laconic Interrogator said as he leapt toward me. His face was so twisted with anger that he seemed to have forgotten himself. The Chaos creature now had only one enemy, and he had to be destroyed. I had no chance to run away, fly away, or counterattack, but I did not want to die helplessly. The gray fire sword came down, but it could not reach me: the protection of the ancients, which the Abyss was able to tune to my body for an insane price, showed itself in all its glory. The energy dome withstood the blow of Chaos!

"What?! Die!"

His stunned surprise lasted only a moment. The Chaos creatures recovered too quickly. I had no way to move, so all I could do was lie on my back and watch as two swords blazing with gray fire stopped ten centimeters from my face and the mana bar dwindled.

Praxis tried its best, but it couldn't withstand such a furious attack. Half of my mana remained. Then twenty percent. Then ten. Then the last crumbs were gone, and with a nasty pop, my defenses burst. The only thing I was lucky about was that the pop pushed the Chaos creatures away from me a little, so they couldn't finish me off right away.

Only a moment later the Interrogator was already at my side. He knew that my shield was down, that I was completely helpless. His anger passed, replaced by hatred:

"Your loved ones will regret what you just did. They will die cursing you and the moment they met you. I want you to know this. So that your death will not be easy. Die!"

The interrogator raised his sword and even started to lower it, but something happened. Before the tip reached its target and ended my life, something fell on my chest and Kimal Sarento's voice rang out. The same one that we all knew and loved, full of sarcasm and a hint of tongue-in-cheek mockery.

"I don't think that's a good idea. Does the esteemed Interrogator really wish to destroy our world?"

The sword froze. The creature of Chaos slowly turned its head to the side. I couldn't see what was going on there: the altar and the pressing force got in the way.

"You have no right to interfere, Nameless One. This is the business of Chaos."

"Really? Yes, exactly, I can't interfere in the affairs of Chaos or humans. Surprisingly. So I'm not going to stand up for Archduke Valevsky. No, respected servants of Chaos. Everything is much more interesting, and…that's it, the point of no return has been passed. Now you have no way to destroy me."

"Archduke Valevsky is ours. He violated orders. You have no right to interfere, Nameless One! You know that. Put down your defenses and let me finish what I started. Archduke Valevsky must die!"

"Well, let's get back to where we started. With Archduke Valevsky, in fact. There is one problem, respected Interrogator, and it is that I cannot allow you to finish what you started. I have become attached to this young man. I want him to live on."

"You have ten seconds, Nameless One, to remove your protection. If you do not, you will be banished! To the same place where the Abyss now resides. You will spend the rest of your days in complete nothingness."

"You dare to threaten me? Good, I can threaten too. Actually, here is my word to you: if

Valevsky dies, at that very moment I will do what none of the active forces had the courage to do. I will kill myself. I swear by the Chaos that revived me, I will do it. My defenses are down. Go ahead, kill your archduke. I have spoken my word."

"You can't! You just received unprecedented power. Your greed, which everyone knows you well for, will not allow you to do this!"

"Do you even hear yourself? Ten minutes ago, I sacrificed my life for the one I consider my adopted son. What has changed? Except that now I have the opportunity to destroy those who would kill him. Destroy Chaos. And stop calling me 'Nameless One.' I have already chosen my name. Order. A great name for the power of the first orbit. My color is green. I have always loved it. Yes, I have no right to protect Valevsky. He is a human and completely devoted to Chaos. But I have the right to dispose of my life. My new power. As I said, the point of no return has been passed, and you know it very well. Kill Valevsky. and let's end all this. Or remove the block. You might strangle my new follower any minute."

The interrogator thought for a long time. But with each second, the pressure he was generating became less and less, until it finally disappeared.

"Your conditions?" the Inquisitor's voice rang out. I could sit down now to assess the situation, but getting involved in the squabbles of higher powers was wrong.

"You leave Valevsky and his family alive. Leave Hearth. Stop pressuring him. Start negotiating if you need anything. Actually, everything else is in the process. I am ready to guarantee the stability of the orbit and the establishment of balance in the world. Not a single bomb of the ancients will explode again. The portals, mechanisms and everything that I received from other forces have already been returned to the world. The Minotaurs have recognized me and are ready to perform their function. You needed this, right? So enjoy the established peace. Why do you need Valevsky?"

"We know how to wait, Order. In a thousand years, the bomb will run out of charge and become no threat. Are you ready to know our wrath? In a thousand years, you will still enjoy living."

"Come see me as soon as the charge runs out," Kimal — Order grinned. I supposed that's what we'd have to call him. "From my perspective, you have work to do. Soon the Archduke will return to his city, by which time you should be gone from that place."

There was a click, and the Interrogator evaporated, along with all the grayness of the surrounding world.

Colors, sounds, even the wind returned. Footsteps were heard, and a creature came out from behind the altar. Outwardly, it resembled Kimal Sarento, but the monstrous green aura showed everyone that this monster had nothing to do with human nature. The gaze of eyes filled with green light stopped on me, and somewhere in the chest area it began to burn.

"Put on the amulet, otherwise you'll burn. A

human can't be near the power of the first orbit. Even its avatar."

It wasn't easy to follow his recommendation, but I managed. The pressure and burning in my chest disappeared, allowing me to sit up.

"First orbit?"

"Why are you surprised? So injecting the power of Skron and Light is easy for you, but thinking about the consequences is too much? Yes, my former mentor, the first. And yes, this is not my real body. This is an avatar. A projection created to communicate with Chaos and especially nimble archdukes. The real me is now settling into my new home."

"Hearth?"

"I see that Chaos has completely burned out your brain. I just told you in human language that my presence will destroy everyone who has no protection. And over a fairly large radius. So I settled in a remote place, ideal for me. In the former lair of ancient geniuses. I liked their interior design sense. So you can forget about the books for now. I will give you dictionaries, but the rest will have to be earned."

"Can't Order's head follower get a library pass?" I couldn't help but be sarcastic. The last thing we needed to be discussing right now was electronic books.

"Order's head follower? Are you talking about yourself? No, my former mentor, you are not fit for this role. Not at all! You are anyone but Head Follower. And you don't need this title anyway — I will appoint someone else to carry out my will. Tarra Loyd, I believe, has been sitting as a chancellor for too long. It's time for her to get promoted. You sit in Hearth, develop yourself and be useful to me."

"And what, you really would have committed suicide if I had been killed?"

"Max...As I already accidentally let slip, all this time I perceived you as the son I never had. At first, of course, I wanted to kill you, more than once, but over time I got used to your quirks and even began to understand them. Yes, I would easily destroy this world if you were killed. And Chaos saw this, that's why they retreated."

"But how is that possible? How can you destroy the world just by dying?"

"The point of no return. After becoming a first-orbital force, I designated my location. As a newcomer, I had such a right, and the other forces had to adjust. Skron and the Light were located at the maximum distance from the Chaos portal and from each other, forming a perfect triangle. When I appeared, the figure should have turned into a three-pointed star with the center as a portal. Since I had the right to a place, Skron and Light had to get off their fat asses and move to a new place, maintaining balance. The point of no return is a state in which they will not have time to return back if I suddenly disappear. Which will lead to an immediate detonation of the charge. Chaos understood this, as well as what will happen in this case. He would die. So, choosing between his life and yours, he chose himself. Everyone wants to live, even the gods."

"And what now?"

"Now? Now I will manage my domain, you will drag essences from the rifts for me, feeding me with their energy, and I will give you books in exchange. Gradually, I will amass followers, my own state. In about three hundred years, we will go to war against the dark ones. Or the light ones, I have not decided yet. But this is if the energy you supply is not enough. So you, my former mentor, will soon have to conquer the rift of the hundredth level to feed me the cream of the crop. But more on that later. First, you should go home and...By the way! You know that there are now three first-orbital forces in the world? By the way, there are now three creatures of Chaos too. The Inquisitor, the Interrogator, and one nameless, whom I will have to give a name."

"If you think you've given me any sensible ideas, you're deeply mistaken. I'm in such shock right now that I can barely think straight."

"Yes, Chaos has definitely sucked all the reason out of you. And I had such high hopes for you...Another color has appeared in the world, respected Archduke of the Autonomous City. There is white, and from it you have Alia. There is dark, and from it you have Naira. Green has appeared. Now do you understand what this means? Okay, I will not keep you in suspense: you have acquired the legal right to take a third wife. Green. And I have an excellent candidate for this role. But let it be a surprise. I hope a pleasant one. Right now you should return home to your wives and tell them that it is all over. This world will survive, and the Valevsky family will rule it. You and I have done everything to earn and secure it. Not a bad finale for a man who a year ago was a simple rank-and-file soldier in the doomed legion, eh? Like a fairy tale. The only way we know how."

The End

Want to be the first to know about our latest LitRPG, sci fi and fantasy titles from your favorite authors?

Subscribe to our **New Releases** newsletter:
http://eepurl.com/b7niIL

Thank you for reading *Condemned!*

If you like what you've read, check out other sci-fi, fantasy and A LitRPG series published by Magic Dome Books:

NEW and UPCOMING RELEASES!

Emperor of the Borderlands
A Historical Progression Fantasy Series
by Eugene Astakhov & Alex Toxic

Thousand Brethren
An Action & Adventure Portal Progression Fantasy Series
by Roman Prokofiev

Backstreet Evolutionist
A Progression Fantasy Adventure Series
by Anton Panarin

We Are Legion
A RealRPG Action Adventure Series
by Dmitry Dornichev & Evgeny Fox

The Doctor from Nowhere
A Historical Progression Fantasy Adventure Series
by Anatoly Drozdov

The Artificer
A Portal Progression Fantasy Series
by Marcus Cass

Guardian's Journey
A Portal Progression Fantasy Series
by Roman Savarovsky

„Earth" Release
A LitRPG Adventure Series
by Vasily Mahanenko & Vladimir Koshcheev

Nanomachines
A Progression Fantasy Adventure Series
by Nikolai Novikov

The Afflicted
A LitRPG Apocalypse Adventure Series
by Konstantin Zubov

The Dark Summoner
A Portal Progression Fantasy Series
by Andrei Tkachev

The Last Paladin
An Action & Adventure Progression Fantasy Series
by Roman Savarovsky

The Other Side
A Progression Fantasy Adventure Series
by Rodion Korablev

Me and My Demons
A Portal Progression Adventure Fantasy Series
by Oleg Sapphire & Alexey Kovtunov

The Blood Code
A Historical Progression Fantasy Adventure Series
by Michael Borz

The Banned
A LitRPG Adventure Series
by Michael Atamanov

Lord of The System
A LitRPG Progression Fantasy Series
by Alex Toxic & Furious Miki

A Shelter in Spacetime
A LitRPG Apocalypse Series
by Dmitry Dornichev

The Coming of God of Death
A Portal Progression Fantasy Series
by Dmitry Dornichev

The Village
A LitRPG Progression Fantasy Series
by Dmitry Dornichev & Alexey Kovtunov

Living Ice
A Portal Progression Fantasy Series
by Dmitry Sheleg

Ghost in the System
An Apocalypse LitRPG Series
by Alexey Kovtunov

The Goldenblood Heir
A Portal Progression Fantasy Series
by Boris Romanovsky

Crossroads of Oblivion
A Portal Progression Fantasy Adventure Series
by Dem Mikhailov

More books and series are coming out soon!

In order to have new books of the series translated faster, we need your help and support! Please consider leaving a review or spread the word by recommending *Condemned* to your friends and posting the link on social media. The more people buy the book, the sooner we'll be able to make new translations available.

Thank you!

Till next time!

9 788807 025805